PSYCHIC PAIR

written by

George O'Har

VIVISPHERE
PUBLISHING

For information address Vivisphere Publishing, a division of NetPub Corporation, 675 Dutchess Turnpike, Poughkeepsie, NY 12603.

ISBN 10: 1-892323-12-5
ISBN 13: 978-1-892323-12-5

Library of Congress Catalogue Number 98-89774

VIVISPHERE
PUBLISHING
www.vivisphere.com

Barbara,

Hope you like
what you read

[signature]

With special thanks to James Merrill
For his kindness and encouragement.

CONTENTS

Time is a child,
Playing a board game
Heraclitus

PSYCHIC PAIR

BOARD TALK

1864

1

Two brigades, one Confederate and one Union, fired remorse-lessly at each other from opposite sides of the creek that ran through the center of the valley. This creek was called Carter's Creek. Under a cloud-filled, smoke-filled sky, they fired across the water with little success until cannon balls fired from a hill above the Union side began to tumble onto the Confederates. In the panic that followed, men stood and ran for cover. Some raced for trees at the rear of the lines and others, inexplicably, ran to the water, where they were cut down. The water, forming into pools near rocks at water's edge, turned red with their blood. The color was visible from a distance. On a knoll beyond the creek, well back from the water, hidden in a copse of pine, a lone horseman in a tattered gray uniform with shining buttons watched the fighting below. The man, a colonel, listened with tired ears to the whistle of cannon balls and the screams and groans of the wounded and dying and reached down to touch the neck of his chestnut mare to calm her when a shell exploded nearby.

"There, there," he said. "It will all be over soon."

His listless eyes studied the proud remnants of his vainly en-trenched brigade and he listened a few minutes more to the shells of the Union artillery and to the clamor of gunfire and to the screams of frightened horses and men and when he saw a boy fall into the si-lently running creek clutching his throat, he spurred his horse and rode back to the top of the knoll and beyond toward a small wooden shack that stood near the entrance of a cave about three miles south of Franklin.

2

He waited in another wood until dusk, a quarter mile the east side of Columbia Pike, not wanting to cross directly through Johnson's troops while the fighting still raged. At the instant of dusk an eerie calm descended. The slender Confederate colonel on the chestnut mare gently touched his spurs to her side and the horse went ahead just south of where Johnson and his men were. The black-haired colonel kept his animal quiet as a ghost and he himself, with that silver streak down the left side of his hair where the Yankee sword had cleft him and left him for dead, not much louder. They traveled unmolested. He was well past Johnson's position when from the gloaming a squadron of gray-clad skirmishers came up before him like an apparition.

"Halt!" demanded a young boy the colonel realized was not much older than sixteen. The boy aimed a rifle at his chest.

"Easy with that gun, son," soothed the colonel. "I might get hurt." He smiled at the youth to put him at ease.

"Damn, William," exclaimed another in the group. "Can't you see he's one of ours? Point that gun at the ground!" He stepped into the twilight and grabbed the barrel from the stunned youth and aimed it toward the ground. "How did it go, sir?" he asked. "How did it go back there?"

"We gave as good as we got in most cases," he replied. "In others we weren't so fortunate."

"The fighting by the creek, sir. I heard it was fierce."

The colonel patted the neck of his horse and looked down at them. There were six of them in all, not one of them above seventeen and each of them in homespun, and most of that in rags.

"The fighting at the creek was terrible, men," he said, knowing that calling these boys men would mean something coming from the lips of an officer. "It was touch and go. Most of the time it looked as if our side was getting the best of it, but towards the end it seemed to change." He removed his hat, brushed his hand through his long black hair, and replaced the hat. "The fighting was worst in Cleburne's division," he droned on, his voice a sad monotone. "I never saw men put in such a position. Some were so exhausted they fell into ditches while the fighting raged about them." He paused to catch his quiet breath. "They chewed their thumbs to pulp listening to the screams and the bullets hissing above them." The words stopped. He looked at them, his eyes empty. Then he continued, with genuine sadness in his voice. "Irish Pat himself is among the missing."

"That can't be, sir," voiced one of the young Confederates. "The Yanks could never kill a man like General Cleburne. He's too good a soldier, sir."

The colonel spurred his mount.

"No one is too good a soldier to catch a bullet." He held the reins loosely. "My advice to you, young men, is to go home to your farms, or what's left of them, and wait this war out." The hand on the reins tightened, tugged. "You'll be much the better for it."

The horse moved forward. The boys stepped aside to let him pass. When they did they could see, just barely, in the dim light and shadows, that silver streak of hair, like a bolt of icy color burned into the left side of the colonel's head.

"My God!" exclaimed the eldest youth when he caught a glimpse of the silver streak. He turned to the boy who had aimed the rifle at the colonel's chest. "Do you know who you almost shot?"

3

He could see the outline of the shack. It appeared unguarded, but he knew that that would not be the case. Someone would be there; someone had to be there. The cave itself was invisible, as it cast no shadow save for that of the hill into which it was dug, but he knew exactly where the cave was and the precise number of steps it took a full-grown man to walk the distance between the shack and the cave. When the sky became completely dark and the stars brighter in the total absence of light from the ground a candle flickered to life in the cabin. The colonel smiled. He stepped down from the mare, patting her nose gently, and tied her carefully to a mimosa bush, the scent of which brought back memories he had thought long dead and unrecallable.

"Be quiet, girl," he whispered. "I won't be long."

He unbuttoned his holster and circled his way around the clearing so that his approach to the cabin would not be observable to anyone watching from the inside. Not that he believed anyone on guard would be looking out the small window or if looking would actually be able to see anything in starlight and even if looking in starlight would certainly not be waiting for him to arrive at the door.

At the door he removed his gun from the holster.

"Damn!" exclaimed a voice from inside.

The colonel smiled and gingerly moved to the window where he bent down and tried to peer into the dimly lit cabin without being seen to determine exactly how many men had been left on guard. The woods were filled with troops from both armies, but in all those numbers only a few knew of the existence of this tiny shack near the mine and of that few only himself and two others were aware of what it was the shack held and of the other two it was more than likely Irish Pat had found himself that bullet some unknown soldier had been aiming at his heart for years. He removed his hat and peeked inside from a corner of the window. The colonel saw one man. He stepped back from the window and walked back to the door and kicked it in with one firm blow from his well-heeled boot.

"Jesus!" exclaimed the soldier, making a grab for his rifle.

"I wouldn't do that," warned the colonel.

The puzzled soldier looked at the gun the colonel held with seeming carelessness in his right hand. He looked up into the colonel's eyes, squinting to get a better glimpse of the face.

"*Sir?*" he asked.

"Are you alone?" demanded the colonel.

The guard was too astonished to answer.

"I want to know if you are alone."

"Yes, sir," replied the youth.

The colonel motioned toward a pile of boxes stacked at the rear of the cabin well away from the crude fireplace built into a wall as an afterthought for heat.

"One of those boxes belongs to me."

The soldier sighed, relieved.

"Oh those," he said, beginning to rise.

"Don't get up."

"Them's just a-ammunition, sir," he stuttered, his voice uneasy and concerned, filled with the puzzlement he still felt at what was happening. "What would you want with that?" He allowed himself a smile and in the dim light of the flickering candle the smile seemed sadder than it probably was. "And some dynamite." He nodded and a look of resolution and understanding crossed his uncertain face. "You're here for the dynamite, aren't you, sir? They said someone would be comin' for that before too long."

The colonel, whose eyes had been straying among the pile of boxes, turned his attention again to the soldier.

"They?" he inquired.

And left it at that. He took a step toward the soldier whose face again filled with fear.

"Sir?"

"Yes," answered the colonel, looking down into the fear-filled eyes, wishing he could calm them and coax the anguish out of them.

"We *are* on the same side."

It was more a question than a statement.

"That we are," replied the colonel, lifting the gun and bringing it down with great force against the head of the sitting soldier. "That we are," he repeated as the soldier slumped to the floor.

A look of great sadness entered the colonel's face when he looked down at the unconscious guard and then knelt to feel for a pulse in the man's wrist. When he found a pulse, he got up and cast about the shadowed room for some bedding or rags and saw in a corner an old straw mattress and some dirty sheets, which he grabbed and dragged to the form slumped on the dirt floor. He wrapped the bedding as best he could about the muzzle of his revolver, cocked the trigger and brought the wrapped muzzle directly against the back of the fallen man's head and fired, the report making more noise than he imagined it would, given the batting and the pounding he felt in his chest.

1965

4

Adrian, in his crisp shirt, eyes glowing, pipes up, "Thanks for having us for high tea, Mr. Sweeney."

Sweeney stifles a smile.

"High tea in England. In America it's just tea."

Dark-eyed Welcome snickers in his seat.

"How old is this house, sir?" He brings the china teacup to his lips. "Look at the ceilings. The room. You could hide an army in here."

"Why would I want to do that?" asks Sweeney. His right eyebrow arches just a bit as he peers into his teacup and catches a glimpse of what he fears is a human hair. "I mean, hide an army."

"You never know, sir," answers Welcome. "It's in the Constitution." Adrian turns on him.

"What're you talking about?"

Welcome looks away, unruffled.

"The part where it says citizens must give succor to the King's horse." He turns to Adrian. "I could quote it exactly. 'A citizen, if true to the Spartan code...'"

Adrian interrupts, addressing Sweeney.

"See what I have to put up with, sir?"

Sweeney acknowledges with a nod, a brief smile.

"Give me a break, Adrian."

Sweeney puts up a hand.

"Boys, boys," He says. "We are at peace in this house." He brings down the hand, fingers gently the ansate cross he wears hidden under his sweater. "Never a soldier, never a quarrel. Not even a horse, King's or otherwise."

Adrian listens, hoping Sweeney will tell them things about the house no one has heard. It is an old house, filled with stories and lives. In the dust in the corners, the creak of the polished wood, tales of lives and more lives, waiting to be told. He takes a long, too audible, sip of tea. To hide his embarrassment, he says, "This tea is delicious."

"Earl Grey, straight off the shelf," declares Sweeney, pleased the boy has noticed. "Glad you approve."

"If I could interrupt, Mr. Sweeney," begins Welcome. "I like the tea too, but... you never answered my question."

"It's a Victorian."

"I knew it," exclaims Adrian.

Sweeney raises an eyebrow.

"Did you? Student of architecture?"

Adrian flushes.

"I knew in my heart, sir. That it was old."

"Your heart? Like the good St. Anselm," says the older man, still wondering about the hair floating in his tea. "Not your head or your spleen or, say, your liver?"

Adrian brings his right hand to his chest, to an area he believes close to his heart.

"The heart, sir."

Sweeney turns slightly in his red wing back chair and looks directly into Adrian Sparks' deep blue eyes, so deep they are almost blue-black. He places his cup in its saucer and puts the saucer on the nearby table.

"Is it better to know something in your heart, Mr. Sparks?" he asks, a smile flickering, then vanishing from his lips. "Or is it better to know in a more rational fashion? With the brain, for instance." He leans forward. "Or is there a difference?"

Adrian thinks before answering.

"The heart, I'd say."

"Why?"

He shrugs. "It's deeper."

Sweeney pursues.

"Explain."

"I don't know if I can, sir."

Sweeney smiles, reaches for his cup and swallows the tea, hair and all.

"You said it." He pauses. "Or are you someone's puppet? A flimsy thing that squawks when the master twitches?"

Welcome interrupts. "He's as flimsy as they come."

Adrian, for once, is relieved at the remark. Sweeney sits back in his chair.

"You may be too impetuous, Mr. Sparks."

Adrian takes this as a kind of compliment.

"Sometimes, I guess."

"No sometimes about it. Wouldn't you say so, Welcome?"

Welcome bobs his head.

"The most impetuous boy on campus."

Adrian flashes him a glance and begins a retort.

"Boys, boys," Sweeney admonishes, getting to his feet. "Nothing to fight about." He sniffs the air. "Do you smell anything burning?"

Welcome points to an ashtray.

"Your pipe, sir. It's gone out."

Sweeney's eyebrow goes up.

"Then it can hardly be burning."

Welcome titters.

"The ash, sir. I think you smell the ash."

5

The desk lamp, tilted so it shines on the board in his lap, glows against the side of his face. His dark eyes glitter with amusement. He hums quietly to himself and stares at the board, wondering if he is doing it correctly, whether it can be done correctly with one person and not two and concerned that it might not work at all if the person involved does not believe. Does he believe? "Is anybody there?" he whispers as softly as he can, but not quietly enough for the sleeping form on the bed on the other side of the room. A grunt, like that of an animal, rises from beneath the sheets, which, momentarily, are hurled back to reveal a head peering at Adrian like a jack-in-the-box.

"*What*," demands the head, "are you doing?"

"I am trying to figure out how this thing works," answers Adrian, not looking up. "I think I might be doing something wrong." He looks over at Boylan. "Do you know how these things work?"

Boylan is not easily put off.

"I don't know what you have there in your lap, Sparks," he mutters, "but whatever it is, put it away. And stop talking to yourself. It's annoying."

Adrian smiles.

"Sorry, Blazes. Didn't mean to wake you."

"Apologies accepted," asserts sleepy-eyed Boylan. His head flops back into the hollow of his pillow. His last words are directed more at the ceiling than at the boy at the desk across from him. "And please, get to sleep. You'll be late again for class."

Adrian nods quietly, still fiddling with the tripod. He moves it from one end of the board to the other. He can feel it skitter beneath the calm control of his hand. Will it move on its own? Adrian frowns.

What does he mean by on its own? What is the force that would move it? An outside force, a ghost, or something from inside himself? That idea sets him thinking. *What is inside me that can make this tripod move in response? My soul? Is that what souls do? Move tripods?* He holds the tripod up to the light and examines it. All he sees is a piece of hand-carved wood. He puts the tripod down on his desk, next to the board. He stares ruefully at the equipment a brief moment and then reaches for the lamp and switches it off. There in the blank darkness he wonders. Is there anything to a Ouija board at all? Are there spirits and can they actually communicate with the living? Why would a spirit want to talk with him? What would he ask it? Is there anything after this? *Would I like it?*

He gets up from his chair and pads silently to his bed, pulls back the cool sheets and settles in for a night of sleep. He covers himself, finds a good place for his head in the pillow and closes his eyes. *What shall I try and dream about tonight?* He is trying to figure out where to begin—back home with Jared?—when his ear is caught by a sound. He listens, sits up.

"Did you hear that, Blazes?"

Boylan is fast asleep.

He leans back on his arms and listens with absolute concentration. He sees shadows, the shapes of things he knows by heart: his desk, the three shelves of books above it, the old chair and the desk lamp. Frozen, hardly daring to breathe, he listens. A chilly breeze comes in through the screen and Adrian remembers having forgotten to close the window. He gets up from bed, walks across the room and kneels at the window, looking out at the stars. He stares up at them dreamily and reaches for the window and is about to begin pulling it down when again his ear is caught by a strange sound.

He closes the window tightly. Still kneeling, Adrian looks at lighted windows, at the church tower; he imagines people about— the night people: the watchmen, the guard at the gate, the cooks in the kitchen getting ready for tomorrow. He stands still, listening.

Do we have a mouse?

He pads back to bed as quietly as he can and dives under sheets already pulled back from before. Where was he before he heard that scraping sound? Ready to dream about back home with his brother?

How was the dream going to start? What would they be doing? He smiles to himself and closes his eyes. They would be playing catch in the driveway. Jared would have on his new mitt and Adrian would be pitching. What would the count be? Who would be the batter? Babe Ruth? No, not Babe Ruth. Even in his dreams he would not be able to strike out the great Babe Ruth. Mantle—the batter would be the Mick. He imagines the cheers of thousands as he goes into his windup. Mantle leans in, batting lefty against the right-handed Adrian Sparks. Adrian glares from the mound. Jared flashes the sign.

A curve.

The count goes full before Mantle goes down swinging. On deck, Moose Skowron steps toward the batter's box. Adrian doesn't see him. There is a sound above the sound of the crowd and he is trying to make it out, but he cannot. It is like something from a blowing wind, something from behind something, like an arm reaching out from a wall of ether.

On the desk the wooden tripod pushes against the hard spine of the Ouija board. It pushes, falls back and pushes again.

6

"You think much about death, Blazes?" asks Adrian, slipping into the requisite blue Justin Martyr blazer.

Boylan, on his way to the shower in a green terry-cloth bathrobe, stops short of the bathroom door and turns.

"All the time."

He heads toward the door.

"You don't have to be sarcastic," says Adrian. "I asked in good faith."

Boylan stops, turns.

"Just the way I answered." He begins walking toward his already dressed roommate. "Like I said. I think about death all the time." He is a foot from Adrian and even at their age the differences that will separate them as men separate them as boys. Boylan is broad-shouldered, square-jawed, a bit too thick at the waist. Adrian speaks of a litheness and eloquence. There is a speed and grace in his every move. "First thing I do in the morning. Open my eyes. That way I know it's daylight. Then I touch my toes. As soon as I can feel them, I say to myself, 'You've done it again. You've gotten through another night.' I throw back the covers, drop to my knees and thank God." He is next to Adrian now. "Goody, goody. Another day for me."

"Better hurry. You'll be late."

Boylan darts a glance at a windup clock.

"Damn!" He points a finger at Adrian. "You did this. You kept me up. You and your goddamn mumbling." He stops at the bathroom door, hand on the knob, and turns around. "You losing it?"

Adrian studies Boylan serenely.

"Welcome and I found a Ouija board at a yard sale day before yesterday. I was giving it a try."

"Ouija board," mutters Boylan, closing the door behind him. "Goddamn maniac," he hollers from the bathroom.

"Want me to wait?"

Boylan cannot hear him with the water running.

"I'll wait," Adrian says to himself, as Boylan begins to sing "Beautiful Dreamer" in a rich tenor voice, a talent Adrian secretly envies. He will never tell Boylan. His roommate is much too sure of himself and Adrian will do nothing that could add to Boylan's certainty. He has never said a word about how well he sings.

Boylan exits the bathroom, still wet, wearing his underpants.

"Did you take those off before you showered?"

Boylan ignores the remark, races to his closet and takes a crumpled shirt from a hanger. He wraps himself in it and selects a tie that doesn't match, which he begins to try and tie with one hand while with the other he reaches for a baggy pair of trousers.

"Have you considered going into fashion?"

Boylan is a study in silence and movement. He pulls on the pants, tucks in the shirt and finishes with his tie. He grabs his blazer, pushes his arms into the sleeves, leaps to the door and looks at his Mickey Mouse watch.

"Again," he says. "Record time."

The boys move together into the empty corridor.

"What time do you have?" asks Adrian.

"Five of."

"We should run."

Boylan smiles.

"We should race."

"I can't run carrying books."

"Speak for yourself, Sparks," says Boylan.

"We have time," declares Adrian, walking alongside Boylan, who at five-seven is two inches shorter. Boylan begins to walk fast, forcing Adrian to catch up. "You interested in going to the psychic fair at the armory next weekend?"

Boylan opens the door to the outside, muttering something unintelligible.

"What?"

"What the hell is a psychic fair?" Boylan works into a trot.

"Tarot cards, palm readers."

Boylan shakes his head. "Who cares about that crap?"

Adrian frowns. "It might be fun."

"I'll bet," comments Boylan, breaking into a run. "Catch me if you can, shithead." Adrian runs, but Boylan, who is fast, has too good a lead. As they race across the lawn Boylan holds the lead.

"I win."

Adrian comes alongside.

"You cheated."

Boylan snorts.

"On time too."

"What about the fair?"

Boylan claps him on the back.

"I'll let you know."

"When?"

"When I make up my mind."

Adrian laughs.

"Don't strain yourself."

Boylan sneers comically, catches Adrian with a stiff punch just above the elbow, laughs aloud and runs off to join the crowd of blue blazers waiting for the bell.

7

Long-nosed Welcome lies stretched out on the bed, listening to Adrian. Adrian is on a jag, so he listens politely to the words that tumble from the lips of the dark-haired boy in the chair, but with no real interest. His ears pick up when he hears his own name, but beyond that he listens in silence. It is like a rule between them: when one talks the others listen. Especially when one of them is Adrian, which is far more apt to be the case, or Boylan with his will-imposing ways. Andrew, the conscience of the group, listens quietly, his eyes upon the ceiling. His body never moves. Adrian, too animated to be contained in a chair, gets up and begins to pace. Welcome recognizes Sparks is in high gear and lowers his eyes to catch the face of his companion. The face will tell him everything.

"Let's do some research," Adrian declares, coming to a stop at the foot of the bed, his blue eyes on the probe.

Eyes lock. Welcome, who has not been paying close enough attention, especially toward the last when Adrian lurched into action, finds himself at bay. He is compelled to ask.

"Into what?" he inquires, his own voice hoarse from minutes and minutes of silence. "Into what, specifically?"

"The use of the Ouija board!" exclaims Adrian. "What have I been talking about?" He stops. "You weren't listening," he says, lowering his voice.

Welcome feels the pressure.

"I've been listening."

"Then what do you say?"

"We both have library cards," Welcome says. "What do you need me for?"

Adrian frowns.

"In case I need help." He sets himself down at the foot of the bed so that their eyes are about the same level. "I thought we were a team, Andrew. You and I."

"What about Boylan?"

Adrian is too eager to be squelched.

"First me and you and then Boylan." He stands. "We won't get him to our side unless we come at him united." He flashes a warm quick smile. "Together!" he yells, raising his right arm in a kind of swirl, like a pirate brandishing a sword.

Welcome, his body still as a corpse, clears his throat.

"Our side?"

Adrian grows frustrated.

"The seance!"

Welcome sits up in bed. He remembers nothing about a seance.

"I agree we should research."

"What have I been saying?" rejoins Adrian.

Welcome ignores him, goes on.

"First things first. We should learn something about the Ouija board." He looks up at Adrian. "We don't even know if it works, or how."

"What do you mean? What's to know?"

"The board could be a dud, a counterfeit. After all, we got it at a yard sale."

"So what?"

"Do you get rid of things that work at yard sale?" inquires Welcome, feeling the high ground within his grasp.

"Not the point," responds Adrian. "You sell things you no longer want. That's all." He pauses. "Besides, you can't sell anything that doesn't work. No one would buy it."

"Have you tried it?"

Adrian sits down.

"Not really," he answers. "We've only had it a few days."

Welcome bores into him.

"You keep confusing your pronouns," he says. "We are still in the 'I' phase here." He beams, a fox outwitting a hound.

"Andy," begins Adrian in a soothing voice, "I *can't* do this alone. You need at least two people to use a Ouija board."

"See your other friend, Boylan."

Adrian jumps to his feet.

"I can't even get him to go to the psychic fair."

Welcome reins in a smile.

"You haven't gotten me to go either."

Adrian stands, halfway between the chair and the bed, eyeing Welcome coldly.

"Don't tell me *you're* not going."

Welcome lifts a hand.

"I didn't say I wasn't going," he declares. "I didn't say I was, either." He looks at Adrian.

"Are you going?" demands Adrian. "I need to know, this minute. Otherwise I go to Boylan."

Welcome laughs.

"Where will that get you?" He lowers himself into a prone position. Eyes on the ceiling, he says to Adrian, "I'll go to the fair with you. I might be interested in that. But this seance, and the board. We have to talk seriously." He sits up again. "It isn't just a game, Adrian."

"I know."

8

"This, I think, is a blurb for your show," declares Boylan, after class, thrusting at Adrian a soggy sheet of paper.

Adrian gingerly accepts the wet flyer.

"What's this?" he asks, looking. "An advertisement. For the fair." Looking up, "Where did you get this? I haven't seen this one," he finishes, reading on.

"In the gutter," answers Boylan. "Stepped on. I only picked it up because I thought I saw a picture of a naked woman."

"Your dirty Irish mind."

"No," says Blazes. "An Irish mind may be filthy, but never dirty. Dirt is unclean. Filth is lust. Lust was what made me bend down." He takes Adrian by the lapels. "See how the Lord makes me pay for my every misdeed?"

Adrian steps out of reach.

"It says Socrates Radio will be there. Who is Socrates Radio?'

"Don't look at me," replies Boylan.

"Ah," exhales Adrian, turning over the sheet of paper. "Here it is. He's a 'trance channeler.'" He looks up. "What's that? And," he continues, eyes on the flyer, "he is going to be on the radio this..." He stops walking. "What is today?"

"Thursday."

"Tonight!" exclaims Adrian. "He'll be on tonight." He pushes aside some maple leaves with an idle foot. "We'll have to listen."

Boylan waggles his tongue.

"What time?"

"Ten o'clock."

Boylan shakes his head, tugs Adrian along.

"You listen, then tell me. I'll be asleep."

Together they walk through the leaves.

"How can you be so..."

Boylan takes a swing, misses.

"So nothing," he says. "Bad enough I'm going to the damn psychic fair with you."

"You're going?"

Boylan bobs his red head.

"Boylan has decided," he says, a grin that will soon be a smile forming at the corners of his lips. "The world is at peace."

9

A clear night and Adrian sits alone in the dark, waiting for the talk show to begin. The show originates in New York, but on occasion the host, a man Adrian has never heard of, takes his show on the road. Tonight he is broadcasting from Hammond Castle in Gloucester, a town just up the road from Justin Martyr School for Boys. Adrian is all ears and he peers through the half light and shadows at the radio, on quietly, where he sees behind the dials amber lights and can hear, just noticeably, a distinct hum. The commercial ends. Another voice is heard, an announcer from Boston welcoming Harry Glick, the talk show host up from New York, and Socrates Radio, whose reputation precedes him. Precedes! All this is new to Adrian.

"I want to welcome you first time listeners to 'Talking Sense'. My name is Harry Glick and my very special guest tonight is Socrates Radio, a man who, at least to myself and his fans, needs no introduction. But for those who don't already know you, could you tell us, Socrates, what a trance channeler is?"

Adrian sits, exasperated. He has never in his life listened to a talk show and the chatter embarrasses him. For once he is glad his roommate Boylan is asleep. He would never hear the end of it. Then above the hum, this voice, this warm voice. Adrian leans forward.

"A trance channeler, such as myself," begins a young voice, "is simply someone through whom others can find a voice."

"What others? You mean dead people," breaks in Glick.

"Well," hesitates Socrates, "I wouldn't exactly use that term. I mean, yes, to those of us who live in this plane they are dead. But we do not live in the Astral Plane."

"Could you explain something about that?"

"Of course," says Socrates calmly, his voice soothing. "There are, to put it as directly as I can, planes of existence. We on earth live in one plane, what I would term the Physical Plane. While we are alive, we can interact with the Astral Plane, astrally project and so on, but for the most part our first experience with the Astral Plane comes after the moment of death. At death we enter the Astral Plane."

Adrian wonders: does he believe this? Is this Christianity calling itself something else? He listens, unsure.

"To come back eventually?" interrupts Glick.

"That would depend," replies Socrates, as serenely as he can, or at least it seems so to Adrian, who is finding the talk show host annoying, "on what stage of Astral existence the individual has reached. There are, I believe, seven stages."

"You mean reincarnation."

"Yes," answers Socrates.

"What about this 'trance channeling'? Let's leave reincarnation for later."

Adrian can almost hear Socrates smile.

"Of course. A 'trance channeler' is a person who goes into what would appear to be a deep sleep, a trance. Once he is in this sleep, others, and by others I do mean bodiless spirits, or souls, can speak through him."

"And you've done this."

"Numerous times."

"Can you give us some names?"

"Well," answers Socrates, "the most famous person who has spoken through me, and this has been documented, is Socrates."

"How?"

"He once supplied me with information about something buried in a hitherto unknown Ionian city. Two years after he spoke through me, the particular urn he described was uncovered in an archaeological dig. Not to mention the city itself."

"Does he speak through you often?"

"Not as much as he used to," answers Socrates Radio. "He has moved deeper into the spirit world, too deep for me to reach. One can never really be certain with the link to the Astral World." There is a pause. "I took my name, as you know, Mr. Glick, from him."

"And been quite successful."

"One doesn't really think in terms of success in my line of work, although I suppose you could see it that way."

"Well, you have your own radio talk show."

"Once a week."

Glick laughs.

"It's better than nothing," he adds. "Probably a lot better than five nights a week. If you know what I mean."

Socrates, radio man to radio man, permits himself an easy chuckle. Adrian imagines him a slight, young dark-haired man, much like himself, who had a childhood that took him abroad, most probably to Greece. If he could ask, the question he would ask would be the most obvious of all: what got you started in this business?

"There are some listeners," he hears Socrates state, "who would be interested in learning how I became involved in this 'trance channeling', as people seem to want to call it these days."

"Why not give them an explanation?" offers Glick. "But after we break for five minutes of local news."

Five minutes of local news! Adrian is aghast.

"And after the news," says Glick, "we'll be taking some calls. 283-9561. Just hang in there, we'll be right back."

Calls? Hang in there? Arian fumes.

10

Boylan sticks his right foot into a pile of leaves, does a quick two-step, a run-through, a return, a squash and a victory dance.

"The Gauls, again, crushed by Caesar," he exults.

Adrian is dying to tell him about the talk show of the night before, but he is determined to outwait him. He wants Boylan to ask. He cannot always be the beseeching party. He waits and has been waiting since he awoke. Boylan, equally determined on his side, refuses to indulge his curiosity. They are at an impasse and each is aware of it and aware that each is aware of it.

Boylan bends down to inspect a large spider walking across a maple leaf. He holds the leaf up to sunlight and the spider moves over to the underside. Boylan puts down the leaf.

"We should take it to class and put it in Flood's desk." He gets to his feet. "What a riot that would be."

"You have a terrific sense of humor."

Boylan snorts.

"Never seemed to bother you before," he says, looking at Adrian. "Something the matter? Get up on the wrong side of bed?"

"Nothing's the matter," says Adrian, walking ahead.

"You're mad," Boylan continues, catching up, "because I haven't asked you a single question about that radio show." He pokes Adrian on the arm. "That's it, isn't it?"

"It's not my problem you have no intellectual curiosity," Adrian rejoins, beginning to walk faster to class.

"Ha!" exclaims Boylan. "We've been *here* before. All right," he says. "I'll be the big man."

"For a change."

"I'll ignore that, Sparks. I'll take a deep breath and count to ten. When I'm done I'll make inquiries."

"I can't wait."

Boylan has taken his deep breath, has begun counting audibly, in a low voice, one, two, three. He reaches and stops at ten.

"There, there," he says. They have reached the hill above Gabriel Hall and see below their mates, all blue blazers and ties. "I am calmed." He turns to Adrian. "All right, what'd he have to say?"

"Who?"

Boylan sighs.

"If I get any larger I'll burst."

"No need to tell me that," retorts Adrian, annoyed with himself and with Boylan, uncertain whether or not he has won this time. Who gave in?

"Say what you want," declares Boylan, walking, "but we'll be in class before long and you'll have to keep it inside all day long. You'll pop." He grins. "Come on, tell me. I'm all ears."

Adrian gives up feigning indifference.

"He calls himself Socrates Radio because Socrates speaks through him. At least he used to."

"How does he know it was Socrates?"

Adrian is taken aback.

"What do you mean?"

"Read my lips," says Boylan. "How did he know it was really Socrates speaking through him? Assuming there ever was such a person as Socrates in the first place. I mean, what proof did he offer?"

Adrian stops walking.

"Tell me you don't believe in Socrates."

Boylan shakes his head. When he does, the thick red hair stays perfect. Not a strand moves.

"Not the point. Fellow gets on a radio station. Says he hears voices. One of them is Socrates." He pauses. "How does he know this voice that claims to be Socrates is really Socrates and not some short circuit?" He taps his head. "You know, a personal problem."

"Oh," nods Adrian. "I get you. Socrates told him about some buried urn that archaeologists found *exactly* where he said it would be," says Adrian. "And this was two years before anyone even knew there was a city there. Above the urn."

"Still doesn't make the voice Socrates."

Adrian is perplexed.

"What do you mean?"

Boylan shrugs.

"Could still be someone *claiming* to be Socrates. Doesn't make the voice Socrates," he declares. "If we accept Socrates, who I think is a lie made up by Plato. You know those dead Greeks."

Adrian, wondering at the 'dead Greeks', grabs Boylan by the arm. "Who could it be then?"

"How the hell would I know?"

Adrian persists, releases Boylan.

"Why would anyone lie?"

"Who? Socrates, or Socrates Radio?"

Adrian begins to walk slowly through the leaves. Boylan, alongside, almost slips on the dew-covered lawn.

"You believe in God, right?" asks Adrian.

Boylan says, a little surprised, "Of course."

"You believe in an afterlife?"

Boylan considers.

"I think I do."

"OK," continues Adrian. "You believe in God. You believe in some kind of life after death." He stops. "What do you think it's like?"

Boylan moves ahead. It is a crisp fall morning. The dew, frozen like glass, crinkles underneath as they walk over the lawn and in the distance, beyond Gabriel Hall, a gossamer mist hovers above the fens, where the ducks live. Adrian catches up to him, waiting for an answer.

"I have no idea," Boylan says. "I mean I don't think it's sitting on a tuffet at the right hand of God. Usually I see green fields, blue skies. Things like that." He looks at Adrian. "What do you think?"

"Same as you, I guess," replies Adrian.

"But you believe in all this other crap," asserts Boylan. "Karma, reincarnation, voices from the dead." He hesitates. "Or is that just your latest jag? You know, a smile for fifth term?"

They are walking side by side down the hill, approaching the edge of the crowd of boys waiting to go inside. They stop just before they join the group.

"I believe the dead still live," Adrian declares, without a trace of levity in his voice. "And I think, when the channels are lined up, they can speak to us."

11

The door opens and Boylan enters wearing a green Mack truck hat, pushed way back on his head. In his hand he carries a burlap sack. He is ruddy and fresh and from him exudes the faint smell of apples and dying leaves. Adrian is at his desk, going through notes he took that day in physics class. Welcome is on the bed, supine, his usual posture when the three of them get together. He has not looked at Boylan, although he has heard the door and can smell the apples and the outside that still clings to Boylan and his clothing because Boylan is late. Welcome intends to punish him with silence.

"Greetings, chums," laughs Boylan.

"You're late," says Adrian.

"What can I say? I'm sorry." He holds up the bag and gives it a shake. "Apples anyone?"

"I'll have an apple," says Adrian.

Boylan reaches in and withdraws a greenish apple that he throws to Adrian at the desk. Adrian catches the apple in his right hand, almost without looking.

"We ready to talk?"

"What about?" asks Boylan. "If that's physics you're looking at, I'd like a look. You take better notes."

Adrian smiles.

"You don't take notes."

Boylan taps his head.

"All in there. Every word." He looks down at Welcome. "Want me to rewind?"

"I want you to die."

Boylan opens his mouth.

"You hear what he just said? You hear it?" He points a finger at Welcome. "You," he says, "are living on borrowed time."

"We don't have all night," says Adrian. "Blazes, what do you think?"

"About what?"

"Come on," frowns Adrian. "You know. The Ouija board."

Boylan shrugs.

"Haven't given it much thought."

Adrian jumps to his feet.

"You said you were going to think about it."

"I forgot."

Welcome laughs.

"Some recorder."

Boylan makes a gun out of his hand, squints, fires, points his finger into the air, blows the smoke away.

"It was self-defense."

"Come on, Blazes. Pay attention."

"I am."

"Then what do you think?"

"I don't know," he replies. "I suppose there's no harm in it." His green eyes study Adrian. "You can buy the boards in a store, so what could happen? I mean, you just push that little thing around and write down the letters."

"You're with us," says Adrian.

"*With us?*" repeats the redhead.

"I mean you'll help."

Boylan nods.

"Yeah, I'll help." He pauses. "Help what?"

Welcome, staring at the ceiling.

"Make contact."

Boylan whirls.

"Contact what?" He stops, then. "OK, I'll sit around and watch, or whatever it is you do when you fool around with the goddamn board. But contact? You gotta be kidding. Who're you gonna contact?" He laughs. "Know any dead people?"

Adrian declares, in a clear, calm voice.

"That's not the question, Blazes. The question is," he explains, "do any dead people know us?"

Boylan rolls his eyes.

"Right," he says. He looks at his watch, then shifts his gaze to the window. "It's getting late."

Adrian follows his gaze. He recalls last night, toward the end of the radio broadcast, going to the window, looking out and hearing an owl, hidden somewhere in a tree or posted in an eave. There were bright stars and high thin clouds scudding past that cast shadows on the lawn and the trees swaying, their leaves rustling on trembling branches, falling to the ground. On the ground the leaves were twisted into piles, like the piles they had walked through that morning.

Adrian turns back from the window to face his two friends. He is serene, his dark blue eyes ethereal. He is remembering the sound the owl made, the way the leaves were swept along the ground. He can see them scattering and collecting, can smell them and feel them with his mind. He waits until he has both Boylan and Welcome in his mind and he can feel them too and he says, "The spirits await."

1963

12

He sat in the red wing-back chair watching the fire. She would have liked this. This house, this fire. Having a place of our own. She would have given the house a name.

What name? He laughed to himself, his eyes reflecting the flames as he paged through his memory in search of suitable names: Usher, Brideshead, Thornfield Hall. He was so immersed in his search he was startled when he finally realized someone was knocking on the door. He looked at the clock above the mantle. It was past ten-thirty. Who could it be? Whoever it was was still pounding away when Sweeney querulously turned the brass knob and pulled in the tall oak door. The hinges creaked and he was in the middle of making a mental note to do something about it when he peered out into the December darkness and saw nothing.

"Who's there?"

There was a long silence, then a voice.

"I am, your honor."

His eyes moved in the direction of the voice and found a vague, smallish form. He switched on the light with his free hand and saw before him a man, a dwarf, who stood a good deal under five feet, squinting in the light.

"Why are you knocking on my door?"

The small man tittered.

"Your name Doucet?" he asked, his voice as thin as a reed, and worn, ignoring the question posed by Sweeney. His eyes reflected red in the house lights and Sweeney looking into them thought it was some kind of disease, or vitamin deficiency.

"No," he replied, keeping his answer short.

"You don't look like one," the dwarf said, but Sweeney's answer gave him pause. He had to think.

"I bought the house from them."

The small man snorted.

"I can see that!" he exclaimed.

His excited reaction made Sweeney step back and when he did his eyes went up to a point beyond the small form before him on the porch to another in shadow at the edge of the long walk that led to the iron gate, which had been left open by the small man and his larger companion. Sweeney tightened his grip on the door knob.

"Is there someone with you?"

The man turned and snarled.

"I told you to keep out of sight."

Sweeney heard a mewling sound, or thought he did. It was all he heard. He stared where the shape had been, but it was gone. It was as if, he said to himself, and remembered saying to himself, the shape had never been or had been more apparition than real.

"Who's with you?"

The dwarf looked up.

"A brother, a friend. Who cares? He won't hurt you." He still seemed perplexed at finding Sweeney and not someone else. "How long have you lived here?"

Sweeney tried to take charge.

"Excuse me, if I may. This is my house. I live here. *You* knocked on *my* door." With his right index finger, he poked his chest. "*I* ask the questions."

The little man grinned.

"Ask away, your honor."

Sweeney considered.

"*Who* are you?"

Scratching his blotchy throat, the dwarf replied.

"My name is Rufus, not that it will mean anything to you. The people who used to live here, they were friends of mine." He smiled quickly, a spasm. "I guess you could say I'm a bit disappointed to find them gone and you here. I've come a long way."

"From where?"

The small man shook his head.

"That matters less than my name," he said. "What does matter is where they went, the Doucets." He looked up. "Do you know?"

Sweeney shook his head.

"I have no idea. I never even spoke with them."

The little man chortled, snapped his fingers.

"Typical," he snorted. "Typical."

Sweeney raised an eyebrow half-consciously.

The little man shook, sputtered with exasperation. When he threw his eyes up Sweeney saw anger in them, and something else he could not name. A vein twitched, pulsed in the side of his head.

"You bought a house from people you never talked to, never even saw, right? That doesn't strike you, your honor?"

Sweeney sniffed.

"I never bought a house before."

Rufus looked up at the taller Sweeney and, still shaking his head, laughed thinly. The laugh seemed to stop before it reached Sweeney, called back by the little man, whose eyes now went behind Sweeney, into the rooms beyond, the stairs. He stepped further back onto the veranda and took a long look at the windows and then turned away and measured the railing and further on the lawn. He turned and showed Sweeney a face composed, calm, although it still contained something unnamable in the eyes, which Sweeney saw for the first time were coal black when the dwarf kept himself far enough from the lights. A smile formed, stopped.

"Well," said Rufus, "you got yourself one sweet piece of real estate, tell you that, Mr.?"

"Sweeney," answered Sweeney, feeling compelled to answer.

The little man bobbed his head.

"Good Irish name, that," he commented, putting on a small round hat he had been concealing a beret of some sort. He moved further into darkness. "Be seeing you, Mr. Sweeney. Good luck with the place."

Sweeney watched him go down the stairs, down the long walk, watched him with his eyes until the night was about to reclaim him. Then he stepped out onto the veranda himself.

"Wait," he called out. "Any message? Perhaps…"

The footsteps ceased. A voice came back, muffled, then clear.

"There'll be no messages, Mr. Sweeney."

Again footsteps, vague movement, nothing.

"Well," he wondered to himself.

He stared into the darkness a long time, listening for further footsteps. He heard nothing. He walked into the house, closed and latched the door and continued walking to the wing back chair. About to sit, he stopped, moved to the fire, grabbed the poker and began shifting the logs. He considered adding a fresh log, but the fire was going and really did not require it. He shut and clasped the grating and returned to his favorite chair, the chair he had been sitting in when he first had heard the knocking.

"What do you think?" he said to himself. Then to the fire. "Mother, tell me. What do you think?"

There was no answer from the flames.

13

She never saw the inside of the house. After he had decided he definitely wanted to buy, he had driven her out to take a look at the place. She had refused to go in. "It won't be right, Jim, until it's ours. We can wait." In three months she was dead. He had lived with his mother his entire adult life, since his father died. She had become, in those years, a part of him, an integral other self. He could not imagine his life without her life and the idea that she could die before he could afford to buy them a place of their own never struck him, not once. She was too full of life. And to die at sixty! He could never fully eradicate the vision from his mind: going home, knocking, getting no answer, using the key, walking down the hallway, turning, looking into the living room, heart filled with dread—she always had dinner waiting—and seeing her there, sitting, almost peaceful, except for the eyes. The eyes were cold empty orbs that stared back and gave nothing, extinguished. Six steps, a deep breath, "Mother, Mother!", another breath to close the eyes and stand above her in silence, picking up the fallen quilt she had been making him for his new house, holding it to himself, weeping. It had been a year—he had moved into the house a year and three months ago—since her death and still he saw her everywhere. He tried to imagine her in the house, but he never quite could. She had not been a part of the place. Instead, he remembered her in the kitchen in Dorchester, making a sauce for the goose or her banana pudding or date nut bread or any of the desserts he loved. In the house he had bought she simply wasn't there. She could not be conjured. When he tried to sit her in the wing back he came up with nothing. Always he had to return to the life in Dorchester they had been planning for years to leave behind.

She died, and left him a prisoner of a house he had wanted to leave, where all the memories lived, and still lived and would live—unless there was a way for him to bring her back and make her part of the new house.

Bring her back! Sweeney laughed and almost dropped his wine-glass. He wondered, sometimes, about his sanity.

The house that would have been her house and his house was just his house, and sadly bereft. Who would make the quilts to go on the beds? Who would make all the nice desserts, the holiday dinners? The answer came back, always, "You will, Sweeney. You will." He *had* learned to cook for himself at forty, he had produced a sound meal or two and was in ownership of a few recipes he was rightly proud of. Sweeney's famous plum pudding, his own date nut bread and Sweeney's own boiled dinner, just like his mother's, only not nearly as good.

Still, fifteen months and grief was yet a part of him. Sometimes the sadness so filled him he could hardly raise himself from bed in the morning. Other times he could not close his eyes. He had considered getting a pet—doctors told him some people did things like that—but he came to the conclusion, rightly, he supposed, that his colleagues at Justin Martyr would think him pathetic. He was *not* pathetic. He would hoard his miserable grief and lock it up inside. No one would see, no one would mock him or say, "There goes pitiful Sweeney with his grief." He would dissemble and go off alone when the waves came—from so many different places!—and quietly clog the tears. He would return anew, eyes glistening, ready.

The thought had occurred to him that he should find himself a wife. Not actually a new thought. It had crossed his mind before, even when his mother was still alive. It had always been a date, or two, sometimes three, and then nothing. After a while he simply stopped trying. He wasn't unhappy at home with his mother. He didn't seem to have any strident sexual urges—some men didn't, like priests—so there was really no need to go looking. What could a wife do that a mother couldn't?

Now there was no mother and his mind had been taking to the idea that perhaps he did need a wife, if for no other reason than to fill up the new house with a presence other than his present dismal own.

When would he snap out of it? Looking back at his life he realized he had failed to plan ahead, with few exceptions. He had always known he would return someday to Justin Martyr and teach, that he would teach English, specialize in Shakespeare and become the best at it. That much had come to pass. He gave little thought to anything else, so it seemed very natural to move back in with his mother once he was finished with college. He would have gone to college in Boston, too, had be known that his father would die while be was away at Princeton. His father's death had been a sad death, but he had been sick with cancer of the prostate for some time and they all knew he was going to die. There was nothing anyone could do. His father had fought courageously, but in the end courage was not enough. It failed him, as it had others. The doctors gave him a year; he lasted a year and a month. Sweeney liked to think the stiff upper lip had gotten him that extra thirty days, but be couldn't fully believe. Mind had no power over matter.

He redevoted himself to scholarship. The house he filled with more books than could be found in many a small town library, most of them on topics related to literature. Then he began to stray. When he looked back and tried to pinpoint the time, the exact moment in the exact day it had begun he found he could not. Time didn't operate like that. It was a fluid that rolled around in a jar, it telescoped and condensed, expanded, shrunk into a pinpoint—his forty years. Wasn't it yesterday, or was it years ago? When, precisely when, did that happen? When did she feed the ducks from the boat in the pond in the Public Gardens? When did he take her to Plum Island and hold her hand along those rickety wooden paths to look for Buffle-heads, Mergansers and rufous-breasted Harriers?

Memory was the enemy. There were times he wished he could pluck what he knew from his head and start fresh. Other times he wanted to hold tight to what it was that made him him. Suffer, yes, but hold on for dear life. If he ever let go of his past, using hypnotism or some clever new method of psychiatrists or pill doctors, who would he be? Would he become someone new, or simply the new Jim Sweeney, but like the old, still whittling away at his Ph.D.? His eyes wandered to a new wall of books, mounting. The shelves he had originally put in to house more texts on literature, but then the change had come, or was it the will to change? He took a deep breath and stared into the fire and wondered at all the strange, sad things that had happened in his life. His father dead before his time, his mother, now him alone in his new house, although hardly new, built in 1880 by Andrew Doucet, he had learned, part of his new research, his new library. His eyes went up to the titles again, seeking consolation.

14

The lawyer told Sweeney that the house had been built "circa" 1880 by Andrew Doucet and had remained in his ownership until 1915, at which time he died and title was passed to his wife, Prudence Doucet. Title to the house changed hands one more time, in 1951, when it was passed on to Marie, the present owner, a granddaughter of Prudence and Andrew. The house had always been in the family. Sweeney was pleased, for reasons unknown, to purchase a house that, at least technically, had had but one owner. He was pleased until the night of the visit of the dwarf and his unseen companion, which had occurred a year and some months after he had moved in and which told him that whoever they might be the dwarf and his friend were no friends of Marie Doucet, whom be now desperately wanted to contact, if not to ease his own mind, then to inform her that two strange men had come calling, presumably looking for her. He was told by the lawyer that such contact was out of the question, that Marie had departed for "parts unknown," most likely an island somewhere or out of the country because she did have in her possession, when last he saw her, a new passport and travel brochures for St. Martin. "Is there any way at all?" Sweeney pressed. "Suppose something had gone wrong with the house?" Miss Doucet has severed all legal obligations between herself and the house of her ancestors, the lawyer assured him. "You'd have to take her to court, assuming you could find her," the lawyer finished, adding a final remark, "She seemed to be in a hurry," before hanging up the telephone. Sweeney spoke into the empty receiver for some seconds before he realized he had been cut off. He was tempted to dial again, but then he decided himself to go to Town Hall in Gloucester, where all records of property transactions in Magnolia were still kept, and do some checking. He found the lawyer had told him the truth: house built "circa" 1880 by Andrew Doucet, passed to wife in 1915, the year of his death, retained by her until 1951, when, for reasons unknown, the title was passed on to Marie. Sweeney stood in the records section of Town Hall, perusing the property transactions in the year 1951 for some minutes before he realized he had a question: if there was a grand-daughter, there were children from the original marriage. "How would I find that out?" he inquired of the elderly woman before him. "Down the hall, turn left. You want the Recorder's Office." A gold mine! Sweeney located a wedding "certificate"—("They didn't have what you would call licenses those days")—that told him of the marriage of Andrew Doucet and Prudence Fischer in 1885. "When are the births recorded and how accurate would such records be?" he asked the young man. "Over there and not very," he was told, and directed to a musty corner of the room. It took him over an hour to find what he wanted: born 1896, Andre Doucet to Andrew and Pru-dence, born 1888, Aveline, likewise to Andrew and Prudence. Sweeney was pleased with this information, but checked in his search. What he had learned was that Marie was possible; he had not learned which of the two Doucet children was her forebear. As the records were kept by years and not cross-referenced in any manner, Sweeney spent weeks going though all recorded births, marriages and deaths in Gloucester—and Magnolia—to no avail. The most recent mention of the Doucets, before Sweeney came along, was 1951, the year the property was transferred. Nothing else. It was as if Andre, Aveline, Prudence and Marie had vanished, or had never lived in the town at all. When he returned to the house, alone, with what little informa-tion he had acquired, he consoled himself with the thought that he had done all he could reasonably be expected to do to find Marie Doucet and warn her, "warn" had become his word for what he tried to do—that two strangers were seeking her. He was afraid they would succeed. It seemed to him that, friend or not, Rufus knew a great deal more about the Doucets than he did. He must have had a reason for coming all the way to Magnolia to a house Sweeney was certain he had at least once been inside; he could tell that from the look in the dwarf's eyes when he scanned the foyer and what else he could see of the house. As if the house should have been his! Sweeney then went over in his mind what he remembered of that brief encounter: a pounding at the door, a little man, gnarled-looking, ruddy-cheeked with a huge throbbing vein in his head that showed he was angry, or worse, furious; a specter in the distance, hiding, capable only of making mewling sounds, huge beyond description. "Typical," the dwarf had fumed. "Typical." "What was typical?" Sweeney asked himself. His behavior, or the Doucets? He had assumed the dwarf was referring to Marie, but perhaps he had meant the remark as an indictment of Sweeney for buying a house from an invisible maid. What was his next step? He had no idea. At the very least, he thought, he could go through this old house from stem to stern, top to bottom, and see what he could find.

So he searched. He had thoroughly cleaned the house before he had actually moved in with his books and furniture, so he spent a good many minutes deciding where to start: the attic, or the cellar? He was halfway down the steps to the basement when he changed his mind and went back up the stairs down the long hall and to the stairs that led eventually to the attic, two floors up. When he reached the attic, which was comprised of two large, empty rooms with a window in each, he looked upon his possession with new eyes. Not here to clean, here to find. His first thought was to tap all the walls to see if any one area sounded different from all the others. He felt foolish at first, like a child almost, and was half certain he wouldn't be able to tell the difference if there were one. But he began knocking and listening, knocking and listening, all about the attic and was quite clear in his own mind that he was becoming some sort of expert at some sort of practice when he found himself brought up short by a hollow sound in one of the panels just off the stairs in the bedroom that faced the front of the house. He tapped again. Hollow, or at least, more hollow sounding than the others, as if there were more space behind this panel, this section of wall than the others. He raced downstairs for his tools and returned with a box containing several varieties of screwdrivers, some chisels, two hammers. He stood looking at the panel, the rich wood, and was about to strike some sort of blow when he stopped himself. He knelt down on the dusty floor, stared and then felt, very carefully, for hidden springs or buttons. Nothing. He pushed. The wall pushed back. He tapped, the wall answered, "Not this way." He sighed, leaned against the panel with some weight and—wonder to behold—the panel slid silently upwards.

He squinted into a small, dark chamber. He saw something, but went first for the flashlight in his pocket and aimed the beam directly into the heart of the hiding place. He saw six objects—the bones of a rodent, two empty brass candle-holders, a doll, worn to rags, a three-legged triangular object, and, with just a thin layer of dust across the faces of the moon and sun, black lettering on brown, a Ouija board.

1864-1880

15

He rode north and gave a wide circle to Nashville and kept riding until daylight, when he knew he had to hide. He could not take the risk of being discovered by troops of either side in heavily trafficked, heavily contested Tennessee. His knowledge of the territory would give him an advantage—an advantage he knew he would need—until he got further north, where the land would be unknown. His plan was simple: north to Paducah, then west to Cairo and the Mississippi. He would stay close to the river and follow it all the way into the new state of Minnesota and from there he would find his way into Canada, where he would stay until the war was over. The trip was going to take months and he had prepared himself for it: a rifle, ammunition, three knives, enough dried food to tide him over when the hunting was bad. He knew, too, he had to watch for Indians in the west, and north.

"And watch for bears," he whispered to himself.

He was a hunter and had been a good hunter in France before coming to America, where he improved his skills by becoming an excellent trapper in the hills around Nashville. He knew he would not go hungry. The Indians could give him trouble because in them he saw his equals. Men, even boys, who could ride and shoot at the same time and who could move through the woods like a ripple or a passing breeze. He knew what they could do to a man and he was not going to let it happen to him. He would rather kill himself, take every last bit of everything with him.

When the sun set he rode again. In three days he made Paducah, again making a wide arc around the city, in four more days he reached Carbondale, two more, St. Louis. He was on his way up river. The woods were filled with rabbits and squirrels and he set his traps at night and in the morning he would find his meal. There were times he would wade into the river and fish, but his luck with fish was much less. He was a hunter who traveled by night. He encountered no others, not in the day, nor in the night. He was getting far from the war and there were no troops and he was careful not to come too close to the cabins whose smoke it seemed he could smell from miles away. He longed to present himself as a stranger passing through, just for the company, for something made by a woman, but he checked himself.

"In due time," he said.

He rode like a whisper and the days went by and the weeks and still he saw no one, not even an Indian, until he crossed into Minnesota from Iowa. He saw them there, a half dozen riders with guns, and he was certain they saw him, but they gave no signal and rode on as if he had been an apparition, or nothing at all. He saw them more now and he rode even more carefully. He was too close and had come too far to be killed by a warrior from a nation whose name he had heard only in conversation from men who had survived, but whose name he knew from the look of them and the spotted ponies they rode: Sioux. He saw more of them the further north he went and always they left him alone. He wondered and he had no answer and finally he came to believe it was the silver streak, the Mark of Cain, that kept the Indians and their guns silent. Maybe they thought he was a god, or a ghost, some entity too big or too little for them to bother.

It made him confident, the way they left him alone, but still he was careful. He slept in places that were difficult to approach quietly, if at all. He kept his fires low and always he kept his rifle less than a second away. What killed him, if anything, would die too. Of that he was certain. Which was the reason it remained a puzzle, always, his crossing into Canada and the bullet that took the mare out from under him. It was late afternoon, nearing sunset. He was some miles south of Rainy Lake Seine when something made him turn back and he looked toward Minnesota and the border he had just crossed and then came the gunshot and the sickening sound the mare made when she fell. He had to shoot her himself to spare her the pain and he used her carcass for cover, waiting for the next invisible bullet, from the invisible gun, but it never came. Was it the Sioux? A parting gift for the ghost they had let ride on into Canada? Or simply an accident, a careless hunter, or was it the hand of God? He never knew. When it was fully dark, too dark for him to even cast a shadow in the moonless night, be crept out from behind the mare, grabbed the saddlebags, his rifle, some bullets, and began walking in the general direction of Ontario.

He wearied quickly on foot. He had found no game for several days before crossing the border and he was hungry and cursed himself for not taking some meat from his dead mount. In the next breath he berated himself for even thinking about eating the flesh of an animal that had served him well, and for years. He could go hungry a few days. It was hunger that had taken him to Tennessee. The nights were colder this far north and when he woke in the mornings his teeth were chattering, and his fingers and toes were numb. He began to worry about frostbite. He had seen it before, in France, when men had been caught in a sudden storm. He remembered the fear in their eyes, imagined the screams when the foot or the leg was being amputated. Would he be like that?

The cold and the hunger were making him delusional and he knew he had to reach civilization, had to stop at the next cabin he found. He was safe now. He had to be safe this far from the war. He could have the warm fire and the home-cooked meal and the conversation. If the cold did not get to him. That or the bullet that said, "Saint-Loup, this is for you. For what you have done." He shifted the heavy saddlebags and crawled, dragging them behind. He came to a stop against a tree, his breathing labored. He was exhausted, but not beaten. He had come too far. He groaned and lifted the saddlebags, their weight, and brought them to his chest.

16

She could not take her eyes from him. This stranger with the silver streak in his hair, who rarely spoke and was never spoken to and who drew her to him like a moth to flame and who awoke in her desires long dormant and made her dream of doing things—she saw herself doing them whenever she passed him, she could not stop herself. She had underestimated her need. The stranger had made her aware of this. She had brushed by him once in the dry goods store and he had looked down and smiled into her eyes and when he did she felt a shudder pass through her.

Who was this man? On this the townsfolk were divided. It was obvious, from the way he spoke, with his slight French accent, and from what little he told people, that he had come to Massachusetts from Ontario. Before that he was from France. It seemed to her he had come in on a wind, on a great gray mare, wearing a capote, and it seemed to her he would move on and go about what he had been going about for years and leave them out of his plans. She was wrong. He stayed in Gloucester and began construction of a great house on a hill south of town surrounded by grass and trees and unkempt forest. Where did his money come from? This was another question people wondered at and the answers, like the answers to all the other questions about the man who called himself Andrew Doucet, were not supplied by the one man who had them. He had brought with him a wagonload of the finest pelts any of them had ever seen and these he traded for the piece of land in the still uncleared forest. The boy and the Indian who brought the wagon stayed for months, helping him clear the land, and like their master, they too were silent. If they knew any more about him than the townspeople, they refused to tell, and many in town fully believed the two knew nothing and had just been hired on to do some driving and some work. The day after the land was cleared they were gone, taking with them the empty wagon they had brought down from Canada.

She could not get him out of her mind. That one look in the dry goods store had sealed her fate—she knew this, although she knew too her fate had been sealed the night he had ridden like a ghost into town. It seemed to Aveline she had felt him arrive in her sleep, that her dream changed suddenly into a dream about a man on a gray horse who had no past and maybe no future and who with one look could either freeze or ignite into flame the very essence of a being. They never spoke. He never said a word to her—and she had seen him eight times in the six months he had been in town. She remembered each time. When her daughter asked her who the stranger was, she said simply, "Andrew."

"I think he's handsome," Prudence said in return.

Handsome he was. Tall, but not so tall, angular. He seemed to project more than he was, like a man as tall as his shadow, or as wide. His blue eyes were not unkind and in them she saw worlds long sealed-up, forgotten. She was a widow. Her husband had been killed in the war. She had a daughter. She was too old for him. This was her litany. When she rode out that day to take a look at what he had been doing in the months since the land had been cleared she did not expect—hope?—to see him, but she did. He was there, working on the foundation of some dream known only to him, or maybe to him and the boy and the Indian. He worked methodically and did not look up when she arrived, although she knew as well as he that he was aware of her. She waited. Should she call out? It had taken all her courage to bake the pie and put it in the wagon and ride out alone into what the townsfolk still called the woods. Was there enough left to call out? He saved her the trouble. He stood up and put down his hammer and walked as steadily over to her as if she *had* called him.

"Morning, Mrs. Fischer," he said.

She was taken aback.

"How do you know my name?"

He smiled up at her.

"How do you know mine?"

She felt a smile grow, she felt years of sadness slough off like a second skin. He helped her down from the wagon and in the touch of his hand she lost her soul. She belonged to him. She would do anything he wanted and when she looked into his eyes she knew this and when he held her gaze with that strange blend of arrogance and pity his eyes always contained she knew he knew it too.

17

She heard them, Prudence, in the night. The sounds they made. She would try to sleep and get what was going on out of her mind, but she could not. It was her mother—and this man. The stranger with the kindness and that other thing that had no name in his eyes that seemed to come from far off, from some place or time that did not belong to the present, but to the past—or the future. He was slender and sometimes his eyes were mirthless and sometimes sad and she could tell from the way her mother looked at him that she was in love and that this was the man of her dreams. When they went by, the townspeople lowered their voices or stopped talking at all. Doucet did not seem to care and her mother did not care because he did not. She would never have been so bold on her own. She began to seem young again, her mother, and for this Prudence was glad. And he was like a father to her, although not the father she knew her father would have been, had he lived. Her mother always said he had been killed in the war, but she knew he had returned, had come home and lived three years, had come home another man with one leg and a haunted took in his eyes. Killed in the war, her mother told her, but that was half the truth. The war let him live three years, until the day he walked into the barn with his gun and did not come out. This was not what her mother told her. She had found that out for herself when she listened and her mother did not know she was cupping her ear to the door to catch the words she always knew had to be true because men don't die from a war three years after it is over. She heard them. She heard her mother groan and cry out and she heard Doucet whisper to calm her. Her mother was now shunned by the townsfolk and none of them came by to see her, to ask for one of her blueberry pies or to buy eggs from them. None of them came. That they did not come did not matter to her mother, as far as she could tell. The man Doucet always seemed to have money and there was plenty of food and he worked around the house and kept things in order. She found herself looking at him when she thought he wasn't aware—although she knew he was. He was that kind of man— and her eyes always came to the silver streak in his hair. How did it get there? He never said. He never said much. All they knew for certain was that he had come down from Ontario, where he had lived as a trapper, and that his dream was to finish the house in the woods.

He was a wonderful rider and that was what she liked most about him: his way with horses. He could calm the most wild of them with a touch and a few short words. It was as if he had some magic known only to himself and the horses. He was worthless with chickens and kept away from them and told them both that an egg farm was a poor way to survive and told them they should invest in land and rent the land out to men who would farm it and pay them to farm it. But where would they get the money to buy the land? All they had was the egg farm, and the homemade goods and no one was buying either. He laughed at her concerns.

"Don't you worry, Prudence."

She did not believe him, but somehow his words soothed her. Was it his eyes? The silver streak? Or was it the fearlessness, the contempt she knew he felt for the others who shunned them. Andrew was not afraid of any man and she knew him to be a marvelous shot, even from horseback. He tried to teach her to shoot, but her mother forbade her to learn and the two of them would sneak off and ride out to his place where he would show her how to shoot apples off a post. And she could. She knew her mother knew she was doing the shooting, but she knew her mother was not able to go against Doucet in anything, not even when it came to her. Her mother was weak when it came to him and in her heart Prudence despised her for it.

What was happening to her? She had always loved her mother, and now because of this man her feelings were changing. She sensed a strange kind of hostility in her mother that seemed to amuse Doucet whenever he came upon it. Not that it was so obvious, but it was there. When she looked at herself in the mirror she could see her mother in her eyes, her mouth. They were the same size, with the same color hair, a reddish brown, only hers was longer than her mother's, and came down to the small of her back. She loved her hair. It was her best feature.

In school, when the others shunned her, it did not matter the way it did when it began years back, when Andrew had started coming around and the others found out. She did not need them. She knew that she and her mother were going to move into the big house and that everything would be taken care of. Andrew was rich and already he was buying more land and renting it out for use. He took a share of crops and some money and he bought them clothes and new horses and when they went riding, the three of them, through his fields, it seemed they didn't have a care in the world. He could make them both laugh when he wanted and when he was riding he wore a grin and looked so slim and elegant in the saddle she almost believed they would be happy together in the tall, wonderful three-story mansion that seemed to rise from the ground by magic, as if Andrew had planted in fall and in spring the house came up from below, on its own, in response to some secret call of nature.

But the house had not been planted, had not risen in reaction to any call of nature. It rose from something else. It rose in response to a mad dream inside the mind of the resolute man who rode into town and took her mother. A mad dream about death and dying and not letting go. She could never forget that grim night Doucet came riding up and went into her mother's bedroom and began to talk and then shout and then whisper and her mother screamed and shouted and swore and tore at his eyes and screamed until she wept and screamed until she could not scream anymore.

A MAD DREAM
ABOUT DEATH
AND DYING AND
NOT LETTING GO

1965

18

"The spirits await?" echoes Boylan. "What the hell are you talking about, Adrian?"

He starts to pace, a small frown creasing his clear forehead. On the bed, Welcome, his eyes following the lazy path of a speck of dust through the air, waits for the explosion, which he is certain will come. They've been at it like this before. He anticipates with a quiet kind of glee. He glances away from the dust mote, peeks at Adrian over at the desk, then at pacing Boylan, who is obviously working at his response to what he suspects will be Adrian's reply. Welcome knows Boylan knows Sparks must be stopped at the outset, before this goes too far.

"Spirits," says Adrian.

"What the hell is a spirit?" counters Boylan. "I mean, what exactly do you mean by it? That thing on the bed?" he points at Welcome, who is puzzled at the remark. "This piece of dust?" He bends down and picks up a ball of dust, drops it to the floor. "The soul? What?"

It seems to Welcome that Boylan has claimed the forensic high ground and in his heart he approves, although he resents somewhat being cryptically labeled a "spirit." He knows little about spirits, but firmly believes he belongs to some other class of being. He removes his glasses from his shirt pocket and puts them on. He will need his eyes. There will be details to notice.

"A spirit is what lives after death."

Boylan sputters.

"How do you know?"

Adrian measures him.

"Know what?"

"That there is any such thing?"

Adrian retorts quickly.

"I don't."

"Then what the hell are you talking about?" insists Boylan.

"Spirits," answers Adrian, calmly, a brief smile crossing his lips. "And how to find them."

From the bed, Welcome mutters.

"Oh, boy."

Boylan doesn't even look at him.

"How?" he demands, walking right up to Adrian. He turns suddenly and points a finger. "You're in this too, Andy. So pay attention."

Welcome squints through his glasses.

"What makes you think I'm not?"

Boylan returns to Adrian.

"You didn't answer my question."

Adrian leans forward and lifts the roll top on his desk, revealing the Ouija board. The planchette sits patiently in the upper left hand corner, near the "Yes."

"With this."

Boylan ignores the board.

"That's a toy," he says. "A game."

Welcome coughs.

"What makes you so sure?"

Boylan turns to face him.

"You too? You're in this together, aren't you? You guys want to play this crap and you want me to go along." He looks at Adrian. "Go ahead. Fool around. You don't need me."

"We're a team," says Welcome. "Besides, you said you'd watch."

Boylan snorts.

"I said watch. Maybe. Not get actively involved."

Adrian leans back against the desk.

"What's your problem, Blazes? If it's a game, it's a game." He looks into Boylan's green eyes. "Suppose it's not, though? Suppose there's something to it."

Boylan stares at the board.

"I can't believe the two of you are taking this seriously," he declares. He looks at Adrian. "I mean, you actually think some spirit is going to talk to you through this thing?"

"We won't know until we try."

"Right," says Boylan. "How do you know it's a spirit and not your own damn fingers? Huh? How do I know the two of you aren't just screwing around to have a laugh at my expense?" He turns to Welcome. "Right four-eyes?"

Welcome moves his hand to his chest.

"Uh," he groans. "I'm wounded."

"Look, Blazes," says Adrian "For starters, let's try it."

Boylan whirls.

"For starters?"

Welcome covers his ears.

"Don't yell," he exclaims.

Boylan looks at Welcome, shakes his head at the covered ears, turns back to Adrian, seated below him.

"I don't know, Adrian. What's this all about? You really believe this stuff? Astral planes, trance channelers. Ghosts? Spirits? What're you doing? Where're you going?"

Adrian smiles.

"Who knows?" he responds. "But listen to this." He winks at Welcome; they have him now. "Andy and I found this Ouija board at a yard sale."

"So? I already know that."

"I think we were meant to find it."

Boylan smacks his head.

"Fruit of the loom," he says, voice raised.

"No, seriously. We were. I know it," asserts Adrian. "I really do. It was no accident. You've got to believe that, Blazes. It wasn't. It was there, waiting."

"What makes you so sure?"

Adrian stands.

"I can feel it. Ever since that board came in here," he says. "Something's changed."

"Your head, more than likely."

Welcome laughs.

"There's a reason Andy and I came by that board," persists Adrian. "We gotta find out."

Boylan looks at the board.

"Can I pick this up?"

Adrian reaches over and hands it to him.

"Looks pretty ordinary to me," comments Blazes, studying the flat piece of wood in his hand. "Heavier than I'd've thought."

"Right," from Adrian. "You see?"

"See what? So it's heavy."

"Most of them are light," counters Adrian.

Boylan shakes his head, hands the board back to Adrian. "What're you? An expert?"

Adrian shrugs, sits back down.

"I've been doing some reading."

Boylan chuckles.

"Good. Keep at it."

He begins to walk away.

"What do you say?" asks Adrian, casting a concerned look in Welcome's direction. Boylan is not interested at all. Failure. He wants the three of them, not two, or one. He needs at least two. But two won't do. Something tells him he needs three, as if three were a kind of talisman or magic number. "OK, screw it," he mutters. "I'll throw the board away."

Welcome, surprised at this, adds a well-thought-out remark of his own. He sits up to deliver it.

"Maybe he's afraid."

Boylan stops at the door. He turns around and walks to the bed and looks down at Welcome, who has not moved an inch and who stares up at him from behind glasses that magnify the size of his brown eyes. Boylan is pinned by pupils the size of billiard balls.

"I was waiting for that," he says. He looks at Adrian and smiles. "Very good. The two of you. Worked well." He shrugs. "How can I refuse?" He laughs. "Either I'm a coward," he declares, "or, what was it you said, Adrian? I have no intellectual curiosity." He frowns. "I got news. I've as much of that as either of you. Or more. And as for guts, ha." He walks to the desk, looks at the board. "Looks like me and you have some business." He turns to Adrian. "I still don't believe a bit of this." He smiles. "When do we start?"

19

Adrian exults: a fair to end all fairs. The three boys stand at the beginning of the long walk that leads to the armory, cutting across the great green- and leaf-covered lawn. At the end of the walk the armory like a gray stone pyramid rises in cynosure, almost medieval. There is something foreboding about this monolith. There are pennants lining the walk and their bright colors offset somewhat the grayness of the building, giving off notes of cheer. They ripple in the autumn breeze. On the lawn there are jugglers, some of them students from MIT, where there is a juggling club, some of them nearby citizens called out from retirement. A long-haired troubadour plays an Irish song on a mandolin, red dogs run, glisten in the sun, children shout and chase after them under a blue October sky that seems to smile in welcome. They walk. People are holding signs, handing out cards. It is like an election. It is an election, a vote for everything lost and gone: magic, alchemy, chiromancy, djinns, haruspices, malocchio, spells, divination, prediction, the life of spirits. The colored flags wave and flap, pointing toward the armory.

"Isn't this something?" inquires Adrian, passing under flying pennants, looking back to see what their message is, if there is one.

"It sure is," says Boylan, surveying the crowd. "You wouldn't think people would come out for something like this. Must be some kind of disease."

Adrian gives him a sharp jab.

"Good behavior, Boylan." He laughs. "Besides, we might learn something here."

"Exactly what I'm afraid of," Boylan says, stepping aside for a small tow-headed child chasing a dog. "The twentieth century." He opens his arms. "Going backwards."

"History could be circular," offers Welcome.

Boylan stops walking, turns around.

"Might even be a lie."

Adrian laughs, excited.

"The truth is all around us."

Boylan raises his eyes to the sky.

"Beyond saving," he says.

They move along. At the door, under the great arch, they each pass two dollars to a gaunt old man in a leather apron with gold teeth in his mouth. They move through the arch. They hear music, more mandolins and a violin and a woman's voice singing in what seems to be French, but then seems to be English. The hall is filled with people and the noise, footsteps and voices, music, clings to the old walls and echoes, caroms down at them. There are two rows of booths, one to the left, one to the right, the length of the armory. Signs point the way: TAPESTRIES, TAROT, PALM READING, NORTH SHORE QUILTERS EXHIBIT, MEEKS AND MAGIC.

"That sounds interesting," says Adrian, pointing at the sign. "I wonder what a meek is."

"What you should be," laughs Blazes.

"All for one and one for all, or do we split up and go off on our own?" asks Welcome, fingering a woolen shawl at the nearest stand. "This is beautiful," he comments, letting go.

"Spun by the fates," says Boylan. "A real bargain. Your life in wool. Go for it."

Welcome eyes him quizzically.

"My life would be worth reading."

Boylan curls his lip into a sneer.

"I doubt it."

The three of them begin to walk down the row of booths to the right. Boylan is in the lead. He touches everything, tries on hats and masks and grins at his reflection in the glass, looking every inch the Irishman with his red hair and green eyes. He plays with castanets, toys with parakeets in their cages, inquires the price and threatens to buy one for Adrian, but only if it "sings." At a game booth he throws fifteen darts for a dollar at red and yellow balloons, behind one of which is a gift certificate for a kiss from a guaranteed princess. "Show me the princess," he says, breaking eleven balloons and drawing a crowd.

"Not your lucky day," smiles the blond behind the counter. "Quite an eye you have."

"He's our star pitcher," says Welcome.

"Oh, really?" she remarks, beginning to replace the balloons Boylan has broken. "Maybe he should try again."

"No thanks," from Boylan.

Adrian steps forward.

"I'll have a turn."

Boylan steps aside to give him room.

"Right with you," she says, finishing up. She gives the wheel behind the balloons a vigorous spin, walks up to Adrian and takes his dollar and gets out of the way. "All yours."

Boylan folds his arms.

Adrian finds it harder to hit the balloons than he thought. He misses the first four, but hits the next three, misses another, hits five in a row, misses, gets the princess on the last.

"Fixed," Boylan hisses. "Prearranged." He nods to the girl. "Tell me you never saw her before in your life."

Adrian grins, accepts the kiss certificate.

"Never."

"I'll bet," from Boylan, flapping his arms.

"Ready for another try, Irish?" she coos.

He shakes his head.

"I know when I'm licked," he says. "Besides, I don't even know what she looks like." He hesitates. "She as pretty as you?"

The woman smiles. "Judge for yourself. It's the Tarot lady."

"Ah," from Boylan.

"Maybe you should have your cards read," she suggests to Blazes. "See if there are any kisses in your future." She smiles. "Or do you plan on becoming a priest?"

Boylan is surprised.

"What makes you say that?"

"You're all from Justin Martyr," she replies. "A lot of boys out there become priests."

"I've been giving it some thought," he declares.

Replacing the balloons, she says: "All the more reason to be kissed. And quick."

"How do you think she knew we were from Justin Martyr?" asks Adrian.

Welcome sighs.

"Look at us. Our hair is short. We sparkle. We smell of knowledge. Where else would we be from?"

"We don't *have* to be from Justin Martyr."

"Sure we do," declares Boylan, wheeling about. "And don't for a minute think you're going to tell us she knew because she had magic power. We look like prep school boys." He thumps Adrian's chest.

They walk around a man dressed as a pardoner, walk around a group of nuns standing before a hurdy-gurdy man.

"Wait," says Boylan.

Boylan goes back, bends down and jabbers at the monkey. The monkey jabbers back, knocking the orange fez from his head. Boylan retrieves the fez, hands it back to the monkey. The monkey takes it, puts it back on and holds out his cup. Boylan roars, drops in a quarter.

"What was that all about?" asks Adrian.

"I had to see if they were really nuns," answers Blazes. "I think they were."

"How can you be sure?" inquires Andrew, who had to admit he was surprised to see three nuns at a psychic fair.

"Their eyes," replies Boylan. "Serenity."

"Ah," from Welcome, who knows the look.

"Come on," suggests Adrian. "There's lots to see."

20

Folk singers, Baroque horns, minstrels, Punch and Judy, rude wandering humorists, food stands, pets for sale: parakeets, canaries, cats, gerbils and tamed skunks for the home, ducks and geese, a mock confessional where all sins are absolved for a dollar, "no questions asked," a one-act play on the Resurrection in a makeshift theater set up at the far end of the hall, a possessed dog and a bogus priest delivering rank heresies from a pulpit, the pardoner buttonholing fair-goers with his tall tales and promises of indulgences for fifty cents.

"A good cause," he says. "Monument to the druids."

"What next?" inquires Boylan.

"I don't know," says Adrian. "What do you want to do?"

"We could see you get that kiss."

"Save that for last," says Welcome. "I think we should end on a high note."

"Right," from Boylan. "Adrian's first kiss."

Adrian swings, misses the artfully dodging red head. Welcome, in the lead, stops at an astrology booth, smiles at the woman sitting in a chair. She smiles back, but he decides against having his sign worked out for him and walks over to a game booth.

"Go ahead, kid," offers a man in an apron. "Get three balls in a basket, win yourself a doll."

Welcome looks at the doll.

"No, thanks."

They move at separate paces now, settling in. Boylan concentrates on the games, at which he does well. Welcome walks around in a dream. He is impressed with the fair, secretly thanks Adrian for suggesting it. He half wishes the armory had a glass roof so at night the stars could shine and make the two rows of booths a medieval village with torches for light, games of chance, revels. He wants it open so the air could come in and make it more real, medieval. All from the past, these discarded beliefs. He wonders: were they as real to them as ours are to us?

"Off on your own."

Andrew turns around, sees Adrian smiling before him. There is happiness in his face.

"Having a good time?" Welcome asks.

"The best," he replies. "Come on. There's something I want you to see."

Adrian tugs on his sleeve, half drags him to a point of vantage where they can see Boylan seated at the Tarot table, studying intently the slender hand putting down the cards. Wands, cups, swords, pentacles—answer to diamonds, cups or spades; swords and wands—answering to clubs; pentacles, answering to hearts. King, queen, knight, knave, all under the watchful weighty eye of bulky Boylan.

"Unbelievable," comments Welcome.

"That's not all. Look at her."

He stares. The two of them stare at a young woman turning over the cards. Dark hair, dark eyes, skin like ivory.

She sees them, looks up, no smile. Her eyes go from Welcome to Adrian, stay with Adrian.

"A goddess," exclaims Welcome under his breath.

Adrian laughs, holds up his certificate for Welcome to see.

"A princess too."

"That's right!" yelps Welcome, racing off.

"Where you going?"

Welcome raises his right hand, makes a frantic motion.

"Darts."

"Palms up."

Adrian extends both hands.

"Which do you use most?"

"Excuse me?" from him.

"Are you right-handed or left-handed?"

"Right."

"Give me your hand."

Adrian delivers his hand to hers. He sees secrets in her hooded eyes, her dress, the perfume that hangs like a barrier between them. She has worried eyes and from her hands he notices she smokes. Her grip is cool, papery, dry. He waits. What will she tell him?

"The finger of fate," he says.

She looks up from his palm. "True enough." Down to the hand. "You have a nice elastic hand." Looking at him. "Do you know what that means?"

"No," he answers.

"It means you are not obstinate, that you have good energy. You have strength in body and mind." She returns to his palm. "Flexible," she utters, moving his fingers individually. "You are agile, intellectually." She looks in his eyes. "Your eyes, that deep blue, say so too." Back to the hand. "Your palm is square, with long, sensitive fingers. The mark of a true intellectual. Do you go to Justin Martyr?"

"Yes."

"I thought as much," she declares. "You take palms seriously." A pause. "More people should. What is written in the palm is what is written in the blood, the genes. And moreover," she points, "after these internal elements have been exposed to life outside." Looking into his eyes. "The palm is the heart plus the world."

"Ah," from Adrian.

"Your palm tells me you are air and water in the same house."

"Is that good?"

"Yes and no," she replies. "It can be controlled." She looks up from his palm. "Do your moods swing a lot?"

Adrian shrugs.

"Sometimes."

"You will have to watch that," she cautions him. "You have a tendency to be impetuous, heedless. Fortunately for you, there is more air in your lines. Much more air. Your head line," she continues, touching him with her finger, "is sensitive. I'd say you are water-governed there. Look," she orders. "See the way the head line,"—she draws with her finger—"curves down toward the mount of the moon?

That's imagination. You have a vivid imagination, which is the best aspect to get from the sensitive hand. Other qualities may come by default, the moodiness, volatility associated with water, as opposed to air, which seeks order, explanation." She looks up from his hand. "I can honestly say I have never seen these two elements so eloquently blended in one hand. A hand, usually, is one or the other."

"What does it mean?"

"You would make a good explorer, but a bad hunter."

"Ah," from Adrian, who does not understand.

"Let's look further," she says, giving his hand a pleasant squeeze. "A good line of life, long. Lots of energy, which springs from the air in you. Your life line begins at the head line, which is good. If it began further up, at the mount of Jupiter," she touches him there, "it would indicate calculation. I am happy to report that is not true in your case." She smiles. "The lines of the head and heart. Your head line is long, lovely. A good sign."

"Of what?" presses Adrian.

"Let us go on," she says, ignoring the question. "The ideal head line is a bit more balanced than yours, although as I said, the line is impressive. Your heart line runs clear and strong between the fingers of Jupiter and Saturn." She looks up. "You will have a good love life. Maybe very good, extraordinary."

"I never had any doubt."

She smiles, looks hard at his palm.

"Now for your line of fate." She traces the line with her index finger. "Your fate line is what I would expect in a hand such as yours, unusual as it may be. See the line? How delicate it is? Clear, long, uninterrupted, but delicate. Ideally it would be stronger, more pronounced. You tend to vacillate, which is in keeping with the water in you. You also do not adapt as well as a person with your intelligence should." She releases the hand. "Overall, an excellent hand, one that well mirrors what is inside you. As do all hands. You are very smart and the air," she declares, recapturing his hand, "which is predominant in you is kept from completely dominating by the presence of water, which I've explained." Letting go. "Watch yourself," she tells him. "Be careful."

"Thank you."

She takes his hand a last time, looks. He does not want to let her go, her touch feels so fine, sensual. Her eyes seem less hooded, more open. There is a clearness he missed. He smiles and takes back his hand.

"A beautiful hand," she sums up, looking up at Adrian who stands looking down at her. "Live up to it."

21

The search for Boylan is on. Beginning at the pet booth, Adrian and Andrew look into one booth after another. When they get half-way through the hall, they agree to split up and meet at the theater. Welcome takes the left, Adrian the right.

Adrian searches for one thing: red hair. If he sees red hair, he pays closer attention. As he scans the crowd, he realizes not many people have red hair, which is a beneficence. Although it is getting late in the day, the armory is still filled with people, noise. He moves deftly from exhibit to exhibit, ducking arms, elbows, sidestepping and avoiding children, listening all the while for the sound of Boylan's booming voice. He hears it when he gets to the hurdy-gurdy man with the orange-capped monkey at the end of a long chain. Boylan is there, pitching pennies at the monkey, who runs for them, chattering, his fez askew, a small crowd urging them on.

"We've been looking for you."

Boylan looks up.

"Well then. You found me."

"We have to meet Andy at the theater."

"And take me from my monkey? Watch this."

He tosses a penny at the cup. It hits the rim, a good shot, but tumbles out and falls to the floor, bouncing before coming to a stop. The monkey cries, moves to it, a tiny ape, picks it up and puts it in the cup. It looks up, tilts its head, chattering at Boylan, who laughs and puts his hand into his pocket looking for change.

"I'm out," he says to Adrian. "Lucky for you." He waves to the hurdy-gurdy man, who nods, grinding away on 'Meet Me in St.

Louis'. "My father used to play that song on a harmonica when I was a kid."

"He did?"

"Would I lie?"

Adrian connects with a jab to the elbow.

"For being smart."

"He was pretty good, my father," continues Blazes. "Nowadays he might have ended up in a band, but back then it was impossible. When I tumbled out of my mother, all his dreams departed."

Adrian lets it pass, looks at Boylan.

"What did the Tarot lady say to you?"

Boylan beams.

"Told me I would not play professional baseball," he replies, then adds glumly, "she also said I was in for some terrible times in the not too distant future."

"How not too distant?"

"Cards didn't say," replies Blazes. "Not for ten years or so, maybe a bit longer."

"That's not the near future," corrects Adrian.

Boylan snaps his fingers.

"Time goes by like that," he declares. "Already I can feel the future breathing down my neck. Time is speeding up. Summers are faster. Everything's shrinking."

"It's all relative," says Adrian.

Boylan disagrees.

"It's absolute as far as I'm concerned." He smiles. "Better practice being nice to me, or I won't help with the Ouija board."

"You can't back out now."

"I'm not saying I will," asserts Boylan. "But you had better be kind. I've just had some bad news."

"You're not telling me you believe it."

Boylan raises his hands, opens them.

"Why not?"

"It's superstitious," says Adrian. "The future can't be predicted. We have free will."

"Sez you. I'm not so sure."

"Since when?"

"Since Marian, the Tarot lady, told me bad things were in store," answers Boylan. "One look into those blue eyes took care of me. Believe me, she has the power."

Adrian studies him, uncertain.

"Bullshit."

Boylan crosses his heart.

"Cross my heart."

"You're a liar."

"I believe," he says. "I believe."

"In what?"

"The cards, the board, anything you want. I've come over to the occult. I'm smitten. Get me some garlic."

Adrian laughs, shakes his head.

They reach the theater and see Welcome sitting in back, watching a magic show with puppets. They stand and watch and when the show is over applaud with the rest and wait for Welcome to notice them. He does and stands and joins them and together the three find empty chairs along the wall and sit down. They have been on their feet all day.

"How'd the cards go?" asks Welcome.

"You don't want to know," answers Blazes.

"He has five days to live," says Adrian. "It's already started. The germ's inside him, growing. His head's going soft." He looks at his watch. "Any minute his hair should start to fall out. In clumps."

"I don't believe it," gasps Welcome.

Adrian, Boylan look in surprise.

"What?"

"There," points Welcome. "Look."

They follow his finger. At the Tarot booth, hugging and talking like long lost friends, Mister Sweeney and Marian, the long-haired, dark-eyed lady with the cards.

22

"What would Sweeney be doing here?" asks Boylan.

Welcome shakes his head, adjusts his glasses.

"Who knows?"

Adrian cannot take his eyes from them. Sweeney, animated now in conversation, making her laugh. He can hear her laugh, like the notes of a bird on a roof. Sweeney takes her hand, pumps it, telling her a story that keeps her laughing.

"I wonder what he's saying to her," he muses.

Boylan gives Adrian a sharp jab.

"Go get your kiss. Find out."

Adrian is glum. He is happy at having won the ticket, uncertain if he ever would have presented it to her, but confused now as to what to do. He has been challenged. He has a right to the kiss.

"I wonder if Sweeney dabbles in magic," offers long-nosed Welcome. He looks at the them. "We haven't seen a single person from school. Only Sweeney!" His eyes, staring hard. "What does that tell you?"

Boylan curls his lip at Welcome.

"How about that they happen to be friends. He heard she was going to be here. He comes to say hello." Smiles. "No magic in that."

Adrian wonders, still watching the two. Boylan could be right, but he could be wrong. He tries to read something in Sweeney's face, then Marian's. Nothing. They do look like friends.

"Do you think they're in love?" he asks.

They watch, then:

"*That's* hard to tell," says Boylan. "She can't be more than thirty, if she's that old. How old is Sweeney?"

"Somewhere in his forties," supplies Welcome.

"Early forties."

Boylan turns.

"I think Adrian's right," he says. "Sweeney tends to look a bit older than he actually is. *And*—he's still working toward his Ph.D."

"Those can take forever."

Boylan laughs at Adrian.

"That kind of time Sweeney doesn't have."

Boylan circles Adrian with his right arm.

"Kiss, kiss." He smacks his lips. "She's all yours. Take her away." He squeezes.

Adrian frees himself. Time to make a move. He steels himself, about to get up, falls back into his chair.

"Well?" from Andrew.

"I don't have to do it *right now*," he says.

"Seems to me," says Boylan, looking him directly in the eyes, "the fair is here today and tomorrow. You plan on coming out again? It's a long walk."

Adrian knits his brow.

"It's now or never," urges Boylan.

Adrian fingers the ticket in his pocket. More truth from Boylan. But does he want to? Does he have to? He is about to get up—what can Sweeney say?—when a sigh from Welcome stops him.

"Saved," says Blazes.

He looks. Marian has been replaced at the Tarot table by the palm reader and Sweeney and Marian, arm in arm, are walking off in the other direction. A handsome couple.

"Don't you think we should say hello to Mr. Sweeney?" asks Welcome. "I don't see why not."

Boylan nods.

"Words of wisdom."

Boylan and Welcome stand.

"Come on, Adrian. Let's go find old Sweeney. Say hello." Blazes winks. "Maybe we can even find out what brought him here. You know, the direct approach." He laughs, turns toward the palm reader.

"You could go up and kiss her." Grabs Adrian by the arm, tugs him to his feet. "Might even turn her into a princess."

They do not find Sweeney, or the woman. It is as if they had vanished, or never been there at all. They are surprised at this. Although the armory is cavernous and filled with exhibits, the crowd has begun to thin. How could Sweeney disappear?

"The gray ghost himself," comments Boylan.

"Where could he have gone?" asks Welcome. "He can't have disappeared."

"There may be more to this than meets the eye," offers Boylan. "Maybe he is some kind of spook. We know she is." Smiles. "The way her eyes kneaded my soul. She had the power, that's for sure. But Sweeney—what does he do? Is he a warlock? Vampire?" Clapping his hands, "That's it! Vampire. That's why he looks older than he is. He's low on blood."

Adrian watches Boylan.

"Could be," says Welcome. "Could very well be."

Adrian looks up at Welcome.

"How tall are you?"

Welcome is puzzled at the line of questioning.

"5'11," he answers.

"Act your height. Stop humoring him."

"Who's humoring?"

Boylan yawns, flops into a chair near the exit.

"Anytime you're ready."

Adrian stands before him, looks down at his friend.

"Admit it," he says. "You had a good time."

Boylan flashes a smile, winks.

"I'll admit it. I had a great time, especially with the monkey."

"The beginning of a beautiful relationship," laughs Welcome.

Boylan swivels to face him.

"The pain you could come to, talking like that. Don't you understand? Aren't you afraid?"

Welcome sniffs, pushes up his glasses.

"You are a potato head. The spuds have made you strong, I'll admit that." Tapping his head, "They've also made you thick. Like bad chowder."

Boylan throws back his head and laughs.

"You are going to die." He leans forward. "A thousand times, Welcome. Each time worse than before." He laughs. "Death. Wait'll we get back. When we're alone."

"Not tonight," says Welcome. "Tonight we fly."

"Oh, right," from Boylan. "Uncharted seas."

Adrian, smiling and listening, has been looking up at the quilts lining the walls. They are so varied, so colorful. He leaves his friends and walks to the wall nearest him and looks up at a quilt. A woman's name, a style—"Clay's Choice"—words he doesn't understand: trapunto, appliqué, a date. He moves to the next, and the next and stops before a third that simply fascinates. A story being told. "Memory Quilt," Prudence Doucet, 1940? He steps up, reads.

23

They wait for Welcome, the scribe. Boylan is in his bed, reading a detective novel, Adrian in his, reading a paperback on the Ouija board. He is learning about circumstances, how important they can be. He puts down the book, turns to Boylan and asks, "Do we have any candles?"

Boylan finishes the sentence he is reading, lets the book glide to his chest. There is a puzzled look on his face.

"I don't think so."

"Damn," mutters Adrian.

"Where is the amanuensis?" asks Blazes, taking up his novel. "Is he afraid of the old *mano a mano*?" He laughs, begins to read. "Calling me a potato head. That took guts."

"Truth hurts," offers Adrian, moving his eyes from the ceiling to the window, where he imagines banners flying, a long walk, an armory rising from the ground like a monolith.

His reverie is interrupted by a knock on the door.

"Abandon all hope," yells Boylan.

"It's open," calls out Adrian.

In comes Welcome, holding a candelabrum.

"Spectacular!" Adrian exclaims. "Right there on the table." He stands up. "What made you think of that?"

Welcome looks out superciliously from behind his horn-rimmed glasses after placing the candelabrum near the Ouija board.

"You can't use the Ouija board without candlelight," he declares sonorously. "First things first."

"If the monks see the flames, we'll get expelled," warns Boylan. "If that happens, Andy, you'll spend the rest of your life in a coma."

Welcome looks at Adrian.

"Is he *really* necessary?"

Boylan jumps up from the bed.

"Of course I am," he hisses at Welcome. "You think anyone would believe you, or Adrian? You need me for balance."

"A flat head like you?"

Boylan shakes his head.

"Death has many faces, my friend."

They laugh. Adrian moves to the window, pulls down the shade. The board is open on the table, the planchette in the center. When the shade is down, he walks to the light switch.

"Light the candles, Andy."

Welcome takes out a pack of matches and lights the three white candles. Sulphur, smoke, three flickers. Adrian shuts off the light. Now there are only candles, shadows on the wall.

"Ready?" asks Adrian.

"Wait," from Boylan. "We have to do this right. Set the mood. I have a tape I want to play."

"Not now," groans Adrian.

"Sit," orders Blazes, stepping up to his reel to reel tape deck. "Just the first two minutes. We don't have to listen to the whole thing." He pushes a button, lights glow softly, on comes Stravinsky's 'Firebird'.

"Jesus," says Welcome, taking a seat. He looks down at the board wide-eyed.

Boylan smiles at the controls.

"Have to make the spirits feel at home."

The bass fiddles, followed by grim horns, play; the candles seem to flicker to the beat of the music. Adrian finds himself keeping time and he wonders at the movement of the flames.

"All right," says Blazes.

He turns off the tape deck and sits down.

"The tripod must have a name," Adrian declares.

"Who says?" from Boylan.

"The book I was reading. If we call it by a name, or think of it by a name, there's a better chance the spirits will respond."

"What's in a name?" smiles Blazes.

"Come on, Blazes," complains Adrian. "This is *serious*. We won't get anywhere if we keep fooling around."

Boylan, eyes on the tripod.

"We could call it Igor."

Welcome smiles. Adrian smiles in spite of himself.

"No," he says. "The name is Melchior."

"Why not Igor?" from Boylan.

Adrian glares at him.

"I think we should think for a minute about what we are doing," he suggests. "Get our heads clear, open our minds. We are trying to reach the other side. We have to believe we can do it."

"Who's driving?" asks Boylan.

Adrian sighs.

"Please, Blazes. You're ruining it."

"All right, all right. I'll just watch."

"Good," from Adrian. "Ready, Andy?"

Welcome shows his pencil, the yellow pad of paper he will use to take down the letters. He nods yes to Adrian, then looks down at the planchette.

Adrian gently touches the small tripod, closing his eyes. He is thinking hard, seeing pennants, colors. He strains to hear a mythic owl, rustling leaves. He takes a deep breath.

"Is anybody there?"

He waits. Nothing happens.

He tries again.

"Is anybody there?"

A tremor, a tightening. The tripod? Adrian? His fingers, light and delicate, lead—are led?—to letters. Eyes closed, he does not see, feels instead the hidden strings of power pulling him, his hands, toward the alphabet. He can hear the sound of the planchette moving—he has heard it before. When? He is aware of the beating of his heart, he senses that his pulse is rising. The tripod stops.

"Andy?" he asks, keeping his eyes closed.

"Yes," answers Welcome, thickly. "Melchior said yes."

A stillness, silence, then:

"Who are you?"

Nothing. Then again the tremor, the sense of being pulled by unseen strings. Many letters this time.

"Andy?"

No response.

Adrian opens his eyes, looks at Andrew, then down at the yellow pad next to the Ouija board. The candles flicker, seem to move to an unfelt breeze. They stare down, incredulous.

O HELLP ME

1964

24

Sweeney watched Marian drink her tea.

"Good?"

She let the cup glide to the saucer.

"Delicious. What is it?"

Sweeney beamed.

"Earl Grey," he answered. "My new discovery. It's English. I suppose that's why it's so good. All that's left of colonialism. Fine blends from faraway places." He picked up the wrapper. "A select blend of black teas and natural bergamont." He looked up. "What's bergamont?"

She shook her head.

"Sounds French."

"In English tea? Marian, they conquered the world for this stuff. Why would they put anything French into it?" He peered down at the label. "Would go against the grain, no?"

She smiled.

"Is that why I'm here? To study tea bags?"

He leaned forward and put his hand on her arm.

"No, of course not. I asked you simply as one friend to another," he replied. "You know that. I want you to see the house. I wanted to see you. We haven't seen each other in how long? Five years? How long has it been? Can you even remember?"

A serious look crossed her face.

"Ah, yes," said Sweeney, catching on immediately. "Not that I forgot." He took his hand from her arm. "Those things you don't forget, *ever*. I just didn't think."

"It's all right, Jim."

"I should've realized," he went on. "It would've been the funeral. What else?" He ran his hand through his gray hair. He forced a smile. "But—before that—when was it?"

"Years," she replied. "New York. We went to that play."

"What play? Do you remember?"

She picked up her cup.

"*My Fair Lady.*"

"You remembered," he exclaimed, a real smile on his face. "My teaching *did* accomplish something."

She disagreed.

"Sorry to puncture your balloon, sir. I always liked the theater." She paused. "On my own. Now, tell me about the house. I want to hear everything. How you stole it from the people you bought it from. How they were crazy enough to leave. How you tricked them." She moved her chair closer to the kitchen table. "Tell me. Everything. What kind of magic you used."

Both of them smiled, at ease with one another. Sweeney had worried, awaiting her arrival, that the visit would not go well. He was the one who had let the contact fade and he blamed himself for it. She was the one who would always call, on his birthday, on Christmas; she was the one who would invite him down to New York, where she worked at an ad agency. He would always decline. But the visit was going well. Not a hitch. They still got along, he could see that. There was this bond, hard to explain but there, between the former teaching fellow at Princeton and his former student. The bond made him happy. It was the bond, after all, that made it possible for him to call, to ask her up. And up she came, this beautiful, long-haired, even mysterious woman.

"Let's move to the living room," he suggested. "I'll get a fire going. We'll talk."

They left the kitchen, taking their tea with them. Sweeney got the fire going in no time, the one thing he thought he did as well as anyone in the world. Sweeney, fire starter. He sat in the red chair, she sat across from him on the couch. A log crackled, the air became pleasantly acrid.

"It's good to see you, Jim," she said.

Sweeney nodded.

"I feel the same way. I'm so glad you could come on such short notice," he said, teacup in hand. "It really means a lot."

Marian smiled, made no reply, let her eyes wander to the shelf of books kept apart from the other volumes lining the walls. The titles she knew by heart, many of them part of her own library, but that Sweeney should have them came as a surprise. He wasn't like her. He didn't believe what she believed. She went down a row: *Incidents of My Life*, D. D. Home; *The Coming of the Faires*, A. Conan Doyle; *Mediumship and Its Development*, W. H. Bach; *Through the Magic Door*, Doyle again; *Some New Evidence for Human Survival*, Drayton Thomas; Podmore's *Modern Spiritualism*; *Apparitions*, by G.N.M. Tyrrell; *Phantasms of the Living*, Guny, Meyer and Podmore. There were others, dozens of them, mostly in old hardcover editions, but some in dog-eared paperback. Her eyes went back to Sweeney.

"What's with the books?"

Sweeney, facing her, turned instinctively to the shelf.

"You noticed." He turned back to her. "I thought you'd be pleased."

She adjusted the teacup in the saucer, then sat back on the couch. When she looked up at him, Sweeney could see her face was filled with questions, that there were clouds gathering.

"This is pathetic," she said, a touch of anger in her voice.

"What?" asked Sweeney, genuinely puzzled.

She looked up at the titles again.

"These books, Jim." She stared at him. "The idea for my visit was really 'spontaneous.' I can see that now. See the house." She paused. "Haven't seen it yet. I don't know what's gotten into you, Jim, but I don't like it."

"What're you talking about, Marian? What's wrong?"

"Let's be honest, Jim. I *do* care about you. That's why I'm upset. I know why you asked me up here." She frowned slightly. "Don't you think I would've come? You might have been direct. There was no need for subterfuge."

"I do want you to see the house," interrupted Sweeney.

"I'm sure you do," she said. "But you want something else." She paused. "It's not hard to figure out, Jim. In the letters you've been telling me how bad it's been."

A shudder passed over Sweeney.

"You've no idea," he said. "I can't seem to get things straight. Half the time I think I'm losing my mind." He reached for a pipe sitting in an ashtray, began to fill it with tobacco from a nearby bag. "I'm so unhappy, Marian. So damn unhappy."

"You've got to expect that," she said, her voice so soothing. "Grief takes a long time. Part of it will never leave."

"I know that," said Sweeney, lighting a match. "I wonder if some of us just can't tackle things like death. Look at me. I feel like a fool, an old fool."

"You are *not* old."

He puffed on the pipe.

"I feel old, Marian. My hair's all gray. My bones are beginning to ache." He leaned forward. "I'm actually starting to resent the boys. For their youth. I love them. I love what I'm doing, but I can't stop these feelings, this sense that life has simply passed me by."

"Didn't this start when your mother passed away?"

He sighed.

"I don't even know that anymore," he declared. "Once your pins get knocked out from under you, you don't know a thing. I used to be something of an absolutist. I feel like a mosaic now, a crazed painting. I half expect one of the students to come up and ask me if I've noticed I've begun to disintegrate."

"You look fine to me, Jim," she said, which wasn't true. When he met her at the airport the first thing she noticed was how worn down he looked.

A small black cat with white paws entered the room and curled up at Marian's feet.

"Oliver," offered Sweeney. "My boon companion."

Marian reached down.

"Come here, sweetie."

Sweeney, puffing his pipe, studied Marian as she petted the cat. He could see that she was still beautiful, with dark eyes and wonderful dark brown hair, so dark it was almost black. Why had she never married? He wondered. A woman that pretty.

"Marian, why do you think it's neurotic in me to manifest an interest in the occult, yet perfectly normal for you?"

"I didn't say it was neurotic."

"You said pathetic," he stated. "The same thing."

She stopped petting the cat.

"This is what happens, Jim. Someone close to us dies, someone we love deeply. Our whole world ends. Nothing has any meaning. We can't get up in the morning, we can't get to sleep at night." She paused, looked into Sweeney's eyes. "You will return to normal. Believe me, you will. Things will balance out. There'll be a change, but you'll be able to manage."

"I don't want to manage," Sweeney said. "I want things to be right. I want to be in control again."

She smiled, still looking into his eyes.

"Be patient."

He frowned.

"Don't you think I have been?" he inquired, his voice tired. He put down the pipe. "Listen. I have a story to tell. You can be the judge of it." He paused, collected his thoughts. "About a year and a half ago, two men, one who went by the name of Rufus, paid me a visit. I only saw the one who came to the door, Rufus. He was a little man, a dwarf. His companion was huge, a great big hulk, but he stayed way back in the shadows at the end of the walk. I never got a good look at him. Anyway, Rufus asked me if I was a Doucet."

"Who's Doucet?"

"The lady I bought the house from."

Marian nodded.

"OK."

"Funny thing about her," continued Sweeney, reaching for the pipe, "is that we never met. A fact that seemed to amuse the dwarf no end." He took a puff on the pipe. "Rufus wanted to talk to her. He told me they were friends." He stopped. "I don't believe him. I think he meant her harm."

"What makes you think that?"

Sweeney leaned forward in the red chair.

"There was something very menacing about those two," he said, "especially the dwarf. A hard little man."

"You don't think you were imagining things."

Sweeney sat back.

"I thought that for a while," he replied. "Who wouldn't? But then," he paused, "other things have happened. I've had the distinct impression the house has been visited when I'm not here. Many times it seemed to me something was just a bit different from the way I left it when I took off for school in the morning." He drew on the pipe, filling the air with smoke. A log crackled in the fire. "It could've been me. Paranoia." He leaned forward again.

"That's probably the explanation."

Sweeney nodded.

"You would've thought. Occam's Razor." He shook his head. "But lately, there's been something else."

"What?"

"At night I hear strange sounds."

She frowned.

"Like what?"

He took a long puff on the pipe.

"Cries," he answered. "Whimpering. Every now and then a groan."

She gave him a puzzled look.

"You think the house is haunted?"

Sweeney shook his head.

"I didn't say that," he declared. "I don't know what's going on." He paused. "I tell you one thing. It can scare the hell out of you."

It was Marian's turn to nod.

"Is that why you asked me up?" She smiled. "To check the house for ghosts?"

Sweeney sighed.

"No, Marian, no." He looked at her. "There's one more thing." He stood up, holding the pipe. He crossed the room and stopped in front of the china cabinet and opened the top drawer. He reached in and removed the Ouija board he had found the year before and walked back and presented it to Marian.

"It's a Ouija board."

"Right," said Sweeney.

She looked at the board, ran her fingers over the smooth surface, and looked back up at Sweeney, who hovered over her.

"This is a very old board."

Sweeney nodded.

"I know," he said. "I found it in the attic." He looked at the letters himself. "In a secret compartment."

Marian looked down again at the board in her lap. She touched the "Yes" and the "No" and then moved her fingers to the moon and the sun. Something was coming up from the board, something she could feel. She looked again at Sweeney and the second she took her eyes from the board she felt a stab of icy coldness in her right hand so severe it almost made her cry out. At her feet, the cat began to growl.

"Jim," she said.

"Yes?" His eyes were cold. "What?"

Her lips were trembling.

"Something is wrong."

25

Sweeney turned at the gate to look back at the house.

"It's a nice house," Marian said.

He nodded, opened the gate. They stepped outside.

"At least it was," said Sweeney.

"Still *is*," she insisted, taking his arm. "Maybe what I felt from the board was a mistake—on my part. That's happened before, I think. I get a picture and it's all wrong."

"What picture did you get from the board?"

"That cold feeling," she remarked. "No picture, really."

"Hmmm," Sweeney mused, disconcerted.

"The cat sensed it too, though," Marian said. "Has that happened before?"

Sweeney shook his head emphatically.

"Not to my knowledge."

"Have you been using that board?"

Sweeney smiled at her.

"Don't you need two people?"

"Not always," she replied.

"I couldn't do it alone. I'd need help," said Sweeney. "I have a suspicion too that my compatriots on the faculty would have refused me, or thought me bonkers. And I couldn't go to a student."

"Why not?"

They walked past a long, tall wall of pine trees. Crows were flying in and out, into the dark branches, hiding. Sweeney raised an eyebrow.

"They're just boys," he declared. "Besides, it would be poor form."

"You have them over for tea, right?"

Sweeney looked down into her kind, dark eyes and gave her arm a squeeze.

"Just the good ones." He raised his right hand. "Think of it, though. Take out a Ouija board when the students are over for tea?" He chuckled. "I like my job. What happens when word gets back to the Jesuits? Faculty member consorting with the dead? Or even thinking he can."

"Swear them to silence."

"These are boys, Marian. They have big mouths."

They walked along.

"Oh, look. A willow tree."

Sweeney frowned.

"Death to the home owner," he commented, making a face at the willow tree, under which was a gathering of small thin yellow leaves. "Especially if you have a septic system, which all these homes do. The willow root seeks water. Any water. They bore through concrete."

"Really? I never knew that."

"Almost any tree will do it," he said. "But the willow is in a class by itself. A real menace."

"Well, then," she laughed. "A pox on willow trees."

"Shh," said Sweeney, bringing a finger to his lips. "Not when we're alongside. Trees are quiet. Not stupid."

She laughed.

"About the board, Jim. You've had it for a year?"

"Yes."

"It's just been sitting there? In the drawer?"

Sweeney grinned.

"Far as I know."

Marian screwed up her eyes.

"What? You think your visitors were after the Ouija board?" she asked. "Then why didn't they find it?"

Sweeney shook his head.

"I didn't say that. But you agree—I've had visitors," he declared. "Good. It's a start. They were looking for something, but I don't think the board. It's been in the drawer. They would've found it."

"Then what?"

They stepped onto Decker Street, turning right.

"That we don't know—yet," he replied. "I want you to take a look at this house up here," he said, getting off the subject. "I do want to use that board." He brushed an imaginary speck from his collar. "You know, it's funny. When I found the board, I was all excited. I thought, God, this is something. But there was no one. Then, you know, school, the department. I got caught up. I never got around to it. Then, oh, a month ago I'd say, I heard this fellow on the radio."

She gave his arm a squeeze.

"Socrates Radio."

He seemed surprised.

"You're familiar with him?"

She shook her head.

"Not very. A while ago he was the talk of the town," she said. "Then he faded, went back to the West Coast. I think I recall he was going to be on one of the talk shows. He has a book out, and he's on the circuit. If he was down in New York, I'm sure he would've found his way up here."

"What do you think of him?"

She looked past his shoulder into a tree branch where there was an empty squirrel's nest. On another branch of the tree a crow sat, looking down.

"Do I believe him, you mean?"

"Yes." He followed her eyes to the tree and saw the crow. "Is he a fraud?" he asked, looking right at the bird.

She answered quickly.

"I wouldn't know."

They began walking again, slowly.

"But you're clairvoyant."

"So? You think that means I can read someone's mind?"

Sweeney looked in her eyes.

"Does it?"

She held his gaze, then looked away.

"No," she replied. "Finish telling me about Socrates Radio." She paused. "Please."

"Well," he began, "he talked about trance channeling and getting across. Voices speaking through him." He took a breath. "He sounded rational. I didn't get the idea he was a crackpot. Anyway, someone asked him about using a Ouija board. A caller. I got the impression there was something to it. He was careful about it. He kept emphasizing set and setting, the right circumstances, and the absolute need for a medium of sorts, a person with ability." Sweeney stopped walking and looked down at her. "Someone like you."

She walked ahead of him.

"Do you think, Jim," she called back, "that Socrates really speaks through him?"

Sweeney chuckled.

"I wouldn't know."

She stopped and faced him.

"For the board to work," she said, almost matter-of-factly, "you're going to have to believe. And not just that. You're going to have to believe that after we die some of us enter a kind of state, maybe not corporeal, maybe not even spiritual. A whole other world. A world cut off from us, but a world intensely involved in ours." She stared at him. "Can you believe that?"

He walked up to her, a stricken look on his face.

"I *do* believe that."

For a while they walked along, not saying anything. Then Sweeney stopped and pointed.

"Take a look."

Marian looked where he pointed and saw a tall dark brooding Victorian with an oculus window way up high in a tower at the front. Before the house, on what once was a lawn, stood a dramatically huge willow tree with long withered empty branches.

"It needs some work."

"Yes, yes," he agreed. "It's a wreck. It's abandoned. But isn't it wonderful? Can't you see the potential?" He smiled down at her. "They just don't make them like that anymore."

She took her eyes from the house, looked at him, and began to walk back down the street away from the house.

"If that's what you wanted me to see," she declared, "we've seen it." She waited for him, staring at the house while he caught up with her. "That place gives me the creeps."

26

Sweeney brought in two Queen Anne chairs from the dining room and placed them on opposite sides of the glass-topped table at which Marian sat surveying the board. She looked up when he sat himself in one of the chairs.

"Why those chairs?"

Sweeney raised an eyebrow.

"I thought if we sat in identical chairs, it might help the serendipity of the moment," he replied. "Better the odds."

Marian smiled.

"You want me to change chairs."

Sweeney nodded.

"If you would. Humor me," he said. "I've waited a long time for this. I want it to be as perfect as possible." He made himself comfortable. "I have a sense antique chairs would help."

Marian, moving into the Queen Anne chair, said, "The spirits won't be talking to the chairs."

Sweeney bowed, shifting in his seat.

"The pathetic fallacy," he said. "I know I'm a novice, but I have done some reading." His eyes went to the books. "Trithemius, Albertus Magnus, the search for the philosopher's stone."

"I've seen the books."

Sweeney nodded.

"Can we ask about the groans?"

Marian looked up from the board.

"I wonder who used this board," she said. "It is old, as I said. At least forty, fifty years." She smiled. "They don't make them like this anymore either." She paused to see if Sweeney understood the remark. He did. "So, that's a good sign."

"Great," said Sweeney.

"We're going to have to be careful," she warned. "I'm not sure about what I felt. The coldness. I don't know what it means. It could be..."

"There's some danger."

Marian, looking very serious, reached down and picked up the tripod.

"There's always some danger."

The Belle Fleur curtains were still and white and silent at the windows, the fireplace whistled away, logs crackling. There was a touch of smoke in the air, an acrid smell. It was dark outside and maybe an owl hooted or a dog barked at the moon, but the two of them heard nothing. Sweeney held the pencil tightly in his hand above the yellow pad, waiting to write down the letters. Marian whispered.

"Is anybody there?"

Her eyes were closed, her breath was even and controlled. Her fingers, lightly touching the tripod, were steady.

"Is anybody there?"

Sweeney sat as still as a cat, staring first at her closed eyes, her lips, her very white teeth. Then he looked at her hands, marveling at how steady she held them. He was watching her hands as a jolt of some kind passed through her. The tripod began to move, aimlessly, going all over the board. Then, finally, it stopped at the "Yes."

"Who?"

Sweeney watched the tripod move away from "Yes" to the first letter of the alphabet, then dart suddenly back to "Yes." Then it began to pick out the letters. He wrote them down, one at a time, not trying to make any sense of them.

"Yes," he whispered, thrilled, and wrote down on his pad the first set of letters, A V E.

"Who are you?"

The curtains began to sway. The fire began to roar. An owl hooted and shadows, fire and moonlight, danced against the walls while Marian, draped in moonlight herself, waited patiently for a reply from the planchette.

"Mother?" asked Sweeney, unable to stop himself.
The tripod shook, darted. Sweeney wrote.

MOTHER WHOSE MOTHER

"Mother?" repeated Sweeney, his eyes bright and feverish. "Is that you? It's Jim, mother. Jim."
Marian, breathing hard, felt her fingers being tugged by the tripod, almost angrily.

WHOS JIM

"Your son!"
The tripod, again.

NO SON OF MINE I AM NOT YOUR MOTHER

"Who?" whispered Marian, her face pale in the moonlight, her dark hair moving slightly in a sudden cool breeze, her eyes shut tightly in concentration. "Who?" she repeated, calmly.
The planchette trembled, picked out letters.

A V E A NO A V E L I N E

1885

27

This is what men wanted. This is what she heard. This being pushed and kneaded and hungered after. She tried to distance herself. She tried to look at herself, at what was happening, as if it were happening to someone else. She imagined herself an angel, hovering, looking down at the bed. She saw the man, naked, strong, his muscles shining in the dim light; she saw herself beneath, her arms at her sides, her hands balling and unballing. She saw her eyes looking into her other eyes in the air. She did not recognize herself. The naked woman under the naked, moving man could not be her. But it was her. She felt the man—he shuddered—and the angel disappeared. The struggle was over.

"In time, Prudence," he said, very quietly. "In time."

She did not say a word.

He sighed. "Was it that terrible for you?"

She did not move. She could not meet his eyes.

"Was it?" he repeated, still softly.

She found his eyes.

"No," she replied.

"Just 'no'?"

She found the place near the ceiling where the angel had been and kept her eyes there. If she kept her eyes on where the angel had been watching, he would stop asking questions for which she had no answer. How could she answer? This had never happened before. She heard it, with her mother. But it had never happened to her. Now it had. Now she had to think. Was there room enough in the house for this to happen again? He, she knew, would make it happen, as much as he could. He liked it. It made him feel good. It made him tremble and she knew from the way he had groaned at the end that he had it in his mind to do it again—and again. That was why he married her. So that he could have her when he wanted.

"You should get dressed," he said.

Her eyes moved from the ceiling.

"Yes," she said.

He was not unkind. He was handsome, strong. He had built this house, for her, he once said. That she did not believe. He had built the house for himself and his mad dream, the dream that said a man did not have to die if he refused the honor, that he could live, if not consciously in the blood of others, his progeny, then through force of will alone. He did not know how much she knew about the dream, how much she had heard, or been told. She knew more than he thought she knew. One day she would tell him. One day she would look in those sad knowing eyes and not be stopped. She would tell him: you did this to yourself. You took a woman who had been good to you and you destroyed her because she could not bear your children. Then you forced yourself upon her daughter, who loved you, or believed she loved you, but not the way you wanted. Then you turned her inside out and made her love the way her mother loved and then you took her for your child bride and brought her to this room and did to her what you had done to her mother so many times.

"We'll have to throw away those sheets."

Half-dressed, she turned and looked.

"Yes."

What was the word he had used? Progeny. Half-mad, half-sad eyes. Progeny. She would give him that. That was what they had just done: the act that brought progeny into the world. In return he would give her a place to live far enough from the townspeople so that their baleful stares and mutterings would not harm her. In this he was foolish. Did he think that the eyes and words of the townspeople bothered her? Would she have given in to him if they had? He should have known that for himself—she would never tell him. That was her price. Part of her price. The other part was never to tell him what he wanted her to tell him.

"Prudence," he said, from the shadows.

She stared across the room at him.

"Yes," she said.

He came to her. She stood before him, looking up into blue troubled eyes. He took her in his arms. She stiffened. He began to stroke her hair. He loved to stroke her hair.

"It had to be this way," he said, still in the same calm voice. "One day you will understand. One day you will come to me and tell me you understand." He paused, looked in her eyes. "Promise me."

"What?"

"When you understand," he said. "You'll tell me."

She looked back at him, her green eyes wide.

"I will never tell you that."

Her price. He was beginning to pay. She could see it in his eyes when she told him she would never tell him. A power. She had a power over him. That too she could see in his eyes. She was young, beautiful. He was strong, but old. Old as her mother, older. Her green eyes looked for and found his older wiser eyes. He looked back. She mocked him. In her heart she mocked him and he saw it in her eyes and she thought *good, so now you know*, and almost said, but stopped herself, that when progeny came, they would be her progeny too and then she prayed, deep in her heart, for green eyes.

28

The midwife left the room.

"You can go in now, Mr. Doucet."

He nodded, moved to the door, which the midwife had closed behind her. His hand on the knob, he asked, "Is it a boy or a girl, Mrs. Savoie?"

The old woman, busy putting away her string, and the two vials she had brought with her, did not look up when she spoke to him.

"A boy, Mr. Doucet. A healthy, baby boy."

He looked, nodded again, opened the door and went inside. He stood just inside the door, looking at the bed where his wife held in her arms a heavily wrapped infant. She smiled at the baby and then stared at him with weary eyes. Her lips were drawn, her skin pale, flushed at the cheeks. She held the child out to him.

"Your son," she said.

At the gesture he walked to the bed and took the child from her. He looked down and saw a wrinkled, scowling face, a tiny thing with clenched fists and strands of dark hair.

"Andre," he said. "His name shall be Andre."

Prudence leaned back into the pillows.

"Like yours," she said.

His eyes went from his son to his wife.

"If you like," he declared.

She laughed at this.

"There he is," she said. "Your progeny."

He looked up from the baby into her haughty mirthless eyes and knew she would never forgive him his use of the word and what he had done. He had hoped for love over time. He still hoped. But there was no love in her eyes, not even now. He did not know what he saw in her eyes. She kept them closed to him. His love for her had grown, but so had her indifference. That was all. There was a wall between them. He understood the reason, or thought he did. But she wouldn't even tell him that. She never told him anything. The price she made him pay, part of the price she made him pay. In his heart he wondered: what more?

"Prudence," he said. "This is *our* son, yours and mine." He looked down at the baby he held. "No matter what you think of me, don't forsake the child." He looked up. "Our son."

Her eyes closed, then opened.

"I'm very tired, Andrew."

Doucet moved to his wife.

"Can I get you anything?" he asked.

She smiled wanly, shook her head. He stared at her red hair, unkempt against the pillow, looked in her eyes and saw the same look he always saw. Was it contempt? He looked away and thought: no, not contempt. Her realization of the power she held over him. In her eyes he saw that she knew. She knew what she meant to him, how much he wanted her. Her power was in knowing he needed her more than she needed him—if she needed him at all. Her eyes said no. Her haughty mirthless eyes.

"I need to rest," she said.

The baby grew restive in his arms.

"What should I do?"

She held out her arms.

"Give him to me," she ordered. "He needs to be fed." She took the baby, looked up. "Leave me alone, Andrew."

He looked a last time into her eyes, bowed gracefully, turned and left the room. He closed the door. The midwife waited in the corridor. When she saw him she got up from her seat, her bag at her side.

"She'll need to be watched," she told him.

"Yes," he agreed.

"Have you made arrangements?"

He felt suddenly tired himself.

"I thought you would stay."

She shook her gray head.

"Can't do that, sir," she said. "There's babies coming all the time. I've work to do. I can stay for a bit. The night perhaps. But first light, I'm off. The Derleths over yonder have a daughter. Ask her. She'll come. I'm sure she'll come." She paused. "Unless..."

He caught her meaning.

"No," he said, quickly.

She bobbed her head, reached for something in her bag. "You'll need to be taking a walk, sir." She smiled briefly. "Tell them I said for her to come." She paused. "It will help."

There was kindness in her eyes.

"Thank you."

"You are welcome, sir," she said.

She opened the door and went inside. He stood outside the door, listening. He heard nothing. The baby had long since stopped crying, his wife was asleep. He brushed his hand through his graying hair, felt the roughness where the saber had cut and left its mark. Now the mark would be swallowed up. So be it. He closed his eyes. He imagined his wife, green-eyed, full-lipped, wanting him the way he wanted her. Was it so much to ask? He found no answer. In its place, the same response. Against his will his eyes went to the ceiling and he heard, or thought he heard, the same sound he had been hearing for years: the rocking chair.

29

She kept her own terrible secret from him. She would never let him know. Not that she had come to understand, because she had not understood. No dream was worth the price he was willing to pay. She could see his need for children. She had that need herself. He did not have to marry her. He could, should, have left, found another woman, in another town, abandoned the house, begun anew with someone else in a place far removed from Gloucester. Why Gloucester? Why her? She knew women, even in Gloucester, who would have married him. But he had to have her. His own grim well-kept secret. He had wanted her all the time. It had never been her mother. It had always been her. He took the mother to bed to take the daughter to bed. A mad scheme. She would never tell him that she knew, or how she had found out—her heart had told her. And—she had seen it in her mother's eyes.

"I hope for another son," he said, coming up behind her and taking her belly in his hands. "I can feel him."

She tried to ignore the effect of his touch, but she could not. Another terrible secret: she loved him. She could not help herself. His touch, the way he made her feel when he took her in his arms and took her to bed.

"A daughter this time," was all she said.

He too felt the change in her. She never told him, but her eyes told him: something had changed. He could feel it in the way she kissed, the way she was in bed. Not like the first night, the first time. Not like the first year. She came ardently to bed, his Prudence. She wanted him the way he wanted her. She would never tell him. That was the price. But he could bear that, and hope someday she would say the words.

"How can you tell?" he asked.

"I can tell," she replied. "I can feel, it's a girl."

He laughed softly and went outside.

Doucet would laugh now in her presence, something he had not allowed himself to do the first year of their marriage. He had kept up his guard, as she had kept up hers. She could feel, gradually, a softening in her. Was it her becoming—a woman? A mother? Or was it him and his making his need her need when he took her upstairs at night, in his arms, and lit small white candles and kissed her as the curtains blew in the breeze and the crickets chorused outside and all the jasmine bloomed? The warmth of him inside her and her warmth and her sounds and his sounds and the sounds of the outside and the sound of the silence when the act was done and together, side by side, they watched for hidden shadows in the dark. It would be perfect, if only one thing had not happened. But it had, and she believed no matter how much she tried not to, that he had made it happen and had known the minute he rode into town like a ghost or some devil, what the future entailed.

She felt a kick and gasped.

"Oh," she said to herself.

She left the kitchen and walked into the nursery where the boy, Andre, was asleep. She stepped up to the crib and reached in and brushed back his dark shiny hair that was so like his father's. She smiled when she thought of his eyes: green like hers.

"Prudence," he called from outside.

She left the baby and walked out onto the porch. She looked out, shielding her eyes from the noon sun, saw him on horseback.

"Yes?"

He looked down at her from the chestnut mare.

"I am going into town," he said. "Is there anything we need?"

She brought down her hand.

"No."

"Shall I stop at the midwife's?"

Another kick. She took in her breath.

"Tell her it will be soon," answered Prudence. "Not right away, but soon. She should ready herself for the weekend."

"I will tell her," he said.

Doucet tipped his hat, spurred the horse and rode off, raising behind him a small cloud of dust. She watched him until she could see him no more. Then she went inside, feeling the weight of the child in her womb. Over eight months. It was getting harder to move all the time. She hoped for an end to it at the weekend. A healthy baby, a girl, and no complications. In the kitchen she suddenly felt weary and took herself into the parlor and sat down. She closed her eyes.

She woke to the creaking of the rocking chair. When she looked at the ceiling she imagined she saw the old woman in the chair, knitting or talking to herself or making those strange sounds. She took a deep breath and stood up, feeling her womb. All was calm. She walked slowly to the foot of the stairs, stopped at the bottom, looked up.

"Mother," she called out.

There was no answer.

She took another deep breath and began to climb the stairs. It was harder than she thought it would be, but not so hard she couldn't make it to the top. She reached the landing, stopped, called out.

"Mother."

Still no answer.

"Oh," she moaned, feeling a pain.

She walked gradually into the shadows at the end of the hall and came to a stop outside her mother's room. She could hear the rocker, and a sort of laughter. She knocked, opened the door.

"Mother."

Her mother did not turn from the window. She rocked, faster and faster, laughing to herself. Prudence stood by the door, waiting for her to stop. But she did not stop. The laughter grew louder, the rocking even faster, until she thought the chair would break or the woman be hurled out of it, and then it stopped. Stillness filled the room. Her mother turned. Prudence could feel the cold, crazy eyes on her unborn daughter.

"Whore," her mother screeched.

She could feel the tears coming.

"Mother," she said. "Don't say that."

The crazy eyes flashed with hatred.

"I have a right to say it!"

Prudence gasped.

"You made me do it," she said. "You and him."

Her mother laughed, then called it back.

"Neither my will nor his will but yours," she shrieked, pointing a bony finger. "Your filthy, disgusting lust."

Prudence shook with sobs.

"No," she moaned. "No."

"Yes," Aveline spit out. "Yes, yes."

Then she turned and stared out the window and the chair began to move. Back and forth, back and forth, faster. Prudence faced her mother, still sobbing, and then turned for the door and pulled on the knob and was out in the hall beyond the woman in the chair when she heard one more time, in a parched voice inescapable as death: "Whore!"

1965

30

Boylan gets up from his seat.

"*Really* clever," he declares, smiling. "Have to hand it to you guys. When you want to clip one to old Boylan, you do a good job." He shakes his head. "For a minute there you had me fooled."

Adrian listens, thinks.

"You think this is a put-on?"

Boylan scowls.

"Come on. You didn't think I'd fall for this, did you? Close, close. But no cigar." He laughs, looking down at still seated Welcome and Sparks. "I really thought your eyes were closed."

Adrian, without hesitation.

"They were."

Boylan throws his hands in the air.

"Come on! It worked, all right. But fun's over."

Welcome, quiet because he does not know what to say and knows that Adrian is telling the truth, adjusts his glasses, which have slipped down along his nose, and looks up at Boylan.

"Adrian's telling the truth."

Boylan makes a fist, directs it at Welcome.

"I *knew* you were in on this together."

Adrian, exasperated, stands up.

"No put-on, Blazes. Dammit! I had my eyes closed. You get up, you ruin the whole thing." He glares at his friend. "Swear to God, I had my eyes closed."

Boylan stares back, analyzes.

"You did?"

"I did."

Pointing to the board, "That thing worked?"

"It did."

Boylan looks down at the board, the still-burning candles. "Well," is all he can say.

"Will you sit down?" asks Adrian. "We must try to go on."

"Must?" from Welcome.

"Someone needs help," replies Adrian, taking his seat. "We have to find out who it is."

Welcome smiles briefly at Adrian.

"Someone? I think some*thing* is what you want to say. You don't know what it is. Could be a demon. A demon," he continues in his deep voice, "would lie. He would say he needed help."

"Why?" asks Adrian, all innocence.

Boylan, sitting down:

"To get our souls."

Adrian laughs at the remark.

"This is the twentieth century."

Boylan catches Welcome's eye, then Adrian's.

"So?"

Adrian scoffs.

"People don't believe in that stuff anymore."

"They don't, huh?" from Boylan. "They don't believe in Ouija boards either. Or ghosts, or go to psychic fairs." He points at the board. "Who the hell do you think communicates through Ouija boards? God?"

"Blasphemer," cautions Welcome.

Boylan whirls.

"You be quiet," he orders. He turns to Adrian. "I'm waiting for your answer."

Adrian answers, his voice very deliberate.

"We don't know what death is. We don't know what happens when we die. No one has come back to tell us." He pauses. "The corpse gets buried, or burned. What happens to the soul? Where does it go?"

"Right," from Welcome, quietly.

Adrian looks at him.

"But where? What's the next state, or plane?" Back to Boylan. "Seems to me we have a chance to find out." Reaching for the tripod, "It could change our lives."

Adrian, blindfolded at Boylan's insistence:
"Is anybody there?"
He holds his breath. He waits. A sudden coolness fills the room. He can feel it, like someone's breath close by. A tingling in his fingers—contact? He feels different, silently thanks Boylan for the blindfold, which has made it easier for him to concentrate.
"Is anybody there?"
The tripod spins from under his fingers, returns. He holds on, lightly, is taken to the alphabet.
Welcome writes:

WHERE DID U GO MES CHERS WE WER WAITING

He tells Adrian, who asks:
"Who are you?"
Welcome, reading now as he records:

WE AR YR FAMILIAARS I AM THE WOLF HAR HAR PREPARE A FUNERAL FOR A VIKING

"Was it you before?"

NO NO THAT WAS A WINGED CREATUR AFTER YR SOULS I DO NOT WANT WHAT U HAV INSID HELP ME SAV

"Save who?" Adrian presses.

THE CHILDRN UF TH WRLD

"Why do they need to be saved?"

EVL SPIRTS AR COMIG TO TAK THEM AWAY STOP THE RAPE AND PLNDR GO GO TO THE HOUSE SAV THE CHLDR HE WILL STEAL

"Who?" from Adrian.

RED O MES CHERS I AM YR FAMILIAR GIVE ME A MIRROR TO SEE YOU BY WE CAN SEE YR REFLXXION IN THE GLAS

"A mirror? You can see us in a mirror?"

WE CN SEE YR SOULS IN THE GLASS U HAV NICE ONES FRM YR TONES WE CD WRK WEL TOGETHR

"Who was the winged creature?"

U WD NOT KNO HER

"An evil spirit?"

HAR HAR THR R NO EVIL SPIRTS ONLY ANGELS SCORES OF ANGELLS THESE WINGED CRETURS AR WAITING REBIRTH THEY HAV LIVES TO LEAD I AM DON I HAV NO LIV SHOW ME YR SOULS N I WILL SAVE U FROM TORMET

"Torment?"

A FIGR OF SPEECH GO TO THE HOUSE BUT DO GO I WILL REWARD YOU

"What house?" asks Adrian.

I WILL WATCH OVR U KEP U FRM HRM BUT GO TIME IS RUNIG OUT

Adrian, taking a deep breath, asks:
"Where is this house?"

HER MES CHERS THS VRY PLCE A STONS THRO

"Does anyone live there?"

NO IT IS NER MY HOUS TH SOURCE OV AL MY PAIN
GO SAV KEP RED AWAY HE WIL BURN ALL MY MEMO-
RIES STOP HIM

"What street is the house on?"

O MY STREETS I HAV NO NED FR STRETS I AM IN TH
DARK WIHT MY WINGED FRNDS IT IS COLD HER WICKS
IS TH NAM THE HOUSE OF WICKS GO I WILL GID U
BRING TH BOARD KEP TH LINES OOPN I AWAT YR NXT
CALL DE BONNE VOLONT

"Wait!"

O MES CHERS UN CHIEN ET LOUP THE DOR S
CLOSIG I FEL THE HOT BRETH OV AVELN GO TAK THE
BORD GO I WEL B YR FAMILIR YR GID YR BONE BON
BOUCHE HAR HAR GO

31

"Time to put the lights back on?" asks Boylan, sitting well back in his chair. He does not know what to think and has, in fact, experienced a vague kind of fear.

"No," says Adrian. "You'll spoil the mood."

"Seems to me the mood is over," counters Blazes, looking hard at Adrian, still wondering if what he saw at the board is some kind of trick worked out by Welcome and Sparks.

"Can I take this off?" asks Adrian.

"If the spirits move you," declares sonorous Welcome.

"Har, har," from Boylan, imitating Welcome's voice when he read the words to Adrian. "Mes chers."

"Well?" from Adrian, his blindfold off.

"Well what?" responds Boylan.

"What do you think?"

"I feel the hot breath upon me," says Boylan, forcing himself to smile. "Go, the mass is ended—and take the board with you," he remarks, to cover his uneasiness.

Adrian tries to ignore him.

"What do you think, Andy?" He pauses. "Honestly."

Welcome shrugs, looks down at the board.

"I'd say something incredible has just happened and it scares the shit out of me." Then to Boylan, "I don't give a damn what you think. You know as well as we do that Adrian and I didn't fake this." He picks up the planchette. "People have believed in Ouija boards for centuries." A pause. "Maybe there is something to it." He puts down the tripod. "I'm willing to suspend my disbelief." He looks again at Adrian. "But I don't know if we should do what the board wants."

"He calls himself the wolf," says Boylan. "And how are you going to get in this house? Ring the bell?"

"I don't see why not," answers Adrian.

Boylan sighs loudly.

"The two of you," he expels. "Listen to yourselves. You're going to walk up to a house, if you can find it, ring the bell and ask whoever lives inside to let you talk to your familiar." He shakes his head. "Give me a break."

Welcome frowns at Blazes.

"Listen to yourself," he counters. "We have been asked to go to a house. The house of Wicks. So we *have* the name. I'd be willing to bet whoever lives there would welcome us."

Boylan laughs, again disguising his uneasiness. He has felt something. "Welcome you as ghost hunters?" He smiles at his choice of words.

Welcome responds:

"Suppose the place isn't occupied?"

Then Adrian:

"Better," he answers. "We wouldn't be interrupted."

"Well," says Boylan, moving from the chair to his bed. "You can count me out." Supine, eyes on the ceiling. "I'm not getting thrown out of here because I talk to a Ouija board."

"It's no crime," offers Welcome.

Boylan stares him down.

"It is if you do it in public," he retorts. "Or if you break into an unoccupied house."

Adrian considers this.

"If you're afraid to go with us, just say so. We won't force you."

Boylan, eyes on the candles, is caught by surprise. The same old trick. Reverse psychology. He wonders. He is trying to be the voice of reason, the one who keeps his feet on the ground. But this? A challenge.

"I'm not afraid."

"Then come," coaxes Adrian. "At least the first time."

A voice beside him.

"First time?" asks Welcome.

Adrian turns.

"We may have to go back."

Welcome sighs, lets his eyes drift to the candelabrum. Boylan, whose eyes are also on the flames, catches Welcome's. An ally? Maybe Adrian has gotten ahead of himself. He probes.

"Why?" he asks.

Adrian stands up.

"I don't know," he replies. "But I really don't know entirely why we'd be going in the first place. He was unclear."

Welcome shakes his head. He looks down at what he has written.

"No, he wasn't," he says. "Bring the board. Save the children. House of Wicks." He looks at Adrian. "Wasn't much of a speller."

Adrian looks down at the writing.

"How do we find the place?"

Boylan laughs.

"Try the phone book."

Adrian's eyes go bright.

"Right!" he exclaims. "The phone book."

Boylan groans. There is pity in his eyes.

32

It is Welcome, two days later, who finds the house.

"It was easy," he declares, sitting in the cafeteria. "All I had to do was think." His round eyes peer at them through thick glasses. "I did look in the phone book," nodding at Boylan, "but I knew there wouldn't be anything there. Not a Wicks in town. Then I said to myself, first things first, Andrew."

"Good for you," Boylan comments, chewing on an overdone hamburger.

Welcome grimaces.

"I went to the source," he declares, beaming. "Father O'Brien. He's an expert on Gloucester and Magnolia, even Salem."

"Right!" exclaims Adrian, smacking himself on the forehead.

"Watch that, Sparks," smiles Blazes. "Not much left to lose."

"Yuk, yuk," from Adrian.

"I think that's har har," smirks Boylan.

"Go on, Andy," Adrian urges.

"Well," says Andrew, "he knew right off."

Adrian frowns.

"What did you tell him?"

"Nothing," answers Welcome. "Told him I had come across the family name in a history book on Gloucester and I was wondering if there were any descendants."

"Are there?" from Boylan.

Welcome shakes his head.

"Apparently all that's left is the house," replies Welcome, picking at his salad. "Abandoned."

"No," utters Adrian.

"Yes," restates Welcome. "And—get this." Pauses for effect. "We all know this house. The one on Decker Street, out by Mr. Sweeney's."

Boylan swallows hard.

"That gloomy wreck with broken windows?"

"And the willow tree," adds Welcome.

"*Wunderbar*," comments Blazes.

Welcome smiles.

"A legitimate remark in German." He turns to Adrian. "A sign that God exists."

Adrian grins.

"Breathing life into the least of his children."

Boylan reaches over, takes Welcome by the wrist.

"Har, har."

Welcome makes a face.

"Watch it," he hisses. "God will have your ear for touching me."

Boylan releases him.

"The Lord is my buddy," he says.

"You shall not want," nods Adrian.

Boylan aims a finger at Welcome.

"You *will* die before your time."

Welcome leans into Adrian.

"Why do we hang around with him?"

Adrian shrugs.

"Gang up all you want," says Boylan. "Might make us even." He pushes his chair out, stands. "But you need me." He taps his head. "Balance. Without me you'd go out to that place and never come back. I'd have to lead a search party."

Welcome gets up next.

"When do we go?"

Adrian looks up at them, finishes his pie and stands.

"We can't go off campus during the week." He stops. "Unless, of course, we bend the rules."

"Break is the word you're looking for," asserts Blazes.

"We can wait until the weekend," agrees Welcome. Looking down at Adrian. "What do you say?"

Adrian considers.

"Sounds good to me. How about Saturday?"

"Fine by me," declares Welcome, reaching down for his littered tray. "What time?"

"Noon?"

He looks at Boylan, waits.

"I don't even know if I'm going."

Adrian raises his eyes to the ceiling.

"Come *on*, Blazes."

Welcome begins to walk toward the door.

"Who needs him?"

Boylan laughs. The gang-up, attack from another quarter, reverse psychology. He knows. But why does it always work?

"I'll think about it," he says. "By the way, do either of you know what day Saturday is?"

Adrian knows, but won't say. Welcome isn't sure.

"What?" he asks.

"Halloween," answers Blazes. "Don't forget to dress up."

33

Life to Adrian is strangely changed. Time moves on tiptoe, with bated breath. The voice from the board has opened a new world to him, a world to be explored. Everything tingles and glows, has hidden dangers, promise. An apple from the cooler of exotic fruit, a pummelo, never before tasted. In bed thinking, reviewing the events of the week, he imagines himself a shadowy figure on an eerie promontory, near craggy bending scrub pine, looking to the roar from below. An ocean of images and ideas that dazzle. In the wind, he becomes the wind. In the sea, the water of life. Nothing will be kept from him, every secret is his for the asking.

In his mind there is a list:

Flashlights
Lantern
Candles?
Table?
Chairs?

Will there be something to sit on in the house? Can he take the chance? Surely an old box, some empty crates, a step on a long winding staircase leading all the way up. What will the weather be like? Will Boylan go if it rains? How can he control these things? He shuts his eyes tightly, wills it not to rain. He opens his eyes. He cannot sleep. Too much energy. He throws back the covers, gets up and goes to his desk.

At the desk he switches on the lamp. The bulb flickers, dies.

"Damn," he mutters.

He walks to Boylan's desk in the darkness. He reaches for the lamp, finds the bulb, unscrews it. Back to his own lamp, where he makes the change. In his mind a new idea: give Boylan the bad bulb. He'll never know. He turns it on, tilts the light away from Boylan.

He decides against switching bulbs, and feels good about it. He has passed a test. He has done unto others. He has challenged himself and made the grade. His eyes return to his own desk, to novels stacked almost carelessly. Two new acquisitions, found in an antique shop— *The Projection of the Astral Body*, by Sylvan J. Muldoon, and another, even more worn volume, standing next to the *Complete Stories and Poems* of E. A. Poe, *The Beginnings of Seership,* by Vincent Turvey. He grabs the Turvey, begins to read.

Adrian reads until he feels his eyes beginning to close. He looks at the clock. It is two-thirty. He closes the book. Does he have it in himself to become a seer? Does he have that kind of belief? Or is there, as Turvey implies, something else, something one is born with? He shuts off the light, sits in darkness, opens his top drawer quietly, runs his hand across the surface of the Ouija board, finds and brushes Melchior. He takes back his hand and closes the drawer. It is then he hears it, outside, in the dark. An owl.

"Hoot."

Has he heard this owl before? Has he ever heard an owl? He slips from his chair, pads to the window, looks out. There are stars in the sky. He scans the trees, half-bare of leaves, and sees nothing. He steadies himself, perches, ready for the long wait. He will see this owl. He lifts the window higher, smells pine in the breeze, dead leaves, swings his eyes to the tall pines and peers into the darkness for the owl. There is nothing. There is no movement. The breeze has slowed. It is silent as the grave and the leaves fall in silence.

"Hoot."

This time he gets a fix. Adrian looks to the oak trees on his right, where the sound came from. He stares and stares until he feels himself beginning to merge with darkness. When an owl wants to hide, it can hide. Then he sees a shape on the ground, skulking. Cat? Too small for a cat. Squirrel? The dark shape moves into the open. Suddenly—he catches the movement from the corner of his eye—it *was* the oak—a flapping, falling, white—it seems white—owl strikes, merges with the ground-born shape, seizes it and takes off.

An owl!

The bird sweeps past the oak. Adrian hears, believes he hears, the beating wings. A screech of something, then nothing. Silence returns. In the dark somewhere an owl feeds its young, feeds itself. He takes a last look out and brings the window down to where it was before, leaving a space for air. They like some air in the room. He moves to the desk and turns on the light.

"Turn it out."

A sullen, muffled command.

He turns it off, wonders why he turned it on, and thinks. He never would have seen, but now he has. The owl.

He returns to bed. He gets under the covers, serene and cool, turns to Boylan, and smiles to himself in the dark. *He* did not see, hear. Adrian shuts his eyes, sees an omen in his sighting of the owl and mentally adds some items to his list.

Garlic
Herbs?
Running shoes

34

Boylan gets up first.

"I was wondering when you'd open your eyes," he says.

Adrian yawns.

"What time is it?"

"Going on ten."

"God," from Adrian, pulling back the covers. "We have to get a move on."

Boylan looks up from his magazine.

"We?"

Adrian is out of bed, rubbing his eyes.

"I made a list of things we might need," he says. "I just have to write it down." He heads toward the bathroom. "Give me a second to shower."

"Take all the time you want."

Adrian showers quickly, dresses in the bathroom, is ready to go, gather items from his list.

"Why were you up so late last night?" asks Boylan. "Having a chat with Melchior?" He says the name distastefully.

Adrian bends down to tie his sneakers.

"I saw an owl."

"Did you?" from Boylan, smartly.

Adrian looks up.

"Why are you being such a pain in the ass?"

Boylan turns a page of his Sports Illustrated.

"Someone turned a light on in my face. Woke me from a good dream." He looks up. "I don't have so many good dreams I can afford to squander them."

"Sorry."

Boylan shakes his head.

"Wrong word," he says. "Try 'it won't happen again.'"

"All right," says Adrian, on his feet. "It won't happen again."

Boylan throws down his magazine.

"Liar."

Adrian ignores him. "Come on, Blazes."

Boylan is still in his underwear.

"I was thinking of going like this," he says, looking at himself. "It's not too cold out."

"Andy's waiting for us," says Adrian, looking for a flashlight. "Let's go."

"Let him wait. He said something bad to me." He stands. "Come to think of it, between the two of you, I can claim to be persecuted." He stops at the closet. "I wonder if there's a statute." He takes down from a hanger his costume and holds it out before him.

"What's that for?" inquires Adrian.

Boylan turns. Adrian can see he's grinning.

"My Halloween costume."

Adrian mutters to himself.

"What?" asks Boylan, dressing in his skeleton costume. "Didn't hear that." He steps up to the mirror. "Jesus," he exclaims. "The grim rictus himself."

"Mixed metaphor," observes Adrian, who scowls at Boylan. "I can't believe you're going to walk out of here in that."

Boylan turns from the mirror, raises his arms, drooping, above his head and groans. "What are you going as?" he asks.

"A human being," replies Adrian.

"Suit yourself," declares Boylan, falling into a chair with laughter. "Har, har." He stops laughing. "Seriously, Adrian. Think about it. We're going to go into this house. That's trespassing. If we go in costume, no one can tell who we are." He gets up. "It's a great idea and this is the one day we can get away with it."

Adrian considers.

"Where would I get a costume now?"

Boylan waves his hand.

"Have no fear, Boylan's here." He steps over to Adrian's bed, rips off the top white sheet and throws it to Adrian. "Use this."

"It's my *sheet*."

Boylan shrugs.

"Sheets can be replaced." He points. "Cut some holes in it and let's get going. Time waits for no one."

Adrian looks ruefully at his sheet, finds the scissors and begins cutting eyeholes. When he is done he places the sheet over his head, locates Boylan at the other end of the room.

"How do I look?"

"What can I say?" replies Boylan. "It's you."

They leave, lock the door behind them. In the tote bag Adrian carries is the candelabrum, three new candles, matches, a small brass lantern his brother gave him and the tripod. Under his other arm is the Ouija board. Halfway down the hall he stops.

"I forgot the garlic."

Boylan stops and peers directly into his eyeholes.

"Did I hear you say garlic?"

Adrian shrugs under the sheet.

"In case there's trouble."

Boylan scratches his head, takes the bag from Adrian with a quick grab of his free band.

"Let's just see what the hell is in here." He sifts through the items, is satisfied and returns the bag to Adrian.

"Everything all right?" asks Adrian.

Boylan nods affirmatively.

"I still don't understand the garlic."

"I read somewhere that garlic is good to have around," explains Adrian. "In case you run into…" He halts. He cannot bring himself to say the word.

"Vampires?" Boylan is incredulous. He taps his finger against the top of Adrian' s head.

"Anybody home? Are you out of your goddamn mind?"

Adrian does feel foolish.

"Guess you're right," he agrees. "Forget the garlic."

Boylan claps him on the shoulder, laughs, and sticks his hand into the pocket of the slacks he wears beneath the costume and takes out a small silver crucifix. He holds it out before him and makes a broad sign of the cross.

"Now God is on our side."

"Good," from Adrian, walking fast.

Boylan catches up.

"Want my blessing?"

Adrian, through his eyeholes:

"Not a chance."

35

Welcome joins them on the walk near his dormitory, a ghost, like Adrian. The three begin the trip across campus that will take them beyond the stone wall and out to Old Beach Road. From there it is a three mile walk to Decker Street. Autumn has settled in. Everywhere they look, leaves cover the ground. The sky is clear blue, with puffy clouds in the south, but the air is filled with the woeful signs of time passing. With every breeze leaves tumble to the ground and gather into drifts, red and gold and yellow on the paths, under the trees. They pass Shroud Theater. Posters announce a new production: *When We Dead Awaken!* The irony is disquieting, but amusing. At the gymnasium they pick up the long walk that circles the great lawn on its way toward the wall and the iron gates that close the campus to all outsiders. All about, behind and beside, gray stone buildings with ivy and inside, creaky stairs, the smell of wax and polish. All old except for the gym, which is new and named for a benefactor, as are all the buildings on campus not named for saints.

They proceed, two ghosts and a skeleton, passing by piles of leaves that are close to the wall, collected there by groundskeepers.

Bare dark trees, trunks and branches, show themselves in the sunshined glass of Xavier Hall. The clouds float by in the windows, images, casting shadows over the lawn. There is movement. They hear laughter, a game in progress, shouts.

"How do we look?" asks Welcome.

"*Wunderbar*," from Blazes.

Welcome flaps his sheet-covered arms.

"An idiot savant. He knows one word in German."

Boylan makes a grab. Welcome is too quick.

"Death has many faces."

Andrew, Adrian laugh together.

"And yours is one of them," says Adrian.

"Har, har, *mes chers*," says the skeleton.

"Har, har yerself," mumbles Adrian.

Boylan runs ahead, then he turns and blocks the walk.

"Can we get serious?" he asks.

"No," replies Adrian, pushing by.

"Wait," calls out Blazes. "I mean it. I have a question and I want to get an answer before we get to the Wicks place."

"What?" from Welcome.

Boylan folds his arms.

"What are the chances the Ouija board talk came from inside your head?" he asks, looking at Adrian. "Your subconscious."

Adrian looks at Andrew before answering.

"It would have to be buried pretty deep," replies Adrian. "I didn't know any of that stuff." Pausing, "And I don't know a word of French."

"You know *rendezvous*."

"So?"

"You may know some more."

Adrian raises his arms, then drops them.

"You *know* I don't speak French."

"You could have known about the Wicks place," Boylan persists. "In fact, the two of you could have." He shifts his gaze to Welcome. "It wouldn't be the first time you tried to trick me." He shrugs his shoulders. "A bit elaborate, but not totally out of the question."

Adrian starts to walk away.

"You know damn well it wasn't a trick." He turns, motions for Welcome and Boylan to follow. "*You're* the one who put on the blindfold. How could I see the letters?"

Boylan steps ahead. Welcome shadows him.

"I haven't figured that out yet."

"There's nothing to figure," asserts Andy. "No plot. Truth, plain and simple. We made contact."

Boylan chuckles shortly.

"You have no idea how good that makes me feel."

Adrian hands him the tote bag.

"Here. Do some work."

Boylan takes the bag without a word.

"Who do you think it is?"

Welcome, still shadowing, says:

"The wolf."

Boylan grabs him by the sheet.

"What is *that* supposed to mean?"

"Unhinge me and I'll tell," replies Andrew, brushing away Boylan's hand. "He calls himself wolf. Like Wolf Larsen." Adrian sucks the sheet into his mouth. He tries to spit it out, but can't. He has to tug with his hand to pull it back out.

"Maybe he *is* a wolf," he suggests.

"Right," mutters Blazes. "And we're the three little pigs."

Welcome spreads his arms.

"Speak for yourself."

Boylan yells. Welcome takes off, pursued by Boylan. Adrian laughs, sees ahead of him, racing, arms and legs flying, two specters among the leaves.

36

"Well," says Blazes. His hands are on the railing. He is looking up at the foreboding house that stands, centered precisely, on top of a sloping rise. "A fine how-do-you-do."

Welcome moves to the gate.

"Once upon a time this was a great place to live," he says.

Boylan snickers.

"Once upon a time."

Adrian keeps silent. He has been studying the house, window by broken window, board by board. It once *was* a good place to live. He can see that. But what happened? He feels strangely out of place, yet strangely at home. He has a sense that this is where he belongs, yet something else tells him that he should not be here. The house has a grim, cold face. He asks himself again. What happened? What is happening? That is what he feels. Not so much dead past, but live present. The house of Wicks, where voices and times meet, behind an iron gate, stone walls and broken windows.

"Getting cold feet?"

Adrian turns his sheeted head to Boylan.

"No," he replies.

"Then let's go," suggests Blazes, taking a step.

"Wait," from Welcome.

Boylan and Sparks look at him.

"Problems, big nose?" inquires Blazes.

Welcome points a sheeted finger.

"I'll settle with you later," he says. "Right now, I think we ought to go trick or treating on this block. Sort of cover our tracks. Make the whole thing legit."

Boylan moves his fingers like a centipede.

"These houses are all a mile apart," he declares. "No one will see us go inside. Besides, what would they care?" He turns, walks toward the stone wall. "I say let's go. Get this over with."

He moves ahead.

"Come on, Andy. He's right," says Adrian. "There's no need for cover." Laughing, "We're covered."

"I think," says Welcome, walking beside him, "I was expecting something a little less dreary."

"We've passed this place before."

"Yeah," agrees Andrew, "but I never took a good look. I mean, Adrian, look at this place."

He does, and sees what he saw before: a wrought-iron gate, rusting, drawing a line between the Wicks property and the street before it. On two sides, stone walls, very old, older perhaps than the house itself, with missing stones, like a broken smile. There is a lawn, leaf-covered. A willow tree, enormous, with implications of water nearby, whose branches sweep the lawn like shaded talons. Further beyond he sees garbage, cans and bottles and leaves, patches of dead grass and dry spots where no lawn has grown for years, weeds along the front of the house, the walk, which is flagstone and extends from the chained gate to the front door, waiting to carry visitors.

"It could use some paint," Adrian says.

"Paint!" exclaims Welcome.

"And some new windows."

Welcome laughs dryly.

"Adrian," he declares in his deep voice, "I can't believe you." He rustles under his sheet.

Boylan windmills an arm at the junction of the wrought-iron gate and the stone wall. A tall pine almost shields him from view.

"Come on!" he hollers.

They catch up and join him.

"Here goes," says Boylan. He jumps over the wall and onto the lawn.

Adrian is second, Welcome last. They walk along the wall, keeping as much in early afternoon shadow as they can. As they proceed, Boylan pops the knuckles of his left hand with the fingers of his right, all the while looking doubtfully up at the house. The wall brings them to the west side of the house, where they stop.

"What's the plan?" asks Boylan.

Adrian speaks from under the sheet, his voice muffled.

"We go in," he answers. "Find a place to sit, set up the board. Put some questions to Melchior."

Boylan laughs.

"You're killing me."

He shakes his head, takes the lead.

"Wait," hisses Welcome.

"What?" from Boylan, exasperated.

"I saw something."

All stop.

"What?" from Blazes.

Welcome points.

"In the window," he answers. "A face."

37

"More schemes, *mes chers*?" responds Boylan, looking up at the window where Welcome claims to have seen a face. "I think not. No face. Just tricks for Boylan." He grabs Welcome in a bear-hug. "If you and your pal get funny inside," he warns, squeezing the air from Andrew's lungs, "you'll die by inches." He lets go. "Hear me?" he asks, raising his hands, squiggling his fingers.

"It was a face."

Adrian looks up at the window.

"I don't see anything."

Welcome insists. "I saw it."

Boylan snorts.

"Come on."

They step toward the house, which seems to grow larger as they approach. In and out of the sunlight they move, their faces shaded by yet another looming pine. Wind whistles through the willow. Adrian turns, his face shadowed, light, dark, light again. A crow, wings flapping, takes squawking to the air. They look, then move ahead, the sun full on them, in their eyes when they look toward the willow.

"Stop," orders Boylan.

Welcome, Sparks come up short and almost collide.

"What?" from Adrian, who nearly drops the board.

Boylan kneels down, poking at something with a stick.

"Look."

"What?" repeats Adrian, stepping around Welcome so he can see what Blazes is doing.

"A trap," answers Boylan, clearing it from the leaves. "For a small animal." He stands. "Could've lost a toe," he says ruefully, conjuring an image of himself without his right toe. "Nasty piece of work."

Welcome kneels down, fingers the trap.

"I thought these things were outlawed," he says.

"They probably are," answers Boylan.

"Then what's it doing here?"

Boylan folds his arms, stares at Welcome.

"Why don't you tell me?"

Andrew stands up.

"Listen," he says. "For the last time. I didn't put that trap there. Neither did Adrian." His eyes go to the window. "Someone did," he says, "but not us." Stepping back from the clearing, "I'm not so sure we ought to be going in there."

Adrian moves toward the house.

"We didn't come this far to turn around," he declares. "In through the window over there," he points. "We'll set up the board and get some answers."

"From Melchior," offers Boylan.

Adrian turns.

"You have the bag, Blazes," he says, without amusement in his voice. "Hand me Melchior," he insists, waiting.

Welcome gives in, walks with Boylan past an old gas lamp with shattered panes of glass toward Adrian. There are weeds, broken bottles, a battered doll, driftwood. They stand where Adrian stands, looking at the beckoning window.

"I'll give it to you inside," says Boylan.

"Fine," says Adrian, overcoming a sudden sense of dread. Looking at the sky. "I hope we make contact."

"We will," comments Welcome.

They form a phalanx, Adrian in the lead. Leaves shake in the wind, flutter to the ground, skitter along at their feet. There is another strong gust of wind, a creaking shutter swings open and shut.

"Here goes," says Adrian.

He steps over the ledge into the house.

"Well?" from Boylan.

"Give me the flashlight."

He reaches in the bag, pulls out the light, hands it to Adrian who takes it and turns it on. A beam of light.

"It's all right," from inside the house.

Boylan steps in next, then Welcome.

"Trick or treat," says Blazes.

"Quiet," orders Adrian.

"I know," says Blazes. "Someone might hear us."

Welcome says, his voice muffled by the sheet:

"The trap."

"Yeah, right. Almost forgot."

"Shhh," comes from Adrian. "Let's find a place to set up. It's not too dark in here." He clicks off the flashlight.

"Maybe you ought to leave that on," suggests Welcome. "There might be holes in the floor."

"Or dead bodies," chuckles Boylan.

Adrian turns on the flashlight. In the beam, dust motes funnel in air opaque from disuse. Dim light comes in through all broken windows. It is a house of permanent dust and shade.

"Place is huge," comments Welcome.

"Sure is," agrees Boylan, his eyes moving to the ceiling, "Room enough for twenty people."

"This must be the dining room."

"So?" retorts Boylan.

"Quiet," again from Adrian.

Boylan brings up the tote bag.

"Want Melchior?"

Adrian takes the board.

"Let's get started," says Welcome. "The sooner we begin, the sooner we get out of here."

Boylan laughs.

"Don't tell me you're scared."

Welcome sniffs.

"Damn right I am," responds Welcome. "This is a crime, Blazes. Breaking and entering."

"Look who's talking," says Boylan.

They choose the kitchen for its French doors and red maple in the backyard. A wall of pine trees at the edge of the yard further secludes the house, finishing the work of the wrought-iron fence and two stone walls, east and west. It is also the only room with a table in it. There are four crates in the room. Two at the table, two near the wall. Welcome brings a third crate to the table. They put down the board, the planchette. Welcome takes two large round scented candles from the bag and sets them at opposite ends of the board and lights them with a match. Cinnamon fills the air. Their faces flicker in the candlelight. They sit on the crates, peering up over the edge of the table at the Ouija board.

"Is anybody there?"

"Wait," barks Boylan. "You're not blindfolded."

"I can't see as it is," he responds. "You won't let us take off the costumes."

Boylan hesitates.

"All right. Go on." Then: "Wait."

"OK," says Welcome. "We're waiting."

"Shouldn't there be two people with their fingers on the planchette?" queries Boylan. "That's the way it was in *13 Ghosts*."

"*13 Ghosts* was a movie," Adrian retorts. "This is real."

Boylan raises a skeptical eyebrow.

"I still think there should be two."

"Which two?" from Adrian.

"Why not you and Andy? I couldn't trust myself."

Adrian shakes his head.

"Andy? Go ahead, put your fingers on Melchior."

Welcome holds out his hands, hesitates, then puts a finger from each hand on the wide edge of the planchette. Adrian does the same on the other end, takes a breath.

"Is anybody there?" he asks.

The candles flicker, as in a breeze. Adrian goes stiff. Welcome gasps. There is a sudden coolness and a chill.

"No," booms Adrian, entranced.

Welcome says nothing.

"Melchior," says Adrian, softly. "Melchior."

His sheet covered arm goes limp, stiff again. Melchior moves, at first without pattern, all about the board, then stops at "Yes."

"YES," reads Boylan, writing it down.

"We are here," says Adrian. "The Wick's place."

The tripod, then Boylan:

I HAD HOPED FOR A GLAS

Boylan stands, reaching into the back pocket of his pants and removes a small mirror, which he leans against one of the candles. He sits back down on one of three crates the boys have moved into position around the small table.

I HAD HOPED FR A BETR GLASS

"Next time," says Adrian. "What is your name?"

I AM YR FAMILIAR MES CHERS THE WOLF

"Are you an animal?" The planchette skitters under two sets of ivory fingers.

HAR HAR I AM NO ANIML WOLF IS MY NAM I WD NT LIE TO U U AR MY FRIENDS U HAV COME TO SAVE ME HELLP

"Do you want us to save you?"

NO NO MES CHERS I NED NO HELLP THE CHILDR IT IS THEY WHO NEED HELP U HAV COME TO SAV THEM U R GOOD I CAN SEE IN THE GLASS U BROUGHT YR SOULS AR GOOD WHAT I CAN SEE OF THEM I NEED A REAL MIRROR NT A DOLLS I SEE NOW ONLE PIECES OF YR SOULS MUCH GOOD IN THEM

"Ask him if we'll get to heaven," urges Boylan.
The tripod swings into action.

ASK YERSELF GREEN EYES

From Boylan: "Do we?"

MAYBE U AR IN HEAVEN

"What do you mean?"

HEAVN IS IN YR EYES HAR HAR I DO NOT KNO OF SUCH THINGS MINE IS KNOWLEGE OF A CERT'N KIND U ASK THE IMPOSSIBL GOD HIMSELF DOES NOT KNOW THE ANSWR

"Then there is a God?"

IN A MANNR OF SPEAKING

"What do you mean?"

THER AR MANY LEVELS I HAVE NOT SEEN HIS EMI-NENCE YET ONLY HIS WINGED EMMESAIRES FOUL CREATURES WITH SMOKE FR BLOOD AND RED EYES I HATE THE COLOR RED IN ALL THINGS IT IS TIME MES CHERS TO GET TO WORK TO SAV THE CHILDREN

"Whose children?"

MINE

"How many children do you have?"

I HAV BUT TWO

"Are they dead?"

I DO NOT LIKE THE WORD

"Then they are alive?"

I DID NOT SAY THAT

"Then what are they?"

LET US STICK TO THE MATTR AT HAND

"Which is?"

STOP THE DAMNABL DWARF

"Is the dwarf alive?"

ALIVE AS U MES CHERS

"In this house?"

I DO NOT KNO WHER HE IS I AM NOT GOD

"Then how do we stop him?"

LISTEN I WILL TEL U UNDERNEATH THIS WICKS HOUS IS A TUNNL GO TO IT AND BREK HIS TOYS

"Where is the tunnel?"

DOWN THE STAIRS

"What do you want us to do?"

BREAK HIS TOYS

"How?"

COME FOLOW ME

38

Adrian stands up, as does Welcome.

"Do we need these?" He points to the candles. "It isn't that dark in here."

"Blow them out," says Welcome. "Someone might see us from the outside. Besides, there's plenty of light."

Adrian blows out the candles.

"How . . ." begins Boylan, still seated. He is puzzled by it all and now that they are in this strange, empty house, his sense of unease is rising. He is ready to admit he is frightened. He is ready to admit he is ready to leave—in a hurry. But something holds him. He is hard at work, trying to determine whether what holds him comes from inside, or from outside. Is he afraid to leave because of what Sparks and Welcome would think? Or is he simply incapable of leaving? What is making him incapable? He is deep in thought when he hears a sound.

"Look!" exclaims Adrian.

Scratches are being carved into the dust-covered floor by some unseen force. The markings look like those of a giant bird.

Adrian begins to move in the direction pointed out by the invisible talons. Welcome hesitates.

"Wait!" yells Boylan, now on his feet. He runs to Adrian, takes hold of him, brings him to an abrupt halt. "Think about this, Adrian. What the hell's going on here? This is insane. Dangerous." He shakes Adrian roughly. "Say something."

Adrian looks at Boylan, his dark eyes filled with excitement and queer serenity. He tries to pull away.

"There's nothing to be afraid of," he says.

Boylan holds him.

"Wait," he barks. "How do you know?"

Welcome breaks in.

"It's a good question, Adrian. How do you?"

They stand in a small circle. Gradually, Boylan releases Adrian and stands back from him. He and Welcome wait for Adrian to respond to the question and both are relieved that Adrian has remained close to them and not run off after the markings. Adrian is quiet. He seems to be thinking. At the same time he appears distracted, as if in his mind he is suddenly able to embrace clear opposites.

"Wake up, Adrian," says Blazes.

Welcome huddles in his sheet.

"I'm *freezing*," he declares.

As soon as he has mentioned it, the others notice. The room temperature has been dropping steadily. They can see their breath when they talk, breathe through their mouths.

"Let's go," says Adrian.

Boylan shakes his head.

"No, no. Let's leave."

Welcome, shivering, speaks up in his deep but tremulous voice. His teeth are chattering."

"Answer him, Adrian. Or we get the hell out of here." He hesitates. "The Ouija board is one thing. This is different."

"How?" asks Adrian. "Why did you come? What did you expect?" He seems angry. There is heat in his voice. "Go ahead. Leave." He stares at his friends from under the sheet. "I can do it alone."

"What? Do what alone?" demands Boylan.

Adrian points to the scratches on the floor.

"Help him."

Welcome is shaking.

"Better do something fast. We'll freeze to death."

The sound comes again. They hear new scratches before they see new scratches being made in the floor. But they see them soon enough, coming toward them.

"Jesus!" yells Boylan.

Adrian grabs him.

"Wait," he whispers.

Boylan shakes him off.

"We could get killed!"

It is too late. A circle is being carved in the floor around them. They form the center. Then another circle, concentric, closer. There is a high-pitched, rough sound as the grooves are cut into the floor. Boylan tries to run, but can't. His feet will not obey. He is in the same position as before, wondering what it is that keeps him there. This time the terror is all-consuming. He is shaking and feels himself about to cry.

"Hold my hand," says Adrian.

Boylan doesn't think, his fear is so complete. He gives Adrian his hand.

"Andy?"

He hardly has to ask. Welcome already has his hand in his.

"I'm scared," says Welcome, his voice shaking.

Boylan turns in costume.

"Join the club."

They edge closer together, Adrian at the center, a bit to the front. On his right stands Boylan, his left Welcome. They all watch the circles being carved into the floor. The second circle is finished. Another circle begins, concentric, one ring closer.

"There's nothing to be afraid of," says Adrian.

The others don't know what to believe. They want to believe him. But they can't control their fear. Welcome is shaking. Boylan can hear his own knees knocking together. Only Adrian seems unafraid and his lack of fear only adds to the terror of the others.

"Says who?" mutters Boylan.

A fourth circle begins, so close it forces them to huddle together. Welcome starts to cry.

"Easy, Andy," soothes Adrian.

The circle stops, is finished. There is silence. Their fear has given way to acceptance. There is nothing left. They hold hands, firmly, shoulders touching. Not one of them tries to move from the center of the circle. Not one of them has the strength.

Welcome points with his free hand.

"Look."

Not a circle this time, letters. Carved in the space between the third and fourth rings, one ragged letter at a time.

FOLOW ME

39

Adrian needs no urging.

"There's no danger," he declares, stepping out from the center. "He could've hurt us, but he didn't." He waits for his friends to move. When they don't, he adds, "He's good."

Welcome and Boylan ignore Adrian and continue to study the crude lettering carved into the circle in the planks. Boylan is first to take his eyes from the floor and look at Adrian.

"Maybe he needs us," he declares. "That doesn't make him good." He pauses. "It makes him weak."

"Weak!" Adrian points to the letters. "That's weak?"

Boylan stands firm.

"Strong enough to do some things," he insists. "Not strong enough to do others." He steps toward Adrian. "I wouldn't make too big a thing about how powerful this guy is. Not if you want me along." He turns to Welcome, who hasn't moved. "Come on, Andy. Adrian's right about one thing. If he wanted to hurt us, he would have."

"Maybe he's biding his time," croaks Welcome.

Boylan reaches in and pulls him from the circle.

"We'll keep that in mind."

They follow the scratchings, slowly. The marks are sometimes Xs, sometimes long gashes in the floor surface. There is no uniformity to them, other than that they lead in a direction, which is out of the kitchen, into the large adjacent room, then through the next and out into a giant hall where strips of water-damaged wallpaper hang down from the walls, unkempt, in great sad shavings up near the ceiling, like broken pennants, worn tongues or dying branches.

Some of the wood near the ceiling is rotten. The hall is damp, and smells of age. They pass under a hole in the ceiling.

"A chandelier, I bet," says Welcome, looking up.

Boylan shivers.

"Place is a dump."

Adrian turns around.

"I agree. Needs some work."

Boylan snorts.

"Needs to be torched."

Adrian halts.

"X marks the spot."

Welcome and Boylan come alongside.

"It's a door," offers Welcome.

Boylan looks at him.

"Is that what it is?"

Welcome shakes his head.

"Drop dead."

Adrian pulls open the door. He sees dark stairs leading down just before a burst of cool air from below breezes past their costumes. He quickly takes the flashlight from the bag and clicks it on.

"Ready?" he asks.

"Maybe one of us should stay upstairs," says Welcome.

Boylan laughs from under his mask.

"Why?"

"In case something happens."

Boylan leans toward him.

"I have news for you, bud. Something already has."

Welcome mutters:

"Something else."

Boylan chuckles.

"Then what? Call the police? Help! Help! I found a ghost. He's got my friends in a headlock?" He grabs Welcome's right arm. "In unity there is strength."

Welcome resists.

"I don't want to go down there. It's too dark."

Adrian begins to descend.

"Come on, Andy. We have light."

Boylan lets him go, starts climbing down the stairs.

"I wouldn't want to be alone in this place," he hollers, his voice muffled. He vanishes in the dark at the bottom of the stairs. "Ugh," he calls back. "Spider webs."

Welcome hesitates, then races down the stairs.

"Now what?" he says, when he gets to the bottom. "Where are you guys?"

He sees the flashlight, moves quickly over the earthen floor in its direction. He links up with Blazes and Adrian.

"What now?" Boylan asks.

"The board?"

"I don't think so," says Adrian.

They stand in a small circle. Adrian aims the flashlight around the cellar, moving it from one place to another.

"Can't see much, can you?" Boylan says.

"Big cellar," comments Adrian. "Beam doesn't even reach the wall over there."

Boylan takes his arm.

"That could be the road to hell."

Welcome yelps.

"You're not funny, Blazes."

There is a boom.

"What the hell was that?" asks Boylan.

Adrian points the light in the direction of the sound.

"A sign."

He begins to move.

"How do you know you're going in the right direction?" asks Welcome.

"I don't," Adrian replies. "But I think I'm right."

"He has good ears," comments Blazes, following Adrian and the light.

"Ah," from Adrian. "I was right. Look."

He points the flashlight at the ground up ahead, where they can see a small cloud of dust.

"What's that?"

Adrian turns around.

"That's how he's going to lead us. He's going to bang the floor, raise some dust. We'll be able to follow."

"Terrific," mumbles Boylan.

They cross the musty, dank cellar floor. Every hollow boom leads them on. Sometimes they can feel the vibration coming up from the floor, sometimes they can't. They can always hear the sound and it, like the gouges in the wood in the floor above, is frightening. It is like a spell being cast. All around are gossamer webs, some with large, motionless spiders at the heart, others empty, ragged, left behind. They keep running into them.

"God, I hate this."

"Shhh," from Boylan. "You'll wake one of them up."

The booms stop and they find themselves standing before a small wooden door that seems to lean against the foundation.

"Oh, boy," groans Andrew.

Adrian takes a deep breath, grabs the handle and pulls. He is startled when the door falls open and drops to the floor.

"Needs hinges," comments Boylan.

Welcome steps forward.

"You're not going in there?" he exclaims.

Adrian waves his hand before him, brushing away cobwebs. He turns around. The flashlight is on in his hand.

"You think it's any safer out here?"

"You're nuts," Welcome insists.

Boylan chimes in.

"Has a ring of truth to it."

Adrian steps into what they all can see is a tunnel. Under his left hand he carries the Ouija board, in the right the flashlight. Boylan holds the tote bag. Welcome follows, alone empty-handed.

"Give me a candle," he says. "We could use more light."

Adrian stops.

"Good idea."

Boylan takes a candle from the bag, hands it to Welcome, who holds it out for him to light.

"Good," says Welcome.

They stand, watching the candle.

"Listen," hisses Boylan.

"To what?" responds Adrian.

"To reason," breaks in Welcome. "And get the hell out of here." He looks at the walls. "This could cave in."

"Jesus," exclaims Boylan. "You're right."

Adrian starts to walk deeper into the tunnel.

"Let's just see where this goes."

Welcome, holding his candle, walks up to a beam.

"This wood is real dry, and old."

"Then get the hell away from it with that candle," warns Boylan. He comes back. "Do I have to watch you too?"

"If you're done," they hear Adrian call from ahead, "there's something up here you should take a look at."

They make a dash toward Adrian.

"What?"

"Over there," Adrian replies. "See? Boxes."

"Crates," corrects Boylan.

"Like the ones in the kitchen," offers Welcome.

"Flash the light over here," orders Boylan, trying to get a closer look at one of the crates. Adrian and Andrew stand close behind him. "Jesus!" exclaims Boylan. He jumps back, almost knocking Adrian off his feet.

"What?"

"They're marked 'Dynamite, Memphis Powder Corporation. 1863.'" He shudders. "Andy's standing next to me with a candle."

"Let's take another look," suggests Adrian. "This time without the candle."

"Fine with me," groans Welcome, a tremor in his voice. He stays back while Adrian and Blazes step up to the crates. He can see the light moving back and forth and can hear the muffled sound of their voices as they bend down. He can hear a crate being opened.

"Don't do that!" he warns.

Adrian and Blazes come back and join him.

"They're empty," says Boylan.

"Thank God," groans Welcome, relieved.

Boylan takes the candle from him and begins to examine something on the floor near the wall of the tunnel.

"Aim that flashlight over here."

Adrian brings the beam where Boylan directs.

"I'll be damned," exclaims Blazes.

They can all see a socket and a wire going off behind it. "I'll follow the wire," says Adrian, moving the light along the length of it. The wire trails along the floor, behind the crates, to the very end of the long, low tunnel, where it takes a turn for the ceiling. The beam moves, then stops where the wire stops. There is a trap door in the earthen ceiling above them and there is concrete around the sides of the door. There is also a wooden ladder, leaning against the wall.

"Unbelievable," exhales Welcome.

"Electricity?" asks Boylan.

Adrian too is puzzled, even disappointed. Empty crates, a wire, a ladder leading up. This is not what he expected to find, although he has no idea what he did expect to find.

"Where do you think it leads?" asks Welcome.

Before Adrian can say "Who knows?" Boylan has leapt at him and covered the hole of his sheet with his palm.

"Shhh," he whispers.

They stand in silence, uneasy, hearing nothing; then they all hear it at once. A voice, not very distinct, at first more a murmur, then clearly, a voice. A dumb show pantomime takes place near the crates. Two ghosts and a skeleton move fingers, eyes, bodies, arms and legs, separately and in cohesion, completely silent. No one knows what to do. The fear they felt upstairs returns in waves. They are about to panic when Welcome blows out the candle. The move inspires. Boylan jabs his thumb toward the trap door, steps to the ladder, motions at Welcome, still visible in the dim carefully hidden beam of Adrian's light. Welcome needs no convincing. He rushes to the ladder, steps on the first wooden rung and begins to ascend. At the top he pushes on the door. Nothing happens. He slides one way, then another. The trap door gives, slides away. Welcome is up, gone. He waves down with his free arm.

"Come on," he whispers.

Boylan is next up the ladder. He climbs quickly and vanishes into the dark. Then his fingers come down, clutching. Adrian understands, picks up the tote bag, moves two steps up the ladder and hands it to Boylan. He hands him next the Ouija board, then stands on the ladder, looking back into the tunnel. Boylan is waving down at him. He nods, can almost hear his heart pounding, or thinks he can. He hears the voice—there is only one—coming closer. He takes a step. The ladder creaks. He freezes, looks back again, and hears, very distinctly.

"Typical," a voice snarls. "Told you to keep that damn door shut, didn't I?" There is a mewling sound.

Adrian gulps and goes up through the hold.

"Typical," he hears again, closer, before Welcome slides back the trap door and Boylan takes the light from him and clicks it off, plunging them into a darkness as complete as that in the tunnel. Each hears his own heart pounding away and from below the muffled ominous sound of a sharp harsh voice raised in anger and a crashing among the crates.

1964

40

"I couldn't sleep at all last night," she said. "I think I finally went to sleep at four or five." Marian wore a light green long dress with small white flowers that swept over the top of the grass. "It's good to go for a walk."

Sweeney was pensive.

"We did make contact."

She nodded vehemently.

"Oh, yes. I'm sure of it." She nodded again, affirming her certainty. "After she gave us her name, something happened. It was as if someone took her away. She was there, then she was gone." Marian shivered. "It was a strain."

"Were you in any danger?"

She gave him a wan smile.

"A little late to think of that."

Sweeney's mouth opened wide.

"You were!" he exclaimed.

She took his shoulder.

"No," she said. "Not from this spirit. I sense only that she is not at ease." She stopped. "There's some kind of trouble."

"Isn't that always the case when the spirits talk to you?" Sweeney inquired. "They get murdered and haunt the castle or come back to life for revenge."

This time Marian did smile.

"Now you're being silly."

Sweeney led her across the great lawn.

"I swear I read it somewhere," he said. "Why, it's even in Shakespeare."

She gave his arm a tug.

"You know as well as I," she declared, "he gave the whole idea of ghosts far too much credence."

Sweeney chuckled.

"But then, so do I," declared Sweeney. "And you too, my dear." He led her along, holding her hand. He would smile and then he would think and a dark look of curiosity and pensiveness would color his face and he would try and catch a glimpse of Marian out of the corner of his eye. He felt filled with an unquenchable need to know and when he turned and looked down at Marian and they stopped in mid-step, his question was serious and meant to be taken seriously. "There *are* ghosts, aren't there?"

She looked up at him and she was serious too.

"That depends on what you mean by ghost, Jim." They began walking. "We've all heard the stories." She stopped. "But whether a ghost can inhabit a physical form, or take on physical form, I don't know. A ghost is an apparition that responds to a call from the here and now. A need if you will."

"Yes," from Sweeney, his barely audible voice evincing hope.

Marian shook her head.

"You can't just make it happen."

"Why not?"

"Give it some thought, Jim."

"Well…"

"No," she said. "People die. They go somewhere, some of them, the ones who can't make it all the way across. The usual story is they died before their time, or died violently, and they are unhappy. They try to set things right." She paused, went under a low branch Sweeney held back for her. "For the most part, though, they are locked in that nether world. They can't come back across, certainly not physically. They need …"

Sweeney broke in.

"Sympathy."

"More than that," said Marian. "Someone who knows what she is doing." She paused. "Which is why you asked me up, isn't it? *I'm* the expert. I do readings. I use Tarot cards. I've been involved in seances."

The word was like magic to Sweeney.

"Seance," he said quietly.

His head went up and down.

"Careful what you ask for, Jim. If a spirit needs something done," she said, "he—or she—gets someone to do it for him. Usually by trickery."

"Why? Why not just ask?"

She shook her head. "You don't understand."

Sweeney almost gaped at her.

"Help me out."

Marian gathered her thoughts.

"If a spirit is unsettled enough to try and make contact with us, there is a reason. A bad reason. What may seem to the spirit to be a simple matter of righting a wrong, may seem to us to be evil." She paused. "A crime."

"Ah," from Sweeney, who bowed his head under a branch. "Murder most foul."

"Something like that," she declared. "The rules of morality bend a bit coming through the channels."

He turned and faced Marian.

"You think this Aveline wants us to harm someone?"

Marian shook her head. She let go of Sweeney's hand and took hold of his arm. She did not speak right away.

"She's not alone," she said. "There's another force. I don't know what kind, if it's controlling her, if it's making her try to reach us." She stopped. "Or if she's trying to break free." She continued. "If there is harm intended, it may not be coming from her."

"She's not the one who wants to set things right," offered Sweeney.

"Possibly," said Marian. She looked up at him. "You told me you believe she was the daughter of the man who once owned the house."

"Owned and built," replied Sweeney, although Marian was not asking a question, only stating what he had told her the night before. "Andrew Doucet built the house around 1880. He had two children. The second was a daughter named Aveline."

"Is she the only Aveline associated with the house?"

Sweeney shrugged.

"As far as I know."

They walked along in silence, over the great lawn in the direction of the main buildings on campus. For the most part, the lawn was empty, the campus quiet.

"Where are the students?" inquired Marian.

"Sleeping, I would imagine," he answered. "It's Saturday. They've been up early all week."

She gave his arm a tug.

"Tell me about them."

Sweeney smiled easily.

"The good ones, or the bad?"

She frowned, briefly. Then her forehead was smooth.

"The good ones." She laughed. "Who wants to hear about the bad? I want good stories," she paused, "with happy endings."

He took a deep breath and turned her around.

"See that island?" He pointed toward Graves Island. "You can see it. Right there." He paused. "It's close enough for the students to get to, if they can find a boat. But there is a current, so there's some danger. Most students don't even try it," he said, smiling a bit. "But some do."

"What makes them do it?"

Sweeney looked down at her.

"The spirit of adventure. The need to know the truth. You see," he said, "there's a story associated with that island. Each new generation of students hears it, one version or another. Each new group of boys decides to find out the truth." He pointed again. "At the far end of the island, near the lighthouse, is a kind of castle. A crenelated building of sorts; an old fort. Legend has it there's a man walled up in that castle."

"No," she laughed. "This place *is* positively medieval."

He nodded and went on with his tale.

"Sometimes the man is a Jesuit, a rebel, like Lucifer, walled up at the behest of a Chillingworth Headmaster. Other times he is a soldier from the Civil War."

She looked at him.

"Did you go?"

"When I was here?" Sweeney asked. "Oh, no. Not my cup of tea."

"Any of your students?"

"None that I know."

She smiled.

"Would you report them if you found out? You would have to report them, no?" She waited for a reply.

Sweeney had to think.

"I don't know," he said. "I don't think so. Circumstances might compel me. If someone got hurt." He looked out at the island. "But, no, I like to think I wouldn't."

Her head went up and down, obviously pleased at his response. When her head moved, her hair moved, and Sweeney watched it.

"Have you any students now who might be tempted to go out to the island? I mean, any candidates?"

He looked at her, curious.

"Are you reading my mind? If you are, stop. I never gave you permission."

"*Tell* me."

"As a matter of fact, there are two. They're in my sophomore English. I'll have them again for Shakespeare. And yes," he said, looking at her, "they might do it."

"What are their names?"

"Sparks and Boylan."

She laughed.

"Good name for a rock band."

Sweeney pondered this, his mind not used to working along such lines. He led her under the branches of a small copse of pine, and once under, they both could feel the coolness in the darkness under the branches. They moved out onto the lawn and looked up at the ivy-covered Gothic buildings with their tall windows. She took his hand and squeezed it.

"Do I get to meet these students?"

"The rock band?"

"Yes."

"Well, I have juniors over for tea."

"And they're sophomores."

"Right," he said. Then he smiled. "There is one thing I wanted to mention that I forgot and now I remember. Next year at the armory

there is going to be a psychic fair. First of its kind in New England."
He stared at her. "I'm sort of a secret organizer. I wouldn't want to
become *publicly* involved, since it is mysticism and this is a Jesuit
institution and they might get upset." He paused. "I'm in charge of
the quilt exhibit. You remember mother was a quilter."

"An expert."

"Yes," agreed Sweeney. "I'm even going to use one of her quilts.
Hang it high so everyone can see it."

"She would have loved that."

He nodded.

"Anyway, if you could come, I'm sure I could arrange for you to
set up a Tarot booth." He looked at her and could see her hesitation.
"Come on, Marian. It might even be fun." He lifted up his right
hand, a gesture of expansion. "It would be this time next year. The
rock band would be juniors."

"You'd have them for tea."

"Yes," he nodded. "I'd have them over before you came, to see
what they were like." He paused. "They could be ruffians. If they
are, I'll get some others."

She smiled.

"They won't be ruffians."

He looked at her and wondered how she could possibly know
and then he knew in an instant that she did and that she would meet
them and then he wondered if in her mind there was some secret
bond between her and one of the boys and then he wondered how
such a thought could have entered his head.

"How can you be so sure?"

She moved her blue eyes to the sky.

"The leaves will be just like this," she declared. "The sky will be
just like this." Her voice went soft. "I'll be there. I'll bring my cards."
She looked at him. "The boys will be good," she said, and she said it
so that Sweeney knew it was true.

41

The sun was setting when the two of them sat down at the table and looked down at the board. Sweeney had his pencil and his yellow pad and Marian, with her blue eyes, was staring at the planchette, hesitating to reach out and touch it. Sweeney waited. The Belle Fleur curtains were as they were the night before, ominous and still, the fireplace again aglow with bright flames and crackling logs and sparks. The cat was at rest near the door.

"I feel very cold, Jim."

"Want me to get a blanket?"

"It might be a good idea."

Sweeney left and returned with a wool blanket, which he draped about her shoulders. There were green and red and black stripes against a white background. She huddled under it.

"Thanks."

Sweeney sat and stared down at the board, thinking that if he stared hard enough and concentrated, he could help Marian in her bid to make contact. She looked over at him. He felt her eyes on him and looked up and looked at her. There was concern in her face.

"There is one danger," she said. "We have to consider it before we go on."

"Go ahead," he rasped. He was surprised at the way his voice sounded.

She gave him a long, steady look.

"People do not come back to life," she said. "But there is something they can do. I mentioned this on our walk. I want to mention it again, Jim." She paused. "If a spirit is strong enough, it can take control of a mind. It can possess you."

Sweeney sat back.

"That can happen here?"

She nodded.

"There is a lot of turmoil in Aveline. Maybe there is hatred," she declared. "Hatred is always a force to be reckoned with. It may be negative, but it's powerful. We must be careful."

Sweeney was troubled, and his face showed it.

"How? Do we stop?"

"No," answered Marian, reaching toward the tripod. "What was it Descartes said? 'Consider that the heavens, the earth, colors, shapes, sounds, and other external things are naught but illusions and dreams.'" She stared at the tripod. "Get ready to go deeper into that world." She looked up. "If you see something start to happen," she paused, "to me. If I start to pass out, or scream. If I start to speak in a voice that isn't mine, if my face begins to change shape." She saw the look on his face. "These things can happen. If they do, I want you to reach across the table and slap me." She paused. "Hard. I want you to knock me out of the seat if you have to. Anything to break contact." She stared at him. "You understand?"

"Yes," he said.

Marian circled her hand above the planchette. Her eyes moved to the board, then back to Sweeney's face. There was fear in his eyes and she saw it. She knew there was some in her own.

"It's good, I think, it was broken off last night. It gave us time to talk. Last night we weren't ready for some of the things that might happen. Tonight," she declared, trying to reassure him, "I think we are. I think *we're* stronger. We know more what to expect." She began to circle her hand faster, closer to the tripod. The tripod began to respond, moving in a mirrored circle beneath her moving open palm. "This spirit is anxious," she said, looking down.

"Good God!" exclaimed Sweeney, tempted to leap up from his chair. "Look!"

"I know, Jim. That can happen." She smiled, a brief flicker that vanished so fast Sweeney doubted it was there in the first place. "It's a good sign."

Sweeney had the pencil poised in his hand.

"Why good?"

"The spirit has something to say," she replied. "It wants to talk. It may even be in a hurry."

Sweeney held the pencil tightly.

"Hurry? Why hurry?"

She fingered the moving tripod.

"We'll find out, won't we?" she asked. She paused. "One more thing, before we go on."

"Yes?"

"No 'mother' questions, Jim," she said, her voice very soothing, almost hypnotic. "This isn't your mother."

He did not say anything. He watched her eyes close, he watched her fingers on the tripod. He watched, and waited.

"Is anybody there?"

He saw, felt in her a strange kind of power. She seemed, before his eyes, to be taking flight, to be soaring. Her skin seemed to shine, to radiate. She seemed serene and powerful and knowing.

"Ah," she groaned, going stiff.

She had felt a jolt from the board. Sweeney watched in terror, remembering her warning. The curtains began to sway, the fire began to beat and swoon in response to a rhythm he could not see or feel. But he felt the cold and he could feel his fear rising. This was not mother. This was Aveline. He looked at Marian. She seemed frozen. He heard an owl. He was certain he heard an owl. Then the tripod made a frenzied move toward the alphabet, the moon.

"Oh," he gasped.

She said:

"Is anybody there?"

42

Sweeney wrote the letters down.

SAVE ME

"Who are you?"

YOU KNOW WHO I AM

"Aveline," said Marian, transfixed. "You call yourself by that name." The tripod trembled, darted.

THAT IS MY NAME

"Why are you calling?"

IT IS YOU WHO CALLED ME I CALL NO ONE

Sweeney whispered the responses, wrote everything down.
"Do you need to be saved?" Marian's hand twitched, just off the tripod. Something seemed to be fighting her. She brought her hand back to the tripod, her eyes still tightly shut.

WE ALL NEED TO BE SAVED

"Are you in danger?"

ALL ARE IN DANGER

"Are we in danger? In this room?"

THIS HOUSE

"Is there another spirit behind you?"

I AM NOT AT LIBERTY TO SAY

"Speak the truth. You *must*. If we are to help."
Sweeney watched in astonishment, scribbled down the letters as fast as he could. His hand was beginning to ache.

WHO ARE YOU TO TELL ME THAT I AM NO ONE TO BE TRIFLED WITH I AM A GRAND DAME OF YORE I HAVE SEEN THINGS ANGELS A GRRAT STAR MOST SPLENDID AND BEAUTIFYL AND WITH IT AN EXCEEDING MULTI-TUDE OF MOST WONDEROUS FALLING STARS LIKE THE SEA THEY WERE THEN THE DARKNESS THE FALL-ING AND ALL THE STARS WENT OUT THEY WERE TURNED INTO COAL AND THEN RED THINS WITH EVIL EYES THAT COULD NOT BLINK FOR FEAR OF GOING BLIND BLACK COALS YOU TWO ARE PLAYING WITH THE WHORES DAUGHTER

The tripod ceased, was becalmed.
"Where are you?"
Sweeney waited for the response, his hand aching.

A BLACK HOLE I THINK

"Where?"

IN THE GROUND IT WOULD SEEM

"When did you die?"

WHAT MAKES YOU THINK I AM DEAD

"Aren't you?"

DEFINE DEATH YOU WHORE

Marian blinked open her eyes. She seemed startled. Her neck stiffened, she gasped, her face went white.

"Who... ?"

The planchette moved on its own now, free of Marian's fingers. She no longer needed to guide it. She just asked questions, keeping her eyes closed, whenever the tripod came to a halt. Sweeney wrote down every letter, following wide-eyed the graceful movements of the little wooden wheel.

AH MES CHERS U MUST WATCH YERSELVES, DO NOT LISTEN TO THE WORDS OF THE MAD BITCH FROM HELL

This was another voice! "Who are you?" Marian asked quickly, waiting to make contact before the first, less powerful spirit returned. "Who?" she repeated.

I AM YR GUID

"What do you want?"

HAR HAR YR SOULS

"Who are you?"

THE BILDER OF THS HOUS

"What is your name?"

U KNO MY NAM

Marian insisted. "We do not!"

THEN I WIL TEL U I AM ANDRE ST LOUP

"That is not the name of the man who built this house," Sweeney interrupted.

WHAT DO U KNO

"This is my house."

SO U THINK

"Is that it? You've come back for what you built?" she asked. "You want your house back?"

WHAT WD I DO WITH IT I HAVE NO BODY I LIVE IN A SEEDIE TEMPL WITH MANE KINDS OF FOWL AT MY BECK AND CALL I SEE MANY LITL WINGS THAT GLOW IN THE DARK U SHD COME AND VISIT

"Who is Aveline?"

GOOD QUESTION

"Who?" Marian repeated, trying to regain control of the tripod. Her hands reached out toward the planchette. It skittered away.

SHE CD BE YR MOTHR

"She is not."

HOW DO YOU KNOW

"I know my mother's voice," answered Marian after Sweeney whispered the response. "She's alive."

MAYBE NT FR LONG

"How can you say that?" Marian demanded. Sweeney could tell from her voice that she was frightened.

I AM SORIE IT WONT HAPN AGAIN AV ELIN IS A MAD THING I BREATHED LIFE BAK INTO

"Then she was dead?"

IN A MANR OF SPEAKING

"Did you kill her?"

O NO

"Who did?"

I DID NT SAY SHE WAS MURDRED

"She was not?"

SHE CN SPEK FR HERSRLF I WIL GET HER U CAN ASK UR QUESTIONS OF HER IT WIL MAK HER GLAD

"Will you let her speak freely?"

DON I ALWYS

"Aveline? Are you there?"

I AM BACK HE TOOK THE LEECHES OFF ME THE FOUL SCUM

"How did you die?"

DID HE TELL YOU THAT

"How?"

HUSH WAIT FOR MHIM TO BE OFF WHEN HE IS CLOSE I CANNOT DO AS OUCH I WANT HE CAN TOUCH ME EVEN FROM THERE THE BASTARD THE FOUL ALL I EVER WANTED TO BE WAS A GOOD SIMPLE MAID A GOOD MOTHER

"You had children?"

OH YES

"How many?"

ONLY ONE

"A boy?"

CURSED BE NO

"A daughter?"

A WHORE

"How can you say that?"

ITS THE TRUTH YOU HAVE HER OWN DAUGHTERS BOARD IN YOUR HAND

"You had a grandchild?"

AGAINST MY WILL

"Who is she?"

AVELINE THE WHORE

"You are Aveline, the mother of Prudence?"

MY GREAT SORROW TO ADMIT

"Why do you hate her?"

SHE KILLED ME

Marian gasped. "Your own child murdered you?"

ARENT WE ALL

"Please."

BY HER LUST THE WHORE BITCH TOOK THE
WHORE MAN TO BED IN HER MOTHERS HOUSE HER
MOTHERS I COULD HEAR THEM IN THE DARK IT WAS
AWFUL I TRIED TO SEE THE LIGHT THE CLOUD OF LIV-
ING LIGHT BUT I COULD NOT I COULD NOT BECAUSE
I COULD HEAR THEIR GROANS DOWN BELOW THEN
WHEN THE GROANS WERENT ENOUGH TO KILL ME
SHE CAME AND DID IT WITH HER FOUL DRAGONS
BREATH

"Your daughter, Prudence?"

DROVE A STAKE THROUGH MY HEART AH HE
COMES I CAN SMELL HIM AND HER BOTH WHORES
AND CRUEL TO A SIMPLE MAID WHO WANTED ONLE
TO BE A GOOD MOTHER AH BE QUICK I CAN SMELL
THE WOLF

"Aveline," Marian yelled. "How did you die? When?"
A sudden chill filled the room. Marian opened her eyes. The two
of them could see their breath. The fire dimmed. The curtains ruffled,
then became still. The fire fluttered, rose again, began to roar.

AH MES CHERS

Marian reached again toward the tripod. The tripod moved away, and when she tried to go after it, she found she could not move her hands. They were frozen, held, in a small space of air above the Ouija board.

BE STIL MEE HEARTIES I ONLY CAM TO SAV THE CHILDRN U CD BE MY VESSELS

"We will be no such thing," shouted Marian. "Let me go."

O YES U R RELEASED

"Thank you."

U R POLITE U GREEN EYED

"I have blue eyes."

IT IS HARD TO SEE THRU THE HAR HAR WINDOW

"Did Prudence kill her mother?"

O NO

"Then who?"

WD SHE NT TEL U

"No."

THN I WIL BRG HER BAK

"No!"

IT IS NO TRBLE I WIL HAV MY MINIONS GET HER

"Leave her alone."

SHE IS HER GO AND ASK

"Aveline," Marian began, quietly breathing deeply, feeling herself part of a strange tug-of-war. "Were you truly murdered?"

AS I HAVE ALREADY TOLD YOU

"How?"

BY THE ROPE I NEVER WOKE SAW STARS THE LIGHT JUST THE UTTER BLANK AND MSERABLE DARKNESS FOR SO LONG I HAD NO EYES NOW I CAN SEE HE MAY BRING THE LIGHT BUT WHY THE BASTARD WATCH OUT FOR HIM OUCH WATCH BEWARE THE WOLF AH HAS A LONG SLEV

1894

43

She felt again the stirrings of new life within her. This time a summer baby, a child with flowers on its breath. To be born in June with roses in the air, all yellow roses like the golden yellow of a good girl's hair. He would people the earth with his children, his seed, sow them throw them into the earth in the mad hope they would rise up an army and believe in his dream. He was good to them, a good father. There was love in him, love too a part of his need, and they both, Andre and Aveline, loved him back. Andre, at eight, was showing signs of becoming a rider as prodigious as his father; Aveline, the six-year-old silent type, had big green eyes that took in the world and gave nothing back. A strange child, her daughter. Something unforgiving in the eyes.

"I waited for you."

He had come up behind her. He would often do that and she could never hear him, as if he were still running north or hiding or still making plans. The dream was the house—or was that part of the lie? Or the dream was the children, the family. He did love them. Her. But did she love him? Was love what she felt? The almost animal hunger for him in the dark when she could sense and respond and see him as if he weren't the shadow he became in bed but the sainted man who rode into town on horseback fourteen years before and took a mother and a daughter into his arms and told them both he loved them and would people the world with their progeny. But the mother could not and the daughter could and she became the vessel through which Andre St. Loup—she knew his real name now, he was telling her things in the dark, building a bond—would implement his need. But what need? Did he not have enough? Was there not more money and land than all of them, the new one included, could expend in lifetimes?

"I know, Andre," she said softly, with just a hint of apology in her voice to let him know that she too felt the same desire. "It was hot, and the baby. This one is a trouble."

"He'll be fine," he said. "Like the others."

She looked up from the chair, shading her eyes from the sun. Even now—how old *was* he?—he was attractive, feral. What her mother saw, she saw, felt. Felt so much sometimes she could almost forget what had happened and her role in it: the mad woman upstairs, locked away of her own will, refusing life. Venom in her eyes. And at night she knew she listened without drawing a breath, like she listened when she, Prudence, could not block out the sounds coming from the bedroom. Now her mother like her, only her mother was mad and she—she was not. She had a man, a house, two fine children, a third on the way. And the townspeople? The townspeople had come along, needing the money or the work St. Loup, known still to them as Doucet, could provide. A crisp greenback or a handful, all that it took to wash away suspicion and scruple and replace it with a belief in the story told by Andre that he had never been carnal with the widow Fischer and had been courting all the time the lovely, long-haired, green-eyed daughter. A good story to believe and it made for a good false camaraderie on holidays and gatherings. Only, of course, she knew otherwise. She had seen her mother's eyes, had heard the sounds, had been outside the door the night Doucet returned and told the poor mad woman he would have her daughter because the good widow was barren and could not form part of the link with the ages. His exact words:

"We are going to have to do something about mother," she said to him. "I can't live with it anymore. The way she rocks, the screams when she starts to imagine. It's not good for me and I know it's not good for the children. It's too much for them. Soon they will want to know on their own."

She paused, looked up into his clear eyes that became cold every time she mentioned Aveline. "She will tell them," she warned, "if she hasn't said something already. I wonder about the girl."

"What is there to wonder about?"

"She is so quiet."

"Many children are quiet."

"Not like her, Andre."

He reached down and ran his hand over her cheek. It felt warm, good to her. In him was kindness, not at the center, but at the edges to dull the glow and ache of the fire in him that fueled the need and the dream that took him from France to America to war and to Canada, an outcast with something to hide and bury, the hunter having become the hunted, at least in his own mind. There was madness too and a kind of sadness that would not go away that came, she knew because he told her, of the one truly dreadful thing he had done in his life. It had brought him to her and that had made it seem more right than wrong but she knew he knew in his heart the ends could never justify what he had done to implement them. He had lived with it for thirty years. He would live with it until he died.

"Prudence," he said, his hand still warm on her cheek. "Your mother is locked away. She cannot get out. The children have never been near her."

"Why am I so less sure of that than you?"

He smiled, his teeth shining briefly.

"You lack my faith in orders," he answered. "I have told Beatrice the old lady is to be kept under constant scrutiny. She has told me it is so." He paused. "I believe her."

She brought her hand up to his.

"Could we send her away?"

He looked down, the sadness again in his eyes. For her too he felt it, although Prudence now would sometimes try and tell herself she did not know fully the truth of the night in the bedroom and the screams of Aveline. Such was the power of his will. *Did* he take the mother wanting the daughter the whole time? Or did he take and want the mother only to find her barren and then take and want the daughter to be close to the mother in the one possible way by marrying one and keeping the other? Was there not a grim logic in that? As long as he did not take the mother to take the daughter the whole time—as he had assured her—she could come to terms with it. But sometimes deep in her mother's eyes, she could see a truth, or part of it, and it was not the truth she wanted to believe or he wanted her to believe. It was vague, though, and unspoken and her mother was mad and she had children to consider. She would believe what she needed to believe, like everyone else in Gloucester.

"Where do you suggest?"

She stood, slowly. She took his hands.

"Not far," she replied. "There is a new place for people like her, further north. They have doctors and nurses. She would be happier there, I am sure of it. Better than for her to spend the rest of her life locked up in that room."

He looked down into the cool green eyes of his wife and knew that what she said was the truth. He too could hardly bear the sound of the rocker scraping and sawing and the screams, muffled and as occasional as they might be. His, though, was the greater guilt. He looked, caught her eyes in his, squeezed her cool firm hands. Good that she had asked. He could do it for her and the children. He bent to kiss her and in response he could sense, even in the shadow of an afternoon, her want and need of him. He leaned away, looked longingly at his wife. If in her clear cool eyes he did not see love, what she gave him was good enough to strike a bargain: mutually carnal need and the peace, if that was the word, that came from it.

"Do you want me to tell her?"

"Yes," she said.

"And when?"

"Soon."

He smiled, still holding her hands.

"Would tomorrow be soon enough?"

Prudence smiled, a cool brief flicker.

"Tomorrow would be fine."

"I shall do it," he said, releasing her, "in the morning. After Andre and I come back from our ride."

"Then," she said, hugging him, "it is finished. The woman is out of our lives.

44

In the morning they went off to ride and she watched them from the verandah, cool and secure, Aveline holding her hand. A floating mist covered the fields and the two cantering chestnut mares— her husband had an almost inexplicable fondness for chestnut mares— and their riders receded very gradually, or so it seemed to Prudence, into the long grass, and the woods beyond the long grass and the open fields. She could see her husband's hat dancing under the low branches on the way out, saw it almost topple once from his head when he had to bend quickly, having been talking to the boy so that the branch came up unexpectedly, quicker than he had anticipated. A deft touch and the hat stayed put and then they were gone from view.

"Would you like to help me with my quilt?"

Aveline looked up, her eyes bright and green, her blond hair in curls about her shoulders. She bobbed her head.

"Yes, mother. Do I get to pick out the piece?"

Prudence smiled, took a last look at where the riders had last been seen, turned and took her daughter by the hand and brought her in off the porch. Behind them the door slammed shut with a bang.

Aveline giggled up at her mother.

"When do I get to go riding?"

Prudence looked up from her bag of fabric. She had selected a number of pieces and was putting them into another bag which she would take back out to the porch with her. She had planned to piece out another row on the quilt before Andre and his father returned and she wanted to do it on the porch, in the shade, before the sun came up and it became too hot to do anything. She smiled at Aveline, pleased that she was doing more talking than usual and taking an interest in quilting. Anything to take her mind from horses, which more and more seemed to be a concern with her, especially since her brother was so praised by the men on his riding ability. Aveline, a graceful, lithe girl, smarter than Andre, saw herself the better rider if she could ever get on a horse. Prudence had never gotten used to Andre beginning to ride at five. She did not ever expect to get used to Aveline on one of the colonel's large mares, not at eight or nine and certainly not at six. She finished stuffing fabric into the bag and took her daughter's hand. Through the kitchen, into the parlor, out through the door, and into the long swing chair from which she could see the new house being built in the empty field across the way, so close to their land as to be on it, but the deed said not.

"Mother, when?"

Prudence frowned.

"Not for a while, dear. Girls don't go riding. Riding is for men." She handed Aveline the bag. "Be a good girl and look through those scraps and find me some blue squares with red. I think they would go nice here." Looking over at Aveline: "What do you think?"

"I want to be riding like Andre."

Prudence chuckled.

"You will, dear. You will. But not just now." She took her eyes from the girl and cast about in the direction where men carried long beams from a wagon toward the foundation. "We can watch them build today, too. Isn't that nice?"

"I don't like that house."

"Oh, why?"

"It's too big."

"It's not big yet."

Aveline jerked her head up and down.

"Yes it is. Father said."

Prudence smiled, grateful for the loquacity. Perhaps her husband was right after all. Aveline was a little girl, prettier than most, and just like other children her age. The silence, perhaps, not unusual for a bright girl, an observer even at six.

"When did he say this?"

"Yesterday," answered the girl. "He went and talked to the tall man."

"You mean old Artemus."

"Yes, Mr. Artemus."

Prudence corrected her daughter.

"He's Mr. Wicks, Artemus Wicks," she said. "It's going to be his house." She looked at the men working. "Quite a place it's going to be, too."

"I don't like him," protested Aveline, looking through the bag, having forgotten about horses now that she was discussing Mr. Wicks and his enormous house. "I found a blue!"

"Good," said Prudence. "If it has red on it we can use it in this line." She took the piece, which did have small red flowers in a field of blue and white. "There, that will go nicely. Now find some more."

Aveline looked up from the bag when the hammers started.

"Mr. Wicks is mean."

Prudence wondered.

"Oh, hush."

"He is."

"How can you say that?"

Aveline frowned, making tiny lines on her forehead.

"He has a big mean dog and he told me to keep away from it if I knew what was good for me."

Prudence laughed, almost sticking herself with a pin. Thinking of the dog, an enormous creature in keeping with the huge house, she said:

"Sounds like pretty good advice to me, Aveline."

The daughter demurred.

"He didn't have to be so mean the way he said it."

Prudence nodded, diligently working the fabric Aveline handed her into an evenly placed row of stars.

"Well, dear," she said without looking up, "perhaps he was a bit quick with his tongue." Smiling, "We'll just have to bake him a cake and take it over and let him know we're all nice people." She paused. "Now what do you think of that for an idea?"

Aveline laughed.

"Could we give some to the dog?"

Prudence nodded yes and smiled and the morning went faster than she would have imagined, given what was on her mind. In no time they had pieced together two rows and were on their way into a third when the sound of shouts and horses made them look up and they saw coming across the field, well past the long grass, Andre and his father. They brought the horses up and the colonel handed the reins to his son and Andre walked them off toward the barn where he would take them around the perimeter twice, slowly, to cool them and then brush and feed and water the mares and leave them in the shade of the barn the rest of the morning. In the afternoon he would take and let them out into the field, brush them again, and put them back inside. The colonel did not like to leave his horses unattended and he liked having them inside, locked away from whatever predators he feared would come for them in the night. A foible of his that amused Prudence. When the boy was gone, Andrew came up to the porch, kissed his wife and daughter on the forehead, nodded curtly to Prudence and took a long deliberate walk down the hall and up the stairs to the attic. He did not come down for some time and Prudence wondered herself, for a long time afterward, what actually took place that afternoon between her husband and her mother. She felt relief when she heard his calm footsteps on the stairs and waited expectantly for him to arrive on the porch. He came out, closed the door quietly behind him, took his daughter and lifted her into his arms.

"How would you like to get your daddy a cold drink from the kitchen, princess?"

Aveline giggled, her curls bouncing in her father's face.

"Only if I can ride tomorrow."

He brought her to the floor.

"We'll have to see about that," he said, eyeing his wife. "First go get me some water. Then maybe we'll talk about it."

Aveline raced off, slamming the door behind her.

"Well?" asked Prudence.

He sighed, nodded.

"It's done."

"What did you tell her?"

"What you asked," he replied. "She had to go. That there's a better place for her with more room, good care. She'd be able to get outside."

"What did she say?"

He stared at Prudence, thought carefully before replying. "Not a word."

"Not a word?"

St. Loup shook his head, his long silver-flocked hair swaying gently above his shoulders. His cold blue eyes colder than usual, his voice calm but cool too, a man grateful for the choice given him, but still resentful at having been made to choose. It was done.

"She stared at me with those damn eyes of hers and didn't say a thing," he continued. "Then she looked out the window and began to rock like she always does." He stopped. "You can hear her now, louder than the cicadas in the heat."

Prudence listened. It was true.

"Did you tell her I would be coming up?"

"No," he replied. He smiled grimly, quickly. "You can surprise her," he declared, giving her the key to the lock on her mother's door.

She took the key, put it in her reticule and went on, without another word to her husband, with her piecing of the fabric. When Aveline returned with the water, she and her father went off to the barn to watch Andre cool the mares, leaving Prudence alone on the porch, sitting in the shade on the long swing chair, listening to the sound of men hammering and cicadas, and, if she stopped to think about it, her mother rocking in the attic.

She did two more rows, taking the better part of the afternoon, before she put up the quilt and got up from the chair and walked into the house and down the hall to the base of the stairs. She stopped when she got there, stared long at the banister, seeing the outlines of her face in the polished wood. She took the first step, thinking about what she would say to her mother. She had no words. The words had already been spoken. She was on the second-floor landing before she knew it and was halfway down the hall when she realized for the first time that the rocker was silent. When had that happened? She took it for a good sign, paused but briefly before the first stair to the

attic, and then bounded up the stairs with an energy she did not
know she possessed in the dull heat of a late spring afternoon. She
stopped when she got to the locked door, and knocked. She always
knocked before entering. Her mother had never responded in any
way to the knocks, but still she knocked. Locked away as she was, it
was still her room and Prudence could not bring herself to unlock
the door and go in without a word.

"Mother," she said, knocking gently. "Mother, it's me, Prudence."

There was no response. There was never any response. She took
the key, put it in the lock, turned and pushed open the door. She saw
immediately that Aveline was out of her chair. But where? Then the
shadow and then she saw, hanging from the beam, the gray-haired
old woman, her unkempt hair, her lifeless probing eyes, unforgiving,
motionless, a pool of something below her, her mouth open and in
it a purple lolling tongue swollen to twice its size. She screamed. She
turned and screamed and ran, fell once, got to the stairs, felt faint,
hot, empty and then she slipped and tumbled and fell, over and over
and over herself, down the stairs, coming to rest against the wall at
the base of the stairs, her head strangely askew and in her belly, a
sharp pain and a sense of something terribly wrong. She screamed,
more a wail now, for help. She heard shouts below, then footsteps.
The footsteps took forever.

A DEMOCRACY
OF GHOSTS

1965

45

A voice, Welcome's, whispers:

"I was right about the window."

"Shhh..."

They sit in the dark, afraid to turn on the flashlight, on a floor they can feel with their hands to be concrete in some parts, dirt in others. There is dirt around the trap door. The air is damp, but dry too; damp, it seems, near the floor but dry higher up. The boys stay still. They listen. They hear a few words from below, whispers actually, they can barely make out. There is some scurrying and for a moment they believe the man—or men—from below will come up. The thought of this makes them sit up in terror. The next thing, Boylan jumps to his feet and makes a grab for Adrian, who needs no urging and is on his feet before Boylan can complete the grab. Welcome follows, reacting to their shadows.

"What?" he whispers in inquiry.

No one knows. This is a strange house. A strange dark room they realize must be a cellar. There are men down below. Welcome is certain they have escaped with their lives, as is Boylan. The two of them begin to creep toward what they can dimly make out to be the base of the stairs in the palpable darkness, feeling about like blind men with their hands. If there is a light switch, they are in no position to find it. Adrian whispers at the others.

"Where are we?"

Boylan hisses back.

"In the dark, dammit."

Adrian persists.

"What did you see when the flashlight was on?"

Boylan, testy this time.

"Why don't you turn the damn thing on?"

"That's not a bad idea, Adrian," says Welcome. "If this is the cellar, it's empty. No one can see us."

Adrian switches on the light.

"Where do you think we are?"

"Another house," answers Welcome.

"That's pretty obvious," says Boylan.

"But whose?" asks Adrian.

He takes the lead and begins to walk, gingerly, toward the stairs, which he has found with the flashlight. He stops, waits when he gets there. Welcome and Boylan, never far behind, come up next to him.

"Maybe no one's home," Welcome suggests.

"Yeah," mutters Blazes, in his ear. "Maybe the door to the upstairs is locked. Maybe we'll have to leave the way we came in."

Adrian claps his hand to his head.

"Oh, God."

"Oh, God, is right," echoes Welcome.

Adrian takes a deep breath and begins to climb, praying the stairs won't creak. There is a creak, the first step, and his heart almost fails him—or so he believes. He nearly turns back. Then he ascends, slowly, a step at a time. Two more of them creak. There is a brief rug covering the top two stairs. He aims the light at the door.

"Should I knock?"

He hears a muffled snort from below.

"Try trick or treat."

Adrian can't help smiling as he reaches for the doorknob. He can feel his knees knocking together and his hand is shaking on the knob. What is the fear? The men in the tunnel, the owner of the house, finding the door locked? He takes a deep breath. The knob turns of its own will it seems. The door is open. Light filters down the stairs, for which Welcome and Boylan mutter praise, but they wait. This is Adrian's job. It was his idea. He can be the first upstairs. They can barely hear him, his movements. A true pioneer, Welcome thinks, waiting for the call to come up.

Boylan is something of the same mind, more certain now of escaping and making it back to the school. He is about to take the first step when Adrian reappears at the top of the stairs.

"You'll never guess whose house this is."

Boylan begins to climb.

"I take it the place is empty."

Adrian nods assent.

"Right," he says. "Besides, there's no danger. The house belongs to Sweeney."

"No!" escapes from Welcome, who is right behind Boylan on the stairs. "I don't believe it."

"Look for yourself," says Adrian. "We sat right in those chairs," pointing to the living room. "Remember?"

"I remember," agrees Welcome, looking in.

Boylan has a dark look on his face.

"I'm glad it's Sweeney's," he says. "But let's get the hell out. We can admire it some other time."

Adrian waves his ghostly arm.

"He'd never know it was us," he crows. "We're disguised."

"He's right," says Welcome, pointing at Boylan. "Let's go."

"OK," from Adrian. "Who's first?"

Boylan steps forward.

"I think that's me."

"Why you?" asks Welcome.

"Because this wasn't my idea," Boylan answers. "Which door? Front? Back?"

"I suppose the back," suggests Welcome, still whispering. "The safest. Nothing out there but trees."

"Good," from Blazes.

Adrian leads the way, having just been to the kitchen. Boylan and Welcome are right behind him. The floor in the kitchen creaks, bringing them all to a stop halfway to the door.

"Damn!" mutters Adrian. "Where's the bag, Blazes?

Boylan looks down at his empty hands.

"I thought you had it."

Adrian scowls. He hands Boylan the light.

"Go back and get it," he orders. "Hurry."

Boylan hesitates, then realizes the fault is his. He turns about, springs from the kitchen and jumps down the stairs. They do not hear him while they wait, inspecting Sweeney's kitchen. Boylan is taking a long time, and Welcome is anxious. He locks his sheet-covered eyes with Adrian's, inclines his head, and starts to say something. He does not get the word out. From below they bear a loud, ghostly groan. They freeze. Is it Boylan? Is he hurt? What do they do?

"Oh, God," exclaims Welcome, unable to stop his voice, to keep it a whisper. His legs begin to shake. Again, he feels himself about to cry. Or worse.

46

They suddenly hear stumbling footsteps on the stairs. Adrian and Andrew open wide their white-covered mouths and stare into the hallway. They wait. There is nothing else to do. They can't leave Boylan.

"Jesus!" exclaims Boylan, careening into the kitchen. He runs right into Welcome and knocks him flat. He bends down to help Welcome to his feet.

"Sorry," he apologizes, handing Adrian the bag with one hand, the flashlight with the other.

"What happened?" Adrian half yells into his ear.

Boylan is busy at the door.

"Damned if I know."

"Someone groaned," says Welcome.

"I know that," retorts Boylan. "Why do you think I ran up the stairs?"

He unlocks the door.

"What was it?"

Boylan looks at Adrian

"Nothing that can't be talked about outside."

"Is someone down there?" from Welcome.

"Not that I noticed," replies Boylan. "Then again, I didn't take time to look."

"Who groaned?" Adrian persists.

Boylan shakes his masked head.

"You mean *what* groaned."

"What?" from Welcome, who is incredulous.

Boylan throws up his hands.

"I told you, I don't know. I heard a groan. It was close. Scared the hell out of me. I ran." Pausing. "I plan to keep on running until I get some distance between me and this place and that place we crawled in from. Far as I know Sweeney is in cahoots with a bunch of crazies." He pulls in the kitchen door. They all feel the outside air. "Maybe he likes digging tunnels."

"Wait," Adrian calls out.

"Jesus," Boylan mutters.

"Where's Melchior?"

Again, the hands go up.

"The bag. Look in the bag."

"I did," says Adrian. "He's not there."

Boylan hesitates.

"Maybe he fell out. I dropped the bag when I heard the groan," he declares. "I didn't hear anything. But it could have fallen out." He steps outside. "You have the flashlight."

"Why should Adrian get it?" asks Welcome. "You dropped it."

"Because, goddamn it, it belongs to him," Boylan declares. "Let him go get it. Far as I'm concerned, we can come and get the damn tripod some other time."

"When?"

"Not my problem," says Boylan.

"What would we tell Sweeney?" asks Welcome.

"That's something we'll have to discuss," answers Boylan.

"He might want to know about the tunnel, assuming he doesn't already."

"What do you think's going on?" asks Adrian.

"Beats me," shrugs Boylan. "He *is* a little strange. Stays with his mother until she dies, then gets himself a cat to replace her." He stops. "Don't forget. We saw him at the psychic fair."

"So?" from Andy.

Boylan ignores the question.

"Better get going," he says to Adrian.

"You won't come down with me?"

Boylan laughs.

"I've been in that cellar two times too many as it is," he says. "I'll be waiting. Outside. Under the trees."

"What if something happens?"

"Nothing's going to happen," says Blazes.

"Suppose something does?"

Boylan chuckles, the fear of his experience in the cellar evaporating. He is back in control. He feels calm, himself again.

"If you're not up in an hour we'll call the police." He smiles. "Anonymously."

Adrian sighs.

"All right," he says. "Any idea where you might have dropped him? Like . . ."

"I was right at the bottom of the stairs when I heard the groan," he says. "Assuming it fell there—and not back in the tunnel—I'd say look off to the right. If not there, in back."

"Andy, you'll wait inside?"

"I am transfixed."

Boylan laughs again, passes through the door and is gone. Adrian takes a last look into Welcome's hooded eyes, then leaves, the flashlight already on in his hand. At the top of the stairs he pauses, then begins a tremulous descent. He cannot help himself. His knees are shaking, there is a knot in his throat and he is covered with sweat. He holds his breath going down, listens to every sound, aims the beam wildly into the dark. Nothing moves. It is a cellar like any other cellar. He sees boxes, tools, paint, a bicycle, a pile of empty picture frames, a rack of some kind, some round hoops, broken windows lined up against the wall. He stands at the base of the stairs until he is sure he knows his way around. Then he moves out. He follows Boylan's first directive and goes off to the right. The beam on the floor, he looks, searches for some sign of Melchior. He goes over the floor, inch by inch. He finds nothing. Everything is undisturbed. He turns to the rear, where there are boxes against the wall. He may have to move them to see in between. He sweeps the beam slowly over to the wall and peers into the first cardboard box. He finds it filled with rags, or fabric. Quilting material. Sweeney quilts? He assumes the rest are filled with the same and ignores them. Not that Melchior would be in a box. He is on the floor. And then he aims the light into a tunnel between the boxes. Aha! he thinks. This is the road taken by Melchior. He knows it. How? Is he being guided? Is Melchior leading him on? He pushes aside the boxes—they are light—and opens an alley for himself. He aims the beam.

"Damn," he mutters.

A low wooden door waits ahead, rotted at the bottom. He knows before he is actually conscious of it where Melchior is hiding. On his hands and knees, now, he crawls ahead and aims the beam into an opening. "Ah!" he exclaims. There sits the tripod, gleaming back. There is also a large spider with red glowing eyes, sitting in the middle of a pulsating web. He sighs, stands, steps back and scans for a stick or one of the tools to pull the tripod out from under the sticky web. If he had a glove, maybe. He takes another look at the spider. Maybe a blowtorch.

He finds a small hoe, brings it back to the opening and tries to get it under the hole. Too big. Unless he can twist it under. Which he tries. In it goes! Victory. Come, Melchior, come. He pulls—and out comes nothing. Again, he pulls. Again, nothing.

"Adrian?" Welcome whispers from the top of the stairs.

He sighs.

"Right up. I found him."

"Good."

He jams in the hoe this time, breaking something—glass? He pulls out harder than he should and out tumbles the whole wooden flap door. Adrian jumps back and gasps. What has he done? He aims the beam on the floor. There sits Melchior. He bends and retrieves the tripod and aims the beam into the new opening at the base of the wall and is startled to see shelves of small jars. Ball jars some of them, and inside the jars—he must get closer—things floating? He gasps. The things are animal heads. A squirrel, a cat. Dogs, more cats. His jaw drops under the sheet. He is suddenly sick to his stomach. Sweeney? He falls to his knees, feeling faint. The beam of the flashlight wavers—with a mind of its own?—and strikes a large strangely bright translucent cylinder of glass. Inside it is colorless liquid and in the liquid, the livid long-haired wide-eyed head of an old man with a bold streak of color up over his ear. The dull lifeless opaque eyes show no new life, but in his hand Adrian feels Melchior quiver.

"Adrian!"

Yes. His name. *His* scream. Welcome has heard him scream.

"Adrian!"

He falls to his knees and throws up. He can hear himself gagging. He spits, tries to stand.

"Oh," he moans. Everything is spinning.

"Adrian!" he hears.

He looks at the head. It floats, stares like Medusa. This time he gets to his feet. He takes a last look at the dark-eyed livid face. The face of some old man. A long life. When did he die? How? Who put his head in the jar? How long has it been there? He stands back, wiping the spit and vomit from around his lips. He is shaking. He is crying. He feels nauseated. He wobbles toward the stairs, drops the flash light, picks it up and begins to climb, trembling every step of the way. At the top he tries to tell Welcome, but when he opens his mouth, no words come out. His voice is gone.

1914

47

The bonfire, like a stook of flame, clawed at the sunset. Tethered horses whinnied, the sparks, the roar too much for them as people encamped about the blaze drank, laughed and cheered on the men loading more logs, withered trees, blasted timber against the spire of flame. The whole town seemed to be out, gathered on the dry flat field where once corn grew, was harvested and set aside. Doucet had been planning the blaze for months and to that end had been piling up wood and scrap and bales of paper and had enlisted neighbors and friends to do the same. Day after day the pile grew, from nothing, until it formed a midden heap made mostly of wood. At first no one noticed. Then they noticed. The sun would set around it, the pile would cast a shadow. It took on a life if its own. Birds flocked to it, mockingbirds, blue jays, blessed it with song in the daylight. At night the owls took to it, hooting, watching the moonlit fields for stirrings over rippling grass. When the day of days, Halloween, came, Doucet was out at the spire, inspecting, adjusting, barking orders, his blue eyes wild with an antic cheer.

"Get it right, gentlemen. Get it right."

They succumbed to the spell. It had never been done like this before: out in the middle of a field, at sunset, with all the children, like little mummers, racing and laughing, taken too by the day and the time and the mood. Mothers watched the kettles where corn and lobsters boiled, seasoning the cool air, cared for the fires on which roasted entire pigs and full sides of beef.

"This is a mad idea, Andre," Prudence said, coming up alongside her husband. "I don't know what's come over you."

His eyes flashed.

"Not mad, Prudence," he said. "Good." He stared out at the fire. "It's good to burn." He smiled and looked down at his wife. "Old-fashioned paganism." He put his arm around her. "My way of making amends."

She stared into his eyes, unsure.

"For what?"

"Everything," he said.

Prudence turned toward the flames.

"We're well beyond that, you and I," she declared, raising her voice above the noise of the fire. "What's done is done."

Still with his arm around her:

"Is that what you really feel?"

She looked up, saw the flames reflected in his clear proud eyes, saw too the old sadness and for the first time, a tight set to his mouth, a grimness not there before.

"It's the way I feel now," she said.

He nodded abruptly.

"Then it's good, the fire." He paused, looked out over the fields. "Aveline, Andre," he said. "Are they here?"

"They were," Prudence answered. She pointed. "Look, there's old man Wicks and that dog of his. The size of them."

The colonel would not be put off.

"I saw Andre before. He's drunk."

"Why tell me?"

Doucet remained quiet. Then:

"What's wrong with him?"

Prudence placed her arm through his. They began to walk closer to the fire, the colonel still tall, thin, with the same silver hair he seemed in her mind to have had since she met him. That was not true: his hair was black, then silver, then white. He was older. He never seemed to change, but he changed. His hair had gone from black to gray, his face had thinned. But his grip was strong and he was strong; there was as yet no lack of need in him for her. A man of stone.

"You haven't answered my question."

She sighed.

"There is no answer," she said. "You gave him too much, you gave him too little. You spoiled him. You were harsh." She stopped. "You tried to make him just like you, Andre, and when you failed you gave up on him." Looking into his dark eyes, "That's why he drinks. He hates himself. You *made* him hate himself."

"That's not true," he argued.

"No," she returned. "Look to your heart." She waited. "You know it's the truth."

Doucet stopped walking and turned to his wife.

"He can change."

He felt her haughty mirthless green eyes before he heard her hollow laugh.

"It's too late."

They walked in silence toward the bonfire. Shrieking children danced past them, some of them in costume. Older children lolled about, drinking hard cider and beer and walked out into the near dark, out toward the barn, where two huge haystacks, well out of reach of the flames, waited for them. A man strummed a guitar, a woman sang, dogs barked. In the clear October sky stars were beginning to shine and just above the bonfire sparks reached up to them and became, ever briefly, a flash in the cosmos. Prudence made for that point. When once she noticed how sparks and stars could match she sought them out. This is me, she thought. This is him. I am so far from him.

"I love the flames," he said.

She felt the heat on her cheeks, the thrill of smoke and flame and the rush of dying burning things. How fast it went. A log became a million sparks and then nothing. The noise it made. The sound of annihilation, a great windy roar, a rising and then a deep blue starry sky where there were no sounds and no flames.

"I do too," she said.

They moved a bit toward the shadows, the heat on their faces pushing them back. A line of jack-o-lanterns had been set up in the field and they followed it, to an old woman, sitting on a box in a circle of candlelit pumpkins. Shapes flickered over her face, her deep eyes going light dark, light dark and her lips, parted in a smile that took in the night. She looked up when she saw them.

"Have your fortunes told?"

Doucet brushed her away with his hand.

"No," he said.

"Madame?" the woman pressed, shuffling and then taking out a face card from the deck and placing it neatly in the center of a small blanket spread out before her. "No harm in it."

"Oh, Andre," said Prudence. "Let's."

Doucet stared down at the cards. He saw a knight, a pentacle, a sword. Then the woman picked them up, shuffled again. He looked into the eyes of the woman, who looked back. There was nothing in her eyes.

"I'm going up to the house," he said, moving his eyes from the fortune teller to his wife. "I'll join you at the pig spit." He looked again at the woman, at the cards in her hand, and stepped stiffly, without a word, into the shadows.

48

He sat on the porch before going in, looking down at the field where the fire burned gloriously, thrilling the night air with sparks, crackles, and sudden groans when large pieces of timber crumpled in the heat. Now and then he heard a crack, like a gunshot. He could hear vague, distant songs from children being led through cadences, could see, dimly, groups of them. Shouts and shrieks too, and a susurrant wind-carried moan from older children and adults listening to ghost stories. The moan rose up in a quiet wave and receded, replaced by shrieks, or an empty wind, and then returned. He waited for it up there on the long chair in the shade, swinging quietly. Come whisper, he thought. Soothe me. It alone among the sounds of the evening brought a land of surcease, a wave of voice and feeling that washed away other voices, feelings. But could it, or anything, forfend? A story, wind-carried, for an old man on an evening, his evening, his gift to the town, to them all. But what story?

The story of eight boxes, a cabin, a shooting and a pounding heart? And what would be the moral? He got up from the swing chair, turned about and went inside, closing the door quietly behind him, the quiet closing his reply to the moral of anything.

He walked down the hall, turned into the kitchen, found himself a glass and poured himself some whiskey from a bottle already opened on the counter. Andre had been there before him. He blamed himself for the boy, the way he turned out. Prudence had spoken the truth. And the girl? The girl in her own quiet way was even more trouble. Aveline had grown up comely, with long yellow hair, but with a reticence she carried like a riding-whip. Something had never taken root in her, she had not molded properly. She was, from the outside, flawless, even beautiful. But inside was a missing piece, or series of pieces: warmth, words, love, response. And he blamed himself for that too. He laughed to himself. The master of his progeny, his own word, tossed back at him by two women and now by his own children, but not with words. Words would have been easier.

He heard a gentle tap at the door.

Doucet, brought back, walked to the oak door and pulled it in, looking into the dark. He saw nothing.

"Yes?" he inquired.

"Evenin', your honor," said a voice, a young voice. "Would you be Mr. Andrew Doucet, owner of this property?"

Doucet followed the voice, saw what it was. A boy, small for his age, well back in the shadows of the porch. He stepped to his left and switched on the light. Saw him better.

"I am," he replied. "What can I do for you?"

The boy forced a thin smile, squinting into the overhead light, from which he shaded his eyes, but not before Doucet could see that they had red points, red centers, where the light hit, like the eyes of a startled animal.

"Actually, sir, it's a business proposition of a sort," the youth said. He tried to smile and seemed uneasy. "I've come a long way. Appreciate if we could talk inside."

Doucet, on guard, spoke out.

"I don't think I'm much interested in talking business tonight," he declared. "Nothing personal. Why don't you come back?" He pointed toward the field. "There's a celebration."

The boy did not turn. "So I see."

"You look young enough to be a mummer yourself."

There was a sudden tightening in the jaw.

"I'm not so young."

Doucet smiled. A smile would put an end to this.

"How old are you?"

The youth grinned maliciously.

"Eighteen, your honor."

Doucet studied the form before him on the porch.

"Bit small for your age."

The boy chortled and brought his hand up quickly to his mouth to keep from guffawing. There were small tears in his eyes.

"Bit of a dwarf, your honor."

Doucet considered this remark.

"You'll grow."

The red-haired boy shook his head slowly.

"Ain't growed in four years, sir." He paused. "No use in dreamin'."

Doucet was tired of the ordeal. He wanted to finish his drink, inside the house, and go back to his wife.

"Well, young man, why don't you go down and eat your fill and come back during the day. We can talk business then," he declared, hoping never to see the young man again. "We have a fire down there. A grand fire." He looked out, saw sparks and flames. "You should enjoy it. Nothing like a good fire."

The boy nodded.

"I'll grant you that," he said. He waited, shifted his weight from one foot to the other, as if he were deliberating. "We have to talk tonight, sir. You and me. Can't be no other time."

The cold blue eyes flashed.

"Listen, boy," he shouted. "I've about listened to all the talk I'm going to listen to from you. Now you get out, or I throw you out." He waited. Softer, "What's it going to be?"

The boy, over a foot shorter than Doucet, tittered.

"Suppose I told you that my business proposition comes from a man by the name of Irish Pat Cleburne." He grinned. "That make a difference to you?"

Doucet felt himself going cold. He could feel a quiet pounding begin. A pain flashed over his eyes.

"General Cleburne is dead," he said.

Cold dark unsmiling eyes glared up at him

"Did I say he wasn't?"

"Then what is this nonsense?" inquired Doucet, still wondering what to say. "The man is dead."

The youth then said, in a voice flat as gun metal:

"Dead he may be, but gone he ain't. You and me, your honor, we got business to tend to. If you want to know more—and I think it's in our mutual best interest if you do—let's go inside." He looked up at the light. "Don't like the air. The bugs." He moved his eyes from the light to the colonel. "Well?"

Doucet knew the boy had to be dealt with.

"Who are you?" he asked, pulling open the door. "Are you a relative of the general's?"

The flat-eyed boy shook his head.

"An heir. Just an heir."

49

They sat across the oak kitchen table, Doucet another drink in his hand, the boy impassive, waiting. Doucet studied the wide, flat face before him, the dark suspicious eyes, the broad nose and the flared nostrils, the thick lips and prominent teeth. He had a shock of unkempt red hair. The face beneath the hair looked strangely dangerous given the size of the youth, and the eyes that looked back at Doucet seemed to suck in the light.

"I'd offer you a drink. . ." he began.

The boy dismissed him.

"I'm not part of the drinkin' South."

Doucet acknowledged.

"I knew you were," he said. "From the South."

The boy chuckled.

"Still obvious, eh?"

Doucet reached for the glass, drank. "Still obvious." He stared into the dark eyes and waited. He put down the glass. "What's the proposition?" he asked. His own voice was flat. "Mr....?"

"Quick, sir," he replied. "Rufus Quick."

"Go on."

"Well, your honor," Quick began, "my grandfather was in the regiment of General Pat Cleburne. He was an adjutant to the great man," he smiled, "and was with him, to make a long story short, the day he died." He paused. "Last man to see him alive."

"Did the general have any parting words?" asked Doucet, suspecting, fearing the response that was there in the flat dark eyes.

"Matter of fact, sir, he did. He told my grandfather, once my grandfather told him he was as good as dead," pointing above his heart, "shot right there." A smile flickered. "Irish Pat told my grand-father about a shack and what was in it. Eight boxes he said." Paus-ing, "Marked dynamite."

Doucet remembered, saw a small cabin rise before his eyes.

Rufus stared implacably.

"General said they wasn't dynamite. They was something a lot more powerful." He grinned. "Gold."

"Eight boxes of gold?"

Quick allowed himself a chuckle.

"Didn't say they was all gold, just one."

Doucet tightened his grip on the glass.

"What does this have to do with me?"

The boy spread out his hands.

"Be patient, colonel. Be patient. I've waited a long time to tell this story. I've gone over it a lot." He flashed a smile, then took it back. His lips twisted smiles the way his eyes swallowed light. "You don't want to go and spoil my fun."

"Enjoy yourself." He gave the boy a curt unfriendly smile.

Rufus nodded.

"You're pretty good yourself, sir," he continued. "You didn't bat an eye when I called you colonel." He paused. "Nobody up here knows you were a colonel in the war, sir." He paused. "Now, do they?" He pointed a small finger. "That was one of my tricks. A test," he said, "to see if you was quick." He winked. "You're a clever man, colonel," hesitating, "St. Loup." He dropped the finger and pulled back in his chair.

"So you know my name."

The dwarf leaned forward.

"Better, colonel. I know your real name."

Doucet shrugged, brought the glass to his lips and drained it.

"What's the point?"

Rufus frowned, balled one hand into a fist and brought it to his lips. He stared at the colonel angrily and took a breath.

"What the general told my grandfather, in addition to what was not in the boxes, was the names of two other men, besides himself, that knew the whereabouts of those boxes and what was inside." He paused. "You, Colonel Andre St. Loup, the wolf, and another man named Demes Fox." He leaned back again. "What about that?"

"So?"

"Fox was killed the same day as Irish Pat," said the boy. "So when my grandfather took a ride out to that shack and found no boxes marked dynamite and a dead man, he knew it was you who done it." He moved forward. "*That's* so."

A smile flickered on the colonel's lips and in his eyes, the old deep sadness. Murder never stopped with murder, a lie with a lie. He stared hard at the boy across from him and thought. Was there no other way?

"Go on," he urged, scattering his thoughts.

"Well," said the boy. "That's the end of the first part of the story." He grinned. "How's it holding up?"

Doucet laughed, briefly, stood up and brought the bottle of whiskey to the table. He sat and poured himself another drink.

"Pretty good so far," he replied. "There any more?"

"You bet," nodded the boy. "The best part."

Doucet worried now that Prudence or one of the others might wander up to the house.

"Go on."

"Did you bury it? Or did you take it right away?" he asked. "My father, he knew the story too, it was him who told it to me, he always thought you took it right away." Rufus shook his head. "That would be a man without a plan. I think you had a plan. You buried it somewhere only you would think to look and then you came back. That's always been my thinking." Looking right at the colonel's face, "I know I'm right. I can see it in your eyes." He warmed, now, to the tale. His dark eyes flashed. Then he went on, in a high, thin, reedy voice. "I also know what you did. The war was still on, so you had to leave the South. Couldn't gather no gold if you was dead." He paused. "Now, where would you go? The North? My father, a ponderous thinker, sir, ponderous, thought you would have gone to the Yankees. I never could understand that," he declared, his high voice ringing with animation. "Suppose the South had won? Then what? You'd'a been shot and hung for treason. You couldn't go there, even though in 1864 there didn't seem to be too much danger of our boys winning the war." He stopped, watched the colonel for a response. "I always knew, I knew, colonel, I knew, you had two choices, and only one of them was worth a damn." He laughed and thumped his tiny fist against the table. "Canada, colonel. Canada. You were French. You could fit in. Who won the war wouldn't matter. You'd be a Canadian. When the time seemed right, you could come back with a wagon and get the rest, what you couldn't carry off alone the night you killed the guard. And headed north." He smiled. "How'm I doin'?"

Doucet nodded warily.

"Just fine."

"I know what you're askin' yourself, colonel. It's as plain as the nose on your face." Pause. "How does Rufus Quick get from 1864 Canada to 1914 America, and Gloucester, America at that." He smiled. "It wasn't easy. Believe me, not a bit. Me and Dad talked for years about this next part." Leaning forward, "You have to understand, colonel, you were a legend in our house. We talked about you and the murder and the gold all the time. I mean, a meal never went by. So," he said, "I was the one to set out. I was the only one who knew, knew, you went to Canada. So it was me. I was the Quick who came after you." He laughed. "Found you too, dammit!"

"When did you start?"

"Five years ago," he replied.

"When you were thirteen?"

"Why wait, colonel? What was the point of waiting? I'd 've gone at ten if the old man would'a let me. I waited long enough." He leaned back, small in the seat. "I figured you would've picked one of the French provinces. Quebec, Manitoba, Ontario. Someplace you would fit in." He aimed his finger. "I was right. Took me five years, but I was right."

Doucet, grimly amused, found himself wanting to hear the rest.

"So, you found me," he declared. "Now what?"

The dwarf frowned.

"Please, sir. Let me finish," he insisted. "I spent a lot of time half frozen to death lookin' for you. I talked to hundreds of people, colonel, hundreds." He paused. "You were no easy bastard to find, I'll grant you that. You kept to yourself. But once I got the trail, I found I could stick to it." He stopped. "And get this, colonel. Canada wasn't the hard part. Getting from there to Gloucester, America. That was hard. Harder than anything. The absolute kicker. To do that, I had to find where you left Canada." He clapped his hands. "I developed a strategy." He leaned forward again. "Can you guess, colonel?"

Doucet shook his head.

"We haven't the time."

Something flashed in the dwarf's eyes.

"I took out a newspaper ad," he declared. "An ad!" he repeated, his voice rising. "The wording, colonel. That was the key," he said, reaching inside his jacket. He took out a small piece of folded newspaper. "I also had posters made." He reached in again. "Have one of those too, I think." Another piece of folded paper, larger, was placed on the table. "I had somethin' else goin' for me, colonel. Can you guess?" Rufus tapped his left hand above his left ear. "The silver streak. The streak and the fact I knew you'd need some help." He paused. "One thing did trouble me, though. I was scared to death you'd dye your hair. Then what would I'a done? Then too, I thought you wouldn't. You would never expect to be followed, much less found." He stopped. "It was a badge of honor. You were a soldier." He smiled. "I bet right, about the help." He stopped. "I was lucky in that idea, because I've come to think you could have done it alone. It worked, though. Beginner's luck." He watched the colonel. "You kind of made a mistake there, Colonel."

Doucet smiled ruefully. The thought had occurred to him when he hired the Indian and the boy. Take the furs down alone. Get the boxes alone. But it was too long a journey to do again alone. There was no absolute need for secrecy. The war was over. No one knew. He trusted them, with what little he let them know, and he had paid them well. But not well enough. He reached forward and picked up the folded poster and spread it out on the table.

REWARD: $500 ANYONE WITH INFORMATION
ON THE WHEREABOUTS OF COL ANDRE ST LOUP
BELIEVED TO HAVE GONE TO THE
UNITED STATES. ST LOUP HAS A SILVER
STREAK IN HIS HAIR ABOVE THE LEFT EAR,
IS FRENCH, TALL, THIN AND GOES BY THE
NAME OF ANDRE DOUCET.

50

Rufus sat back in his chair, leaned forward, tried to put his elbows down on the table so he could lean on them, but he found it difficult. He sat back and slowly folded his hands in his lap and took a long look at Doucet, who sat right across from him, waiting. Doucet had not said a word in a long time.

"Have to admit, colonel," the boy remarked, "I tell quite a story."

Doucet nodded. "That you do."

The eyes of the boy took on some kind of glow.

"I can still see that mark. Where the Yankee carved you and left you for dead." He paused. "Chickamauga, right!"

The colonel stared back impassively.

"Chickamauga," he echoed, and before him memories, like dead men, rose from the past.

The boy seemed suddenly unhappy.

"Come on, now, colonel," he urged. "We won some, we lost some. If we coulda held out, we just might've won that damn war." He smiled at some memory. "Back in Tennessee, folks still talk of the uprising." He stopped. "It ain't over. Not yet."

This time Doucet did smile, at the recollection of rebel tenacity, rebel romance. It was not new to him, but that it should come from this boy across from him. That was new. He chuckled to himself, wrapped his hand around his half-empty glass of whiskey.

"Somethin' funny, colonel?"

Doucet shook his head.

"Nothing you'd understand," he replied. "A fine tale you tell, young man. Very fine. Even if it isn't true." He waited. There was nothing from the boy across the table. "But what of it? Suppose it was true, what you said? Where's the body? The evidence? Any witnesses?" He stopped and stared out with flat blue eyes. "Where's the gold? Tell me, boy. Where's the gold?"

Rufus didn't say a word, not for a full minute, and it seemed longer. This was the moment. A vein twitched nervously in his neck. He rubbed two fingers together in each hand. He remembered the words, what he had come to declare and he delivered them to the man across the table.

"That's where you come in, sir," he replied. "I don't want it all. Just my third." He stopped and let the light slip from his eyes. "My share."

Doucet thought: his share? By what right? He was the one who risked his life to ride alone through the west and up north, where he did live alone and did wait out the war and a good many years afterward. Until he was sure it was safe to come back and take another risk and hire the Indian and the boy and get the wagon and take the pelts and get the boxes and go east.

"Suppose there's nothing left?"

A simian smile eclipsed the flash of anger in the boy's dark eyes.

"It don't much matter, colonel, what you say about that. I kinda figured you would," he replied. "You got a lot of land here. Land's as good as gold and you own half the town." He squeezed his right hand into a fist and opened it when he became aware he was doing it. The vein in his neck, which had subsided, began to twitch again. "You got plenty to spare." Then he smiled. "We could be neighbors." He paused. "I haven't given up on the gold either. There was a lot, the way I understand." He paused. "Heavy enough to leave and bury and come get with three men." He smiled. "Seems to me that gold always needed three good men." He leaned as far across the table as he could, "And, colonel, sir," he said, his eyes dark and cold. "Here comes Rufus Quick to claim a share of it. In the name of old Pat Cleburne."

Doucet drained the glass. He decided not to have another. He had come to a decision.

"Get the hell out of here," he ordered.

The boy was startled and blinked.

"What?"

"You heard me," said Doucet. "Get out."

The boy still seemed surprised.

"Colonel, I've come a long way." He stared back at the colonel, still blinking, but the vein had stopped twitching. "I aim to have my share."

Doucet snorted.

"Your share of what? There is no gold."

"Then land," said Rufus. "A deed." He continued, his high thin voice etched with some kind of pain. "I don't believe you about the gold. You would've held onto that." He took a deep breath. "You had furs, other money." Stopped. "No, you kept the gold. I know you. You'd keep some." He leaned forward, brought down his head and twisted it up at the colonel. "I followed your trail!"

Doucet stared with his own cold eyes at this thing come from the past. He had listened long enough. There was a question, but there was no answer, and none he would get from the boy on the other side of the table. Was he alone? Had he told? There was no time. He could hear again the fire, the cracking of logs, the voices as a whisper on the wind. He heard shrieks and the dull sound of people far off all talking at once, a kind of dream in the dark. If he could look right through the dwarf, out through the back of his head and then through the wall, he would be able to see sparks and flames and stars. He was sure of it.

"Get out," he ordered, his voice rising.

The boy did not move.

"Can't do that, colonel."

He had no choice.

"Last chance, boy," barked the colonel, already sliding down his right arm to the boot where the derringer always was. He moved fast, the old move, and had the gun at table level.

Rufus jumped up,

"No! Don't do it!"

A grim sad smile cut the colonel's lips. It never left. Not when the boy, through some magic of his own, threw the knife that came from nowhere—where had it been?—and caught the colonel just above the heart. The gun clattered to the floor. The cold blue eyes shadowed and dimmed. There was no pain. Briefly, yes, but then nothing. His eyes cleared. He looked up with lifeless, lusterless dark eyes at the dwarf, who now stood over him.

"No, colonel, no," the boy cried. "Don't you die on me." He rubbed a sleeve across his eyes. "Damn you! Damn you! Why'd you do it? Colonel, why?" He stood, he looked, he did not know what to do with his hands. "You got somethin' to tell me, colonel. Don't you? The gold. Tell me where you hid it." A spasm of rage and the hands clutched, but still they did nothing. There was so much blood on the colonel's shirt. "Colonel," he moaned. "You have somethin' to tell me. Don't you?"

Doucet felt a sudden sharp pain and a throbbing and his mind going in and out. The face of the dwarf became other faces, a long line of faces. A soldier, a boy, a dead man, his wife. A dead woman with a rope. Then the dwarf came back and the colonel, with the same grim smile he could not control, with great effort lifted his head and whispered.

"*Je suis un homme mort.*"

Rufus screamed.

"Die! You're not gonna die. You can't!" He threw his hands in the air and brought them down, taking the colonel by the hair. "The gold, you bastard. Tell me about the gold!"

The blue eyes blanked and saw no one. He heard, or thought he heard, at the last, a sea of tiny voices come up from down below, where the fire raged.

1965

51

"A head? A *human* head?"

Boylan is pacing in a circle around Adrian, listening to him go over, for the third time, details of what happened to him in the cellar. He can believe Adrian about the jars and has himself put together a line of reasoning in regard to that. The traps they had seen outside the Wicks house were in some way connected to the jars Adrian found in Sweeney's basement. Those traps would not catch a human or hold him for long if he had been caught. They would do fine for the squirrels and cats Adrian saw in the Ball jars. But what put the old man's head there? Where was the rest of the body? What was Sweeney's role in it?

"A head," insists Adrian, his voice tired. When he talked, he circled Boylan. "With long hair, dark eyes and a big cut." He makes a mark with his hand above his left ear. "There."

Welcome is propped up against a pillow on Adrian's bed.

"His death wound," he comments.

Boylan turns to him.

"We don't know that." He faces Adrian. "A line in the hair, right?"

Adrian nods.

"He could've dyed it."

"Why?" asks Welcome.

Boylan sighs.

"How do I know?" He circles around Adrian. "How do you know it wasn't a dummy? You know, a mannequin."

"Because of the eyes," answers Adrian. "It had human eyes."

Welcome asks a question from the bed.

"How does Sweeney figure in all this?"

The question brings a silence. There is no logical way to factor in Sweeney. Could he be involved? And if he were, what could they do? What should they do?

"I can't see it," declares Boylan. "He's too old."

"To murder?" asks Adrian.

Boylan sighs again.

"Jesus, Adrian. He's an intellectual."

Welcome snickers.

"Right," he says. "Intellectuals don't commit murder."

Boylan nods.

"For once, shithead, you have a point."

Welcome clutches his heart.

"Another dart."

"Come on," presses Adrian. "This isn't funny. We have to decide what to do."

Boylan interrupts him.

"Use *I* when you talk."

Adrian, walking an intermittent circle, shakes his head and ignores Boylan. "The wood was all rotten."

"There a long time," says Welcome.

"Right," agrees Adrian. "There was a smell. Like biology lab."

"Formaldehyde," offers Boylan.

"Right," says Adrian, thinking aloud. "Everything was covered with dust." He stops. "What does that tell us?"

Welcome sits up.

"No one had been there for a while."

"Right." Adrian snaps his fingers. "But how long? How long does it take a layer of dust to build up?"

Boylan stares down at the floor of the room.

"Not very long."

Adrian looks at him, follows his eyes to the floor and agrees. He can see the layer of dust. There is more gathered in the corners, even some on the bookshelves.

"Won't tell us anything," he says.

"You got it," says Boylan.

Welcome watches the two of them from the bed. On his face is the expression of permanently amused irony that characterizes him.

His round eyes always seem to wonder and his thick glasses always seem to magnify that wonder and mold it into irony. He runs his hand through his thick dark hair. He has his own ideas and one of them is that Sweeney has nothing to do with anything in his basement. Sweeney could never murder. He knows that. But who? He has his suspicions in that regard, but keeps them to himself. Better to let the others first acquit Sweeney.

"What about a mad Jesuit cabal?" Boylan wonders. "I mean, blood isn't news to these guys." He looks at Welcome. "What about that monk walled up on the island?"

"That's not a fact," says Welcome.

"It is as far as I'm concerned," insists Boylan. "We could've stumbled upon a coven."

"You said cabal."

"I meant coven," answers Boylan. "Think of it. We have a psychic fair. A dark lady. A teacher. Loons and wackos from all over the country, right here. In our midst." He stops talking. "It could be. It could very well be, dammit," he exclaims. "The head could be what's left of the sacrifice. They always have to sacrifice."

Welcome shakes his head.

"It has to be a virgin."

Adrian raises his arms.

"This is not a joke." He begins to pace. On his face is a slight frown. "We have to find out who that is, the head, I mean."

Boylan touches him on the shoulder.

"I, I, I," he chants. "Get used to it, please."

Adrian ignores him.

"A crime's been committed," he asserts. "A man's been murdered." He stops. His eyes take in both of his friends. "We found the head. I say we find out who put it there."

Boylan falls into his chair.

"Maybe the poor guy lost a bet," he suggests, smiling.

"A *big* bet," offers Welcome.

Adrian moves over to his own chair. As soon as he is seated, a wave of exhaustion comes over him.

"God, I'm tired," he says. He stares at his two companions. "Has it occurred to you that Sweeney may be in danger? From these guys?

And who the hell are they, digging a tunnel? I mean, Jesus. Right under his house! Why?"

"Good question," says Boylan, staring back. Adrian nods his head.

"We have to warn him."

Boylan raises an eyebrow.

"We?"

"How?" from Welcome.

Adrian tries to look as calm as he can.

"What do *you* think?"

He is looking at Welcome, who groans from the bed.

"I know what you're going to say," he says to Adrian. "So I'll say it first." He points to the bag on the floor next to Boylan's chair. "Ask Melchior."

52

They are back at the board. It is late afternoon. The three are suffused with a manic energy that comes in part from the terrors they experienced earlier in the day and a grimly curious, tired need to learn the truth about the house, Sweeney, the tunnel, the voices in the tunnel. In each of their minds is an image of the old house with a brackish leaf-covered pond feeding a tall old willow whose long low branches lash the lawn. Each sees a high ceiling and broken windows, a long hall, a kitchen and table, empty open cabinets, a French door. Each sees a long dark tunnel, hears voices, sees scratches being carved in a hardwood floor. One of them sees more. He sees a head in a jar. He sees the eyes. His is one of the hands on the tripod. The other belongs to Welcome.

"Melchior?" asks Adrian, his eyes closed, breathing evenly to keep himself calm. He is curious, like the others. He is afraid. In this he is like them too.

"Into the breach," mutters Blazes.

"Shhhh."

Boylan grinds his teeth.

"Is anybody there?" asks Adrian.

The tripod sits, lifeless, under the guiding hands of two boys. There is no link. Adrian opens his eyes, gets up.

"Where's the mirror?"

Boylan points.

"I'm going to set it up in the chair," Adrian says, walking to the long piece of glass propped against the wall which he and Boylan sometimes use as a mirror. "It might help."

The other two nod in agreement. Adrian places the mirror in the fourth, empty chair, which is opposite him. He looks at the glass and sees himself. Boylan leans forward and makes a face. Adrian moves around the table to his chair and sits down. He and Welcome brush fingers above the tripod and then get down to business. Both close their eyes.

"Melchior?" asks Adrian, again the speaker.

Nothing happens.

"Want the blindfold?" asks Boylan.

Adrian shakes his head.

"Is anybody there?"

There is a tremble under their fingers. The tripod moves to "Yes." Boylan reports this. They proceed.

"What is your name?"

A hesitation, then a sea of letters that Boylan has difficulty getting down on his pad.

IT IS I MES CHERS TH WHOF

"Why do you call yourself the wolf?"

IT IS MY NAM

"Mr. Wolf?" asks Adrian, fingers on the skittering planchette.

AS IN ST LOUP

"Is your name wolf in French?"

MY HOLLOW TONGUE

"Why did you send us to the Wicks place?"

SO U CD SEE NOW HE IS AFRAID OF U MUCH REMANS TO B DON

"What?"

MANY THIGS

Adrian takes a chance.
"Was the voice in the tunnel the dwarf?"

THE VERY SAME

"How can we stop him?"

SMOK HIM OUT

"Start a fire?"

O MES CHERS U WIL NT HAVE 2 DO THAT I EMPLOY
A FIGER OF SPEECH ENOUGH THE DWARF IS ON THE
RUN LET HIM SUFR I HAV HIM NOW O IN MY CLUTCH
O MES CHERS O WE HAV HIM

"Is the dwarf dangerous?"

NO MORE THAN MOST

"Most what?"

OF HIS KINE

"Why do you hate him?"

WE DO NOT HATE

"What is the feeling?"

THER AR NO FEELINGS HERE

"That must be sad, in a way," says Adrian.

AN OUTRAGE

"Is the dwarf evil?"

IS THE SNO WHITE

"What did he do?"

MANY MOONS AGO AN THER WAS A TERRIBL ACCI-DENT

Adrian, thinking, remembers Melchior's flutter in the cellar. "Is that you, St. Loup, in the jar?"

IT GRIEVES ME TO SAY

"What should we do?"

DIG ME A LITTLE HOLE THEN WE CAN SAV THE CHILDR.

"Where are your children?"

SADLY DISPERSED

"Are they alive?"

IN A MANR OF SPEAKING GET ME MARIE HELLP O SAV MARIE

"Where is she?"

IN A SAD HOUS BY THE SEA

"Where?"

A STONS THROW

"Is she in Magnolia?"

I HAV HERD THE NAM I WILL SEND MY BIRD TO HELP WHEN THE TIME COMES I THANK U 4 THE GLAS SUCH LIMBER SOULS AND SMILING A RED ONE LIK THE DWARF HIS COLOR IS SORE TERBL 4 ME TO SEE I COULD PAINT HIM FOR U

"He is one of us," replies Welcome. He looks at Boylan. "There, I've saved your life."

WE MUST STOP THIS DWARF I WIL HELP

"Will we see you?"

AH

"Is it possible for us to see you?"

IT WOUD NOT BE EASY

"What do you mean?"

HELP O SAV MARIE I WIL B UR GID YR FAMILIAR ALL U HAV 2 DO IS ASK THE WOLF WIL B THER

Adrian is insistent. "*Can* we see you?"

YES

"How?"

HAR HAR DIE

They stand and watch Sweeney's house for lights. They see a light, somewhere in the back. Other lights come on. They can see a person moving in the living room.

"Is that Sweeney?" asks Boylan.

Welcome responds.

"Hard to tell."

Boylan twists around.

"True," he says, "with your eyes."

Adrian raises his hand. "We know what we have to do," he declares, his eyes on the house across the street and down a bit from where they stand.

"Right," says Blazes. "Tell Sweeney there's a head in his basement."

Adrian ignores Boylan, keeps waiting. The others follow close behind. In a minute they are there, standing at the edge of Sweeney's bush-lined wall. They see lights on inside the house, although there is no movement, at least none they detect. Only the lights tell them someone is inside.

"Sure you saw someone?" wonders Welcome.

Boylan points to his eyes.

"Like an eagle's."

It is beginning to get dark and the impending darkness makes the three boys uneasy. They want to get it over with, but they want to get it over with without going inside, which they know is impossible. They are close enough now, on the walk, to see the huge door, much larger than they remember it, with a large brass knocker.

"Ring or bang?" asks Boylan.

They stand in a cluster at the base of the stairs.

"What do you think?" asks Adrian, his empty hand up for advice. "Ring?"

"Ring," counsels Welcome, who favors the quieter approach himself.

Adrian goes up the stairs, crosses the veranda and rings the bell. There is a loud chime from somewhere deep within the house.

"What do we say?" he calls back.

Boylan flashes his teeth.

"Trick or treat."

Adrian, his heart pounding, waits for someone to come to the door. After a few seconds, he begins to suspect that no one is home, that there really was no one in the window, that the lights are on a timer. He feels relieved. Then he hears footsteps. Then something else, sliding. The door slowly opens, filling the porch with light. He stands illuminated, anxious.

"Yes?"

His eyes go wide. It isn't Sweeney. It's the woman from the fair, who up close, even in shadows, is prettier than she was at the Tarot booth. He can't make out the color of her eyes, can't remember what color they were at the fair, or if he even took note of it. All he can sense is that he is being measured by eyes that are steady and dark. He is completely at a loss for words. Suddenly he sticks his hand into his pocket and gropes for the ticket he won at the fair. He holds it out to her.

"I came for my kiss."

1930

53

He could not believe his eyes. The tawny hair, like snakes about her the way it went down her back, the sound of them under the window on the old mattress. Was this where they did it? Why here? Why not her room? The thought of them in his sister's bed made it worse and he understood—yes, understood—the need for the attic, her acknowledgment. Not my bed because this is wrong. But here. Up here where the old woman had to be cut down with a knife, where quiet and the stillness of death—still in the room—made wrong better, more pleasing. He heard his sister moan and saw, too, that the boy could see him, was watching him in the doorway, fear in his eyes.

"Get out," he said.

Aveline turned at the sound of his voice.

"What are you doing there?" she yelled, making an attempt to cover at least her upper half with a shirt belonging to the boy.

"Get out," he repeated.

This time with menace in his voice. The boy slipped out from under his sister, naked, too astonished to think about anything but getting to the door, away from Andre. Aveline saw his fear. She took the shirt, stood naked before her brother, the boy, gave the boy the shirt, reached down for his trousers, handed them to him, then motioned him away with a calm wave of her hand. He hurried with his clothes, never saying a word, his eyes all the time moving between the sister and brother. Then he moved, out, around the figure in the door—but not quite. Doucet took him by the neck, lifted him, held him up against the wall.

"Andre!" screamed his sister.

"I'll kill you," he said, his voice flat, even serene. "Kill you if you come here again."

He lowered, released the boy, who ran, tumbling, down the stairs, the hall, the other stairs. The front door slammed. Aveline, dressed now, reached for a cigarette, lit it, sat curled up on the mattress behind a cloud of acrid smoke. Light through the window touched her face, made her hair golden again. Her face was empty, closed to the world.

"How old is he?" Andre asked, still at the door. This time there was a tremor in his voice. "Twelve?"

Aveline stared back, contemptuously.

"Chrissakes, Aveline," he half-shouted at her, "you're forty years old." He took a deep breath.

"So what?"

His hand shaking in rage, Andre took a step toward the mattress. She watched him, smiled, then moved her eyes to a point somewhere at the other end of the room, away from her brother.

"Big, isn't he?" she asked.

Andre stared down at her.

"Right," he spit out. "And slower than he's big." He stopped, wanting to strike her, to beat sense into her. He caught himself in time—this time. "Can he talk yet?"

Aveline eyed him suspiciously.

"If you're insinuating he's retarded, I don't care. I'm not much interested in his brain." She smiled.

"You could go to jail."

She glared at him.

"So what?"

He tried to reason.

"Artemus is twelve, thirteen years old," Andre declared. "This is child molestation, for Chrissakes. They'll throw you away."

She dropped the cigarette into a glass of whiskey.

"Listen, Andre," she said, her eyes on the whiskey glass. "I may be a whore, but you," she pointed, looking up into his eyes, "you're nothing but a goddamn drunk. You stink of booze even now." She sighed and leaned against the wall.

The sun filled her hair. "What I do," she said, "I do. You have nothing to say about it. And don't tell me you're going to run and tell mother, because you won't." She moved her eyes down to the glass. "Things didn't just get bad around here, Andre. They've been bad." She looked up at him. "And we all know *exactly* when it started." She grabbed the pack of cigarettes.

"That's not true."

"Don't hand me that," she said.

Andre knew. His sister spoke the truth. The night their father disappeared. That was the beginning. After that, nothing was the same. Not him, nor her, nor their mother. And worse. It could not be changed. She was a whore, he was a drunk.

"Still doesn't make it right to take a child to bed, Aveline." He paused. "Because that's what he is. A boy."

She smiled. When she did he could see she was still a beauty.

"Maybe, Andre, I like them young."

He tried for something.

"But a Wicks? We don't like them."

She laughed.

"Artemus is all right," she said. "Bit big for his age, and dumb. He does what I want." She looked up. "When he stops doing what I want, I'll send him away." She paused, measuring her brother. "But not before."

Andre raised his hand.

"Go ahead. Hit me."

He held it, then brought it down. He could not. He saw the look in her eyes when he didn't hit her. Contempt. He stepped back, looked at her, there under the window, filled with sun. His own sister.

Contempt.

54

There were fireflies. She could see from where she sat in the dark. They tended to hang just beyond the porch, above the roses. On and off, the brief cool lights. It was peaceful there, watching them, listening for sounds. The breeze cut through the July warmth, for which Prudence gave thanks. Nearing sixty, she could no longer stand the heat and found herself, more and more, driving out to the beach at Magnolia, where she would sit, under her parasol in the sun. More and more, too, at the beach or on the porch, whenever she found a moment, she would go over things. This life. What it meant, if anything. She had long since given over trying to find definite meaning. What she looked for now was a simple reason to explain what had happened. No God to justify. No better afterlife. Just an answer.

"Where are you going?" she asked, turning into the light when the door opened.

"A ride," he said.

"Where?"

He walked to the railing and leaned down on it.

"Fireflies," he said. "Look."

"I know, Andre. Where are you going?"

He turned and saw his mother all shadow sitting in the dark.

"Marblehead."

"Go where you want to go, Andre," she said. "But walk. You've been drinking."

He laughed quietly.

"Mother, I'm always drinking." He turned away from her. "Want to come along? You like the beach."

"Not at night."

"Don't say I never ask."

Prudence let out a long sigh.

"Where's Aveline?"

She could see him shrug, even in the shadows.

"Upstairs."

Prudence thought: these children. Progeny. For this the tall man left Canada for Goucester. To build his house and his family and all the while the dream eating away until one day he could no longer stand it and he stepped out into the night and never came back. Bitter progeny. If he had just said one word and then gone on. But to simply leave? Like that? On Halloween?

The top down, the wind blasted against his face. The air was cool against him and in the July night he thought he could hear the sounds of music, some song from long ago, coming from the radio, but he could not tell for sure, the wind was so loud. Above the lights he could pick out sea gulls, standing, watching the cars. Boat lights bobbed on the water. It was a clear starry night. There was a full moon. Andre roared along. *He left because of me. I failed him. I could not become what he wanted me to become.* But what was that? He never said. And Aveline. His own sister. With a gruesome ape-like child, hands down at his sides, and dumb empty dull eyes and Aveline a rare beauty, even at forty. He felt a cool gust from the sea as he turned and moved the car into an incline and then felt it sweep around a curve and out onto the road that would take him past the Yankee Fleet and out toward the ocean where the water would soothe him. The lights of the boats flashed in and out now, like fireflies themselves. He shouted to the night at the top of his lungs. The cool air. Life was worth living because the air was cool and made his face feel like water, smooth and moist and alive. He sang. He gunned the engine and screeched and finally, thinking of Aveline, he roared to-ward the ocean. He could see the lights of the boats, coming up, could see rocks and foam. The water seemed strange, choppy and filled with swells. He screeched again. In his headlights he saw bright foam, rocks sparkling, and the wind, the wind so cool against his face he forgot for a moment that he had no father and that the horses had been sold and that his sister despised him. Then he remembered. The elegant rider with the streak in his hair going out in the morning, all mist and dew. He bounced, once, leaving the road, but took to the air again and hit the big rock, all foam and light, full on. There was a flash. And then nothing.

55

Like yesterday, the whole sad business. A man rides into town, stays too long. Courts the mother, takes the daughter, the mother dies. In time they are at peace, and then: the man leaves, the boy dies, the girl begins to consort with the devil. Prudence sat with her quilting. It was still summer, late August. If she listened, she could hear birds, a mockingbird in a maple, on a lower branch, and some black-topped chickadees, all singing. Out in the grass were cicadas, a chipmunk. The first square would be the man. He would be seated on a dark horse and there would be a line of gray in his hair. The second, this house. Three floors. The house would be red with gold trim and the porch would be surrounded by a white fence. Square three. Baby Andre. Baby Aveline the next. A head of gold. And then—the bonfire. A huge man and a huge dog and a woman at the end of a line of pumpkins. Prudence remembered. The cards had gone down and the woman had looked her square in the eyes.

"Ah," she said. "This is not good."

"How do you mean?"

The woman, as if she had made a mistake, gathered up the cards, shuffled them, put them back on the blanket.

"I see death."

She remembered. The look in the woman's eyes had told her. A death in the family. But whose? The colonel? Had the colonel gone off to die like some old dog? That she could not believe. He left. A *kind* of death? Was that the card? Or was it Andre? The next square— Andre in the ocean.

"When?"

The woman considered.

"The cards say soon."

"Who?"

"Not you. That is all I can tell you."

"Could it be someone who has already died?"

"No. Someone else. Soon."

Sometimes when she thought of her husband she thought he had died. There was no understanding how. It could have been that someone from the past, one of the others involved in the gold, had come for him. But why kill him? If it had to do with the gold, there was still some gold. It had not moved. No, the colonel had gone. There was another part to his mad dream. A corollary. If the progeny of the first mother prove tainted, children of a second mother must be provided. The first mother, like her mother before her, should be deserted.

"You will have a long life."

"How long?"

"The cards cannot say."

"Will I be happy?"

The old woman had frowned, as if she had known the mad truth.

"The cards say no."

There, she thought. Six of the nine squares of the memory quilt all mapped out. What would the others be? She would wait for events. If something happened tomorrow, good. It would go right in. If not, she was content to wait years. One thing she did know: the end of the quilt. That had come in a dream and she could do it as soon as she had something for the other two open squares.

"Is anybody there?"

She turned and saw that Aveline had come up onto the porch.

"Stop that," she said.

Aveline went on.

"Just a board game, mother."

Prudence looked up from the map of her quilt. Her eyes were filled with shadows, partly from the shade on the porch, partly from within. She stared a long time at Aveline.

"Why do you do that?"

Aveline was toying with the tripod.

"I like it," she replied. She looked at her mother, her own eyes circled in mystery, hooded from the world.

"Why?"

"Do you know that father talks to me?" she asked.

Prudence, angry at Aveline.

"Don't be stupid."

Aveline moved the tripod to the center of the board, began to move and twist it about. She pushed it to YES, the sun side.

"He does," she insisted, her voice ringing with certainty. "Did you know he was murdered?"

Prudence got up from the swing chair.

"Damn you, Aveline," she swore. "Stop being a..."

"Whore, mother?" she finished.

Prudence walked to the railing, her blue dress still about her. There was no breeze. It was warm and still and silent.

"It's immoral," she said. "What you do."

Aveline looked out past the railing, toward the lawn, out at the tall grass her father and her brother used to ride through to get to the open fields.

"Well, mother," she said. "If it is, it is. I don't care."

Prudence snapped.

"It's about time you cared about something in your life, Aveline," she yelled, surprising herself. She took a deep breath, shielded her eyes from the noonday sun. "I'm sorry."

Aveline hummed to herself.

"No need, mother." She smiled softly. "If it helps, I do care about some things."

Prudence, quickly.

"For instance?"

"Oh," from Aveline. "You'll find out."

She hummed, moved the tripod, watched the tall still grass, parched from the sun. Father, she thought, and Andre. Her eyes followed a line of squawking crows. She touched the tripod and when she stretched her arm she felt stirring within...the child.

"Is anybody there?"

Prudence watched her.

"I do wish you'd stop that."

Aveline sent her a brief, mocking smile.

"Is anybody there?" she said.

She turned her eyes to the field, where the crows were, and she saw, leaning against a wall, Artemus, the tall dumb child. She knew her mother, too, could see him and she wished, for just one moment, to be alone in the world, so she could watch, from the shade of the porch, the strange dumb boy with the straw hat.

1965

56

"Won't you come in?"

They step inside and wait for her to close the door. She waves her hand to let them know they should follow her and the three of them do, two steps behind. They realize she is viewing them with some amusement. She is as tall as Boylan, the shortest of the three, which makes her tall for a woman. Boylan keeps catching Adrian's eye. Adrian tries to avoid him. He knows what Boylan is thinking. What is the connection between Sweeney and the woman? Isn't he too old for her? They turn the corner into the living room to find Sweeney, pipe in hand, sitting in the wingback chair. He stands when he sees them.

"Marian hoped you were trick-or-treaters," is all he says. He walks over to them. They can see he is annoyed. They can tell from the set to his mouth and his eyes. His eyes are cold. None of them has ever known Sweeney to have cold eyes. "Is this trick or treat?" He brings the pipe to his lips. "But what about costumes?" He smiles tightly.

He is waiting for a reply, an explanation. The boys are tongue-tied. They are upset at finding him in a bad frame of mind and feel they *have* interrupted something. But what? She is in slacks and Sweeney is casually and completely dressed.

Sweeney looks down at Boylan. "I get it," he says. "This is your idea. You thought it would be funny to come here on Halloween and stand in my living room. Struck dumb."

Boylan lifts his head at Adrian.

"It's his idea, sir."

Adrian is too surprised to say a word. He stands looking up at Sweeney, who stands looking down quizzically at him.

"Well, Mr. Sparks?"

Adrian opens his mouth to speak. Nothing is happening the way he thought it would. In his mind he had visions of knocking on Sweeney's door, being asked in, sitting down and telling his story. In his mind, Sweeney was grateful, even abject in his gratitude. When he looks in Sweeney's eyes he sees no gratitude. He is not sure he even sees any of the usual ironic detachment.

"Jim," says the tall young lady, coming up alongside him and taking his arm, "why don't we all sit down?"

Sweeney is not readily persuaded, but he seems to respond to something in her demeanor that urges him to let the boys enter the living room and sit down. They all wonder at the familiarity between the two. Is this intimacy?

"Yes," agrees Sweeney. "Sit, boys, come inside." He smiles. "Or rather, since you're already here, come further inside." He points his right index finger. "One over there, please. Two of you in the Queen Anne chairs." He himself sits back down in the red wing back chair. "Now, if we're all settled," he says, "maybe one of you, Mr. Sparks, I would assume, can tell me why you're here." He brings the pipe to his mouth. "Or is that asking too much?"

Adrian, sitting next to Marian on the couch, is put off by Sweeney's tone and the way he is talking. He can't get the words to come out the way he wants. He can't seem to get his mind to work at all and he is wondering at that, too, when he smells the perfume on Marian. *That's* it. He is sitting too close to her for his head to work.

"Anytime, Mr. Sparks."

Adrian nods.

"Yes, sir."

"Oh," interjects Sweeney as an afterthought. "Has everyone been introduced?"

"Yes, Jim. The boys told me who they were on the porch." She pauses. "You don't think I would open the door to just anyone."

The way she says the word *anyone* gives Adrian a shudder. He has a sense something larger is meant, out of reach of the words being used. A kind of code.

Sweeney holds the pipe aloft.

"Well?"

Adrian is filled with emotion. He is upset that Welcome and Boylan refuse to help. Upset that Sweeney keeps poking at him with that pipe and his questions. He is also deeply confused. His eyes, which have been wandering about the room, have noticed a section of books he did not notice on their previous visit for tea. The titles unnerve him. Is Sweeney really up to something? Books on the macabre, a mysterious woman who reads Tarot cards. The grisly floating head. His eyebrows go up, an unconscious imitation of Sweeney—all the boys in his class do it—when he sees, draped over two chairs in the dining room the quilt from the psychic fair. He jumps to his feet.

"Sir," he exclaims.

He sees that Sweeney's own eyebrows have gone up and that even Welcome and Boylan are looking at him strangely.

"Yes?"

"Isn't that the quilt from the fair?" He points.

Sweeney does not have to look.

"One of them, yes."

He looks down at Sweeney.

"May I have a look at it?"

Sweeney shakes his head.

"No, Mr. Sparks. First, tell me why you're here." He motions with his free hand for Adrian to sit down. "Then we'll talk about the quilt."

Adrian sits down.

"Calm down, Adrian," the woman says. "Just tell us why you're here. There's nothing to be afraid of."

Adrian looks at her. Why did she say that? Isn't that what they say in the movies? *Horror* movies?

"I'm fine," he responds. He takes a deep breath and turns to face Sweeney. "This is going to sound impossible to believe, sir. But if you would, could you please just listen?" He hesitates. "Even if it sounds crazy." He thinks of the books. Now he finds them reassuring. "I know it will, sir. Sound crazy."

"Sound as crazy as you like, Mr. Sparks," offers Sweeney. "Life is a pyramid of ironies." He pauses. "This could be one of them."

Adrian thinks: whatever *that* means.

"Go ahead, Adrian. Tell him."

Blazes, deciding he has had enough of this hesitation, is now determined to stand with his friend in the face of what he considers to be collusion between Sweeney and the dark-haired lady. He is annoyed at himself for not being able to take his eyes from her, further annoyed she keeps catching him at it and smiling. What's on her mind? What's really going on in this house? He too has noticed the books and is beginning to wonder if they haven't let Sweeney off the hook too quickly. Maybe he does know something. Maybe he is involved. His right hand moves toward his pocket. It is there. His razor-sharp fishing knife. He looks at Sweeney. He looks at her, sees her eyes boring into Adrian. What's she looking at? He takes his hand from the knife. He catches Adrian's eye and nods encouragement. Adrian flashes a terse smile.

"Well, Mr. Sweeney," Adrian begins, "a few weeks back, Andy and I bought—I know this is going to sound crazy—but, please, just listen. We bought a Ouija board. At a yard sale." He sees a change in Sweeney's eyes. He wishes he could think about what he sees, but knows he must continue. "It was a whim, sir. We just bought it." He stops. "I don't even know why."

He hears a deep voice.

"It was cheap."

Welcome has decided to help. He too has been watching. He too has sensed some bond between Sweeney and the woman. Not a sexual bond, some other bond. Of long standing. He has watched her watching Adrian, and has felt she wants to touch him and not just because he said he had come for the kiss. Something more. He looks at her and admits to himself that she is very attractive. He cannot tell how old she is. She seems too young for Sweeney. Too sexy for Sweeney. And too old for Adrian. But on that count he is less certain.

"Right," echoes Adrian. "It was cheap, and second hand."

"Obviously," Sweeney comments. "If you bought it at a yard sale."

Adrian thinks: why does he sound so serious? He does not know what to make of Sweeney. His mood has certainly changed. But for the better? At least he *sounds* interested.

"Yes, sir," he says. He gathers his thoughts. "One night, I started to fool around with it. Nothing serious. Just me and the board. But, funny thing is, I felt something happening."

"Happening?" Marian asks. She gives him a warm smile. "Tell us what you mean. Exactly what you mean."

Adrian is surprised again. The look in her eyes does not entirely match her tone of voice. What is going on?

"I don't know if I can," he replies. "I thought I heard something, but maybe I didn't. I mean, the tripod didn't move or anything. I thought I should have some help. I couldn't really do it alone." He stops when he realizes he is explaining himself to her and not Sweeney. "Do you know anything about Ouija boards?"

Marian laughs. It is a warm laugh and for some reason it thrills Adrian. He almost laughs himself.

"A little."

"You know what I'm talking about," he declares, searching for further support.

"Maybe," she says. "Maybe I do." She takes his arm. "But you haven't really told us anything, have you?"

Adrian nods.

"I needed help, so I went to Blazes and Andy. I figured if there were three of us, we could give the board a good try. At least find out if there was anything to it at all."

"What did you find out?" Sweeney inquires, his voice almost hoarse. The pipe in his right hand has gone out. He clears his throat and tries to smile. "Did anyone talk to you?"

The smile does not put Adrian off. Sweeney is interested. More than interested. All the boys can see it. This is not the Sweeney they know. This is another Sweeney. A new one, but somehow, older than the old one.

"Yes, sir," responds Adrian.

"Who?"

Adrian looks at Welcome and Boylan. There is not a trace of humor in their faces. They too have been changed. He turns his head to Sweeney so he can see him. Can see his eyes.

"He calls himself St. Loup."

57

It is as if a switch has suddenly been turned on. Light from a lonely streetlight comes in and falls on Sweeney in the chair, illuminating half his face. The other half is a little more in shadow. Sweeney reaches over and turns on the lamp on the end table near to him. He has not said a word. He carefully empties the used tobacco from the pipe, dully refills it. He tamps it down with a finger, then lights it. When it is going and he is obscured by a cloud of smoke he permits his eyes to return to Adrian who, like Boylan and Welcome, has noticed an even deeper change in the man in the red chair, an even more palpable response and more than simply the tremor in the hand holding tightly to the pipe, as if seeking a kind of hopeless ballast, a counterweight to keep this world from merging completely with another.

"Always been too dark in this room," Sweeney says, just after turning on the lamp. His eyes are watching Adrian. "St. Loup, you say." There is no question in his voice.

"That's what he called himself."

Adrian half wonders why Sweeney hasn't offered some objection to his using a Ouija board at a Catholic school. Shouldn't Sweeney be saying it's all a lot of nonsense? He feels himself go cold and he hopes no one can see what he feels in his blood. What if Sweeney has something to hide? He casts a desperate glance at Boylan, but Boylan is watching Sweeney.

Sweeney clears his throat.

"Has this St. Loup said anything?" he asks simply.

Adrian is taken aback. He has assembled in his mind all the arguments he had planned to use in defense of the Ouija board. But where is the attack?

"Adrian," Marian presses. "Has he?"

"Yes," he replies, somewhat confused. He looks at Sweeney. "It's not my hand making it move, sir. I'm sure of it."

Sweeney smiles.

"No one said it was."

"You believe me?"

Sweeney glances at Marian.

"Why does that surprise you?" he asks. "I may be a teacher, Adrian. But I'm not God. I'm not enough of a fool to think I have all the answers. Some," he finishes. "They just let me know some."

Adrian thinks: they?

"Go on, Adrian," Marian urges.

Adrian nods his head.

"Well, sir, his main concern is that we help him stop," he lets his voice fall, "the dwarf."

Sweeney leans forward.

"Say that again."

"The dwarf, sir. He wants to stop the dwarf."

Welcome interrupts.

"That isn't all."

Sweeney turns to him and nods and then turns back to Adrian, on the couch next to Marian. He studies the boy. He does not know what to think. Nor does he know what to say. He feels like sitting back and going to sleep. But he is excited. He can feel a secret surging that tires and excites him at the same time. Is this proof of another life on the other side of some unfathomable wall?

"Go ahead," he hears his own voice say. "Tell us the rest." He pauses. "Try not to leave anything out."

"Yes, sir," Adrian responds, thinking. "The main thing is like I said. Stop the dwarf." He hesitates before beginning the rest of the tale. "He also said to 'save Marie.'" He looks at Sweeney. It is clear the name means nothing to him. "We ask questions and get responses. Sometimes, though, it's hard to tell."

"Hard?" inquires Sweeney.

Boylan answers.

"He can't spell."

Sweeney turns.

"St. Loup, sir," Boylan tells him.

"That happens a lot," explains Marian. "Sometimes the channels don't get lined up. They have to be pretty exact. The voice speaking to you is not deliberately misspelling. It can't be helped."

Adrian looks at her.

"Oh," he says, his voice soft.

"Adrian," says Sweeney. "Finish the story."

Adrian nods.

"He's given us instructions. We followed them."

Sweeney nods himself, says, "Ah."

Marian looks at Adrian and wonders how much courage it took for him, for them, to come and tell Sweeney this tale. She sees in his eyes something she has always known in her own: an insatiable curiosity and willingness to learn, to experiment. When she touched his arm she felt a goodness and a kind of power and she understood why the board would talk through him. He was like her. There was a link between them that transcended mere knowing and she was pleased with herself for having realized its existence the second she had heard his name from Sweeney a year ago.

"He told us to ..."

Sweeney suddenly interrupts. "This dwarf."

"Yes."

"Has St. Loup said anything about him?"

"In what way, sir?"

"Is he dead? Is he alive?"

Adrian nods in comprehension.

"Alive, sir. Definitely alive."'

Sweeney frowns.

"How can you be so certain?"

Adrian sits back.

"Because, sir. We heard him."

"Heard him?"

"Yes, sir. In the tunnel."

Even Marian is surprised.

"Tunnel?" she asks.

Sweeney, not knowing what to think at hearing the word tunnel, sighs and leans back. The pipe almost falls from his hand.

"So he's back."

58

"You *know* him?" asks Boylan. He realizes that a bridge has been crossed and they are all on the same side of *something*, although what that something is would be difficult for him to explain. "I mean, you've actually *seen* him?" He has a number of questions he wants to ask Sweeney, or Marian, but he stops.

"Oh, yes," Sweeney replies. "If we are talking about the same man." He pauses. "And I believe we must be. It would be too much of a coincidence otherwise."

"Is he a friend of yours?" asks Boylan.

Sweeney shakes his head.

"I really don't know him. A year or so back he came here looking for the previous owners. I wasn't much help on that."

Marian interrupts.

"Adrian," she says. "Go on with the story."

"Right," he says. "Well, St. Loup wanted us to find this house…"

"*This* house?" Sweeney inquires, his eyebrows up.

Adrian is embarrassed.

"I meant *a* house."

"A generic house," comments Sweeney.

"Right."

"Did you find it?"

Marian breaks in.

"Jim," she says. "Let *him* tell it."

Sweeney brings the pipe to his mouth and puffs.

"Anyway," Adrian continues. "He wanted us to find a place called the Wicks house."

Sweeney's jaw drops.

"It's right over there."

"Yes, sir," says Adrian. "It is." He pauses. "This afternoon, the three of us, in costume, walked from the campus to the Wicks house." He stops. "And went inside."

"You broke in?" asks Sweeney, vaguely aware that some crime may have been committed and that as a faculty member, he has some need to know these details. "How'd you get in?"

"Through an open first-floor window," Adrian answers. "It had no glass."

Sweeney nods approval.

"Go on," he urges.

"We had the board with us, and some candles."

"Candles?"

"For effect, sir," rejoins Boylan.

"Ah," from Sweeney.

"We set up in the kitchen," declares Adrian, "and we started asking it questions." He looks at Marian. "We got a response. St. Loup wanted us to follow him."

"How do you mean?" Marian asks.

"Well," responds Adrian. "He made scratching marks in the floor." He swallows. "I know it sounds impossible. But it happened. Ask Andy and Blazes."

"He's telling the truth," says Welcome.

At this news Marian's face darkens. She now knows for certain they are dealing with a spirit of considerable power, even more power than she feared when her hand was held immobile above the Ouija board. She stares at Adrian, relieved that the boys have come back to tell the tale. It tells her St. Loup is powerful, but probably not evil.

"Then what happened?"

"We followed the markings. They took us downstairs, to the cellar. In the cellar we were led to a tunnel."

"And?" from Sweeney, anxious. His suspicions have been thoroughly aroused and in his mind he assembles into a composite whole groans in the night, eerie visitations. He knows before he is told where the tunnel leads.

"The tunnel leads to your house, sir. Right underneath your basement." Adrian stands up. "That isn't all, sir. There are empty boxes at the end of the tunnel." He stops. "Marked 'Dynamite'. We were examining them, sir, when we heard the voices."

"Voices?" is all Sweeney can think to say.

"Actually just one voice," corrects Adrian.

Boylan interjects.

"So, you see, Mr. Sweeney," he says. "We had no choice."

Sweeney faces him.

"Choice?"

"We had to get out," Boylan continues. "There was a trap door. A ladder. We went up."

Sweeney waits.

"Yes?"

Boylan grins nervously.

"It took us to your basement."

Sweeney gets to his feet.

"I expected you to say that."

"You did?" asks Adrian in some surprise.

"Is there more?"

Adrian gulps. He gathers his thoughts.

"I'm afraid so, sir."

Sweeney is becoming impatient.

"Get on with it."

Adrian begins to pace.

"As soon as we got upstairs, we realized we left the bag with the board in it downstairs. Blazes went down to get it. When he was down there, something groaned."

"Scared me to death," interjects Boylan.

"Anyway, he ran up the stairs with the bag," continues Adrian, "but the tripod fell out. I had to go down and get it. It was pretty dark. I had to use the flashlight. I was looking around those boxes you have.'"

Sweeney nods.

"The quilting material."

Adrian looks up at him.

"Did you know there's a low door in the wall behind the boxes, Mr. Sweeney?"

Sweeney frowns.

"No."

Adrian sighs.

"Good," he says. "That's where I found them."

"What?" demands Sweeney.

Adrian studies his eyes.

"The heads, sir."

Sweeney is incredulous and Adrian can see he is sincere, that he is not concealing anything. He is relieved. Whatever is going on in the basement and the tunnel beneath has nothing to do with Sweeney. He is innocent. Adrian smiles at Marian. His head is spinning. He feels himself becoming giddy. He realizes he is exhausted, but he must finish telling Sweeney the story.

"Heads, sir," he says. "Animal heads. Squirrels and cats. In jars. With formaldehyde."

An expression of disgust from Sweeney.

Adrian takes a deep breath. He will need strength for the final revelation.

"There's something more." He glances quickly at Boylan and Welcome, sensing he needs their support. He sees it is there. He turns again to the man standing before him. He looks into his eyes. "Among the jars, sir, is another jar. Much bigger. Like a cylinder of glass."

Marian gets up and moves to Sweeney's side. She gently takes his arm. She knows she is about to hear some terrible detail, something horrible kept to last. The real reason the boys came.

"There's a man's head in that jar."

Sweeney gasps.

"Good God!"

Marian holds his arm firmly. She sees that Adrian's face has gone pale, knows too that her own probably is. She can tell without looking at Sweeney that he is white as a ghost.

"Is there more?" she asks.

Adrian nods.

"Yes."

Sweeney's eyes bore into him.

"What?" he demands, although his voice is shaky.

Adrian looks up.

"The head, sir. It belongs to St. Loup."

59

It is dark outside. A moon is beginning to show itself, the sky is filled with stars. There is a wind. But there is a stillness in the living room. Everyone is seated. Sweeney is in shock. He does not know whether he believes what he has just been told by Adrian. He has believed everything up to that point, but murder, which is what he knows must be the case, is another matter. It represents the grim side of the nether world, the evil side of the unknown. He sits holding the stem of his cooling meerschaum. He has been sitting for some time. He hears the leaves rustling, the wind blowing. He is afraid.

"Did St. Loup say he was murdered?" he hears a voice ask. It is his own voice. It sounds hollow.

The bass voice of Welcome responds.

"He said it was an accident."

"An accident his head wound up inside a jar?" Sweeney retorts. "That's a little hard to believe."

"Accident?" inquires Marian. "What kind of accident?"

"He didn't say," answers Boylan. "He seemed to blame the dwarf."

"The dwarf has a name. If it is the same man who visited me," interjects Sweeney. "Rufus."

"Does he have red hair?" asks Welcome.

"That I couldn't tell you," answers Sweeney. "Either I couldn't tell, or I can't remember." He pauses, "Why?"

"St. Loup calls him 'red.' I was thinking it could be the color of his hair."

Sweeney nods in approval.

"Could be," he comments. "Could be too that Rufus means red in Latin."

The boys mull over this bit of news. They may know now why the dwarf is called red. They may not. It does not seem to be a significant detail. Especially to Adrian.

"I don't see that it matters," he declares. He stares at his teacher, sitting in the chair across from him. "Do you think St. Loup was murdered?"

Sweeney raises an eyebrow.

"Seems to me he didn't kill himself."

Boylan leans forward and clasps his hands.

"Couldn't it be, though, that St. Loup *was* dead. Murdered or a suicide, and that Rufus found the body and just cut the head off and put it in a jar." He smiles quickly. "A kind of joke."

"Doesn't say much for his sense of humor," Sweeney offers. He is not smiling. He is trying, almost desperately, to decide what to do next. "He didn't strike me as a man with a keen sense of humor when he came here." He stops. "All in all, I thought him rather menacing."

This sends a shudder through the boys and confirms their suspicions about the voice they heard from below. It was thin, cold, high and horrifying and it belonged to someone capable of anything. It is unsettling that Sweeney has confirmed this.

"What do you think killed him?" Welcome asks. "Or who? I mean, sir, do you have any ideas?"

Sweeney sits in contemplation. His gaze wanders to Marian, who is sitting, very quietly, in a posture of serenity that belies the look of concern and fear in her eyes. She is as still as a statue and when Sweeney looks at her, he cannot determine whether or not she is paying attention.

When he speaks, his voice seems very quiet to him, inaudible. It is the way his voice gets when he has doubts about what it is he is going to say, the well-practiced refuge of a man used to public speaking. To him, the wind is louder than his voice. The rustle of the leaves drowns him out. The hoot of an owl outside covers up every word he says.

"We don't know who," he says, his voice rising. "If we can believe your board, we know the dwarf has something to do with it. Exactly what, we don't know. We could assume Rufus murdered St. Loup," he pauses, "and we might be right. We could be wrong." He takes a deep, audible breath. "I suppose what we have to do is go down, get the head, and take it to the police." He looks at Marian. "It seems to be a matter for them."

Marian decides to speak. She has caught Sweeney's gaze and realized he has in as circumspect a way as possible sought out her opinion on what next to do. He has posed a solution. But he has left the final decision to her.

"Adrian," she begins, her voice calm, even. "Tell me your impression of St. Loup." She turns to Boylan and Welcome. "You too. If you disagree with Adrian, let me know." She looks back to Adrian, touches him on the arm. "Think now. Can you tell me anything?"

Adrian does not answer right away, although he knows immediately what his response is going to be. He is going to act on his convictions and his convictions do not render themselves to logic or even to reason much of the time.

"I don't think he's evil."

"What makes you say that?"

"He never tried to hurt us."

"What makes you think he has that power?" she inquires.

Adrian hesitates.

"Those claw marks. He could have gouged right through us, if he wanted." He stops. "I mean, they were pretty deep."

"Why do you think he picked you?"

"Me?"

"You," she insists. "You're the one he's speaking through. You're the voice." She smiles. "You are functioning as a medium." She brings her hand back to his arm. "Have you any experience with the occult? Do you have any powers?" She stares into his eyes. "Do you know what I mean?"

"Yes," he blurts out. "I mean, I know what you mean. But I don't have powers."

Marian acknowledges his outburst with a smile.

"Is it your impression he means harm to the dwarf?" she asks. "Do you think him capable of that?"

Adrian, again, considers.

"I'm not sure how to answer," he replies. "He wants us to stop him. He didn't say kill." He pauses. "He is powerful, though. I get the idea he could do pretty much what he wants."

Marian shakes her head.

"There you're wrong, Adrian. He isn't *that* powerful. At least, not yet. He is a powerful spirit. Maybe even very powerful." Her eyes move to Sweeney, then back to Adrian. "He has been able to do something *physically* and that is something few spirits can do." She stares hard at Adrian. "Those that do, Adrian, are usually evil."

"No," Adrian half-shouts. "Not St. Loup. He's got a sense of humor. He's funny."

Marian gives him a sad smile.

"That would have nothing to do with his intentions," she explains. "Has he asked to see you?"

Adrian nods.

"Yes," he replies. "He asked us to bring a mirror."

"Did you?"

"Yes."

She frowns.

"You shouldn't have done that."

"What's wrong?"

Marian shakes her head. She is not going to explain her reasoning to Adrian. She is looking for answers.

"Maybe nothing, Adrian," she says. She looks right into Adrian's eyes. "Did you ask if you could see him?"

Adrian is very uncomfortable.

"I think, yes. Someone did."

Boylan coughs.

"You," he says. "Not someone."

"What did he say?" says Marian.

Adrian gulps.

"He said we had to die."

"His exact words," muses Boylan, "were *'har har* die'." Marian releases Adrian's arm. She sits back in the seat, is obviously thinking over what she is going to say. When she is satisfied she has it right, she begins.

"I think, boys, we can assume that what we have is a spirit out for revenge. He is very disturbed, otherwise he wouldn't be reaching out. And he is strong, very strong." She stops. "But not as strong as he is going to get, if you don't stop listening to him." She looks at Adrian. "You see, right now he needs you. He isn't strong enough to do what he wants on his own." She takes his hand. "The danger, Adrian, is that he is drawing strength from you. All of you, but especially you. When you let him see you, he looked into your souls. That's the source of *your* power." She waits. "If he could add your power to his, we might never be able to stop him. That's why you must *never* use the board again."

Adrian is crestfallen, deeply disappointed. He had hoped to find a kindred spirit in Marian and had felt for certain that he had. But she wants to make him stop. This was not at all what he expected. He doesn't know what to do. St. Loup is powerful and frightening. But not dangerous. Not to him.

"Never?"

Marian shakes her head.

"Not for a long time," she answers. "Not ever around here." She lets go of his hand. "Spirits are usually linked to a particular place. St. Loup is connected to here." She leans forward, brushes her hair back. "He won't follow you. He can't leave Gloucester."

60

Boylan has sat in the Queen Anne chair, for the most part quietly, all evening. He has listened. He has watched Marian and Sweeney. He has watched Adrian. He saw the look on his friend's face when Marian told him to give up the board. He cannot keep silent any longer.

"Excuse me," he says. "But, you know, we came here to tell Mr. Sweeney he might be in danger. That's why we came. We took a risk." He looks at Sweeney. "We didn't know if we were going to get thrown out of here, or expelled, or whatever." He takes a deep breath, gathering courage. "I just don't think you have a right to tell us to stop. Or to tell us what to do."

Adrian flashes him a look of approval.

"I agree with Blazes," says Welcome. He stares at Marian, holds her eyes with his own. "Something else. You seem to know a lot about this stuff." He pauses. "I just have one question." He turns and faces Sweeney. "Will you, please, tell us who St. Loup is?" He swallows. "I think you know."

Sweeney moves his eyes from Welcome to Marian. He does not say a word. He empties and refills his pipe and gets it ready to smoke. He is considering. He knows the boys should be sent back to school and forbidden to use the Ouija board. He knows he has the authority to do this. But there is something else at work. He likes these three. He has liked them since he first met them in class the year before. They are good boys, very intelligent, filled with the kind of promise a teacher spends his nights dreaming about. And they have brought him something: a confirmation. There *is* another life, another country. His mother is there. He will be there. They will all be there. So he feels he owes them. He himself, if he were in their place, would refuse to go away. But he also knows there is a risk, there is a danger, a kind of danger he could not save them from. These boys have been entrusted to him. He has an obligation to their parents, to Justin Martyr, to do the right thing. Which may not be what he wants. But what he must.

"Andre St. Loup," he hears his voice again, "is the man who built this house."

"No!" exclaims Adrian.

Marian takes her cue from Sweeney. She knows, as he does, that the boys must be kept from the Ouija board. She knows, too, they must be given something that will enable them to leave this room as friends. To be able to play a part in this makes her happy.

"You asked about the quilt before," she says. She stands and walks to the dining room to get the quilt. She comes back and Sweeney stands and together they hold it out for the boys to inspect. "This type of quilt is called a memory quilt," she explains. "Its purpose is to chronicle events in the life of the person who makes it." She stops. "In this case, as you know, if you saw the quilt at the fair, it was made by Prudence Doucet, the wife of Andre Doucet, the man who built this house." She looks from behind the quilt. "For some reason, the man who calls himself St. Loup changed his name to Doucet."

"Ah," from Adrian.

"We don't know the meaning of most of these squares," she continues. "This one here," she points to the upper middle square, "is obviously this house."

"Right," exclaims Welcome. "Exactly."

"This is a bonfire," she says, pointing out another. "We have no idea why that would be important. Something must have happened that night. These two are birth squares." She looks at them. "There were two children from the marriage."

Adrian stands up. He moves closer to the quilt, a look of shock on his face. "This one," he points. "The first square in the first row. It's St. Loup. I can tell from the silver streak. The head in the jar has a streak."

Sweeney opens his mouth, about to comment, but changes his mind. Marian continues.

"Notice in the birth squares that the birth dates are stitched in: 1886 for the son, another Andre, 1888 for the daughter. Her name, I believe, was Aveline."

"Incredible," escapes from Boylan's lips.

"What about this one?" Adrian points.

Marian takes a look.

"We have no idea," she answers, "A car and some water, probably, given the area, the ocean." She looks for another square. "Look at this one. A square half night, half day. The sun and the moon and a year stitched in black on the bottom. 1930."

"What does that mean?"

"We don't know," answers Sweeney.

"Where did you find this quilt?" asks Adrian. "Was it in the house?"

Sweeney shakes his head.

"I bought it at an antique shop outside Bangor," he says. "I had no idea it had anything to do with the house. At least I don't think I did." He smiles. "Just plain luck." Then frowns. He is not sure anymore.

"Finally," Marian begins, her finger ready to point out another square. She never finishes her sentence.

"What was that?" asks Sweeney.

Boylan runs his hands through his hair. He is excited. All the boys are excited. They know the sound.

"That's the groan I heard," says Boylan.

Marian looks at Sweeney, takes the quilt from his hand and brings it back to the chair in the dining room.

"Jim and I are going to take a look downstairs," she declares. "You boys stay up here."

The three of them look at one another. They are not happy, but they can wait. There is no real desire on any of their parts to go back down there.

Sweeney and Marian usher them to their seats and then together leave the living room, walk down the hall and open the cellar door. There is a pause. Sweeney finds the light. Then they hear footsteps going down. Then nothing. Nothing for a long time. They are beginning to become anxious.

"What's going on?" asks Adrian.

The others shrug.

"We should see what's going on," says Adrian. He stands up. "They might be in trouble."

Boylan smirks.

"Not half the trouble you're going to be in if you go down there after Sweeney told you to stay put."

"What do you think they're looking for?" Adrian asks.

Boylan stands.

"Nothing horrible," he says. "They went down unarmed."

Welcome tries to smile.

"You can't shoot a ghost."

Adrian looks down at him.

"There's no ghost downstairs," he declares. "Remember the wires we saw?"

"I thought that was to steal electricity from Sweeney to put light in the tunnel," responds Boylan, revealing to the others his most recent perception in that regard.

Adrian nods.

"Right," he agrees. "Electricity. Suppose there's a tape recorder, or something like that. Ghosts don't need wires. If that dwarf was in the tunnel and the tunnel leads to Sweeney's basement, maybe he's trying to frighten him away."

Welcome gets up and starts to pace.

"They're taking a long time."

There is a pause. Adrian heads for the stairs.

"Let's go," he calls back.

The other two are right behind him. They stop at the top of the stairs. They want to run down. They want to wait. They want to obey their teacher. No one wants to see the head.

"Are you all right?" Adrian calls down.

They hear nothing. Then finally a faraway voice.

"It's all right. Come on down."

Sweeney's voice. They waste no time. Soon they are at the bottom of the stairs. They can see Sweeney and Marian over at the boxes of quilting material. The sight makes Adrian shudder.

"We're looking for a tape recorder, or speakers," Marian tells them. "These screams or groans are not the work of some unhappy spirit. They're the work of an unhappy man. Or a sick one." She moves a box. "A clever one too. We haven't found a thing."

"There were wires in the tunnel."

"Thanks for telling me before," says Sweeney. "I still can't find any trap door."

Marian takes his arm.

"Not with the boys here."

Sweeney stops.

"Oh, right. I almost forgot myself." He stands with his hands at his sides. "Just point out more or less where it is," he requests. "I'll take a look on my own."

Adrian leads him to the trap door, the sight of which causes Sweeney to gasp. He finds when he gets there he has no desire to open it. They return, after a brief inspection, to the boxes of fabric.

"Find anything?" Sweeney asks.

"Nothing, sir," from Boylan.

Marian looks at Adrian, singles him out.

"What about that little door?"

Adrian feels his mouth go dry.

"I don't know if I can."

"Just point it out," she coaxes. "I'll do the rest."

Adrian steps slowly up to the boxes.

"In there. Between the boxes."

"Down there?"

"Yes."

The boxes are moved aside. When the space is completely cleared, they can all see the low door.

"I can't believe that's been there all the time," says Sweeney. "I don't see how I could've missed it."

Marian bends down.

"Maybe it hasn't been."

Adrian steps forward.

"Wait," he says.

Marian turns and looks up.

"What?"

"The door is closed."

"So?"from Sweeney.

"I left it open," answers Adrian.

Everyone is frozen. Even the thoughts in their heads come to an end. No one wants to open the door. Then Sweeney decides. It is his house, his basement. He will take charge. He steps forward, bends down, lifts up and pulls open the door. It springs loose. Sweeney falls back.

"Ah," he exhales.

Even in the dim light from the bulb they can all see the jars and inside the jars the heads of small animals. Everything is still, even in suspension. The creatures grimace and look out with eyes that are dead and opaque.

"Where is he, Adrian?" asks Marian.

Adrian stares into the opening. He bends down to get a better look. He feels himself begin to tremble. His mouth is dry as parchment. He steps back.

"Adrian?" asks Marian, concerned.

His jaw drops. His face goes pale.

"St. Loup is gone!"

1951

61

The old woman in the chair could hear the other old woman in the other chair upstairs in the attic, rocking back and forth, like her mother used to rock in that same room in that same chair. Prudence could not stand the sound of the rocking chair. Not when it was her daughter doing what her mother once did. And that other thing, which was worse even than the rocking chair. It was obsessive. Aveline really believed in it, the power of the board to reach the spirit world. She had tried, shortly after Andre died, to convince her of the power, but for Prudence the board never held the fascination it held for Aveline. It was a piece of wood with numbers and letters and the faces of the moon and sun. It said OUIJA and GOODBYE.

Prudence wondered about the state of her daughter's mind. Ever since the accident—the coroner had been kind enough to call it that, although all knew what had happened—Aveline had labored over the board, had tried to reach Andre, her father. Twenty years, almost. She had grown old at it. And the girl. Was she a fit mother for the girl? More and more Aveline took to the rocker with the board, retreating further from a world she had never truly been a part of. She had always been too quiet, born with suspicious, unwavering eyes and hair too golden to be real. It was the golden hair that had drawn Artemus Wicks, then a boy, to her. The hair. What drew her to him? A contrary nature? And now the poor child. But loved. Marie was well loved. Prudence got up, slowly, from the chair, put down the quilt and walked down the hall and out to the porch, where she took up her position on the swinging chair. A summer evening. Fireflies again. Always fireflies.

"Father, are you there? Answer me."

Aveline sat, motionless now, in the rocker. Twilight and moon came into the room, an eerie kind of half-light.

"Father?"

The tripod moved under her fingers. She read out the words as they became clear, talking aloud, but soft voiced.

MA FILLE

"What am I to do?"

I SAID B 4 SHOOT HIM

"I can't do that."

IF NT 4 ME THN MARIE

"It would be murder."

JUS DESSERTS

"What should I do with Marie?"

LUV HER I WIL TAK CARE OF THE HIDEOUS CREATUR MYSELF

"Can you do something to make him stay away?"

SHRINK HIM

"Father, how could you do a thing like that?"

1ST TOAST HIM LET HIM COOL THEN LET THE SNAKES LOOSE ON HIM HE WILL NEVR RECOVR FRM THE SNAKES THEY WILL BRING ME HIS EYES I WILL USE THM 4 MARBLS

"You can be cruel."

ACH U WING ME I ONLE MEAN TO HELLP U AND
THE POR CHILDE MARIE LIGHT OF LIGHTS N WITH A
MONSTER FOR A DADDY IT BREKS MY HERT WHAT U
DID AVELIN

"I used him, father," she said.

NEVR USE PEOPL ITS PARLOUS DUTY

"Oh, Father," said Aveline. "It's time, I think, for me to go to
bed."

ALON I HOPE

"You know as well as I."

I DO NT THES DAMN WINDOWS BEND UR HEAD
INTO THE GLAS LET ME C UR RAVING HARE UR SWET
PRETTY LOCKS

Aveline bent into the mirror.

IT WARMS ME

She stood, brought the board to a small opening in the wall.
She placed the Ouija board, the cup, and a doll, once Marie's before
she had grown, in the compartment. Already inside were the brass
candle holders that she used when she tried to reach her father in
the dark. She took a last look at the board before she closed it up
and sealed her secret hideaway. She walked to the window and looked
out at the moon. It was full. She looked out toward the Wicks Place,
looming so large in the twilight. A horrid house, she thought. So
huge. With big empty windows that stared and stared at the world
and never showed any light. And poor dumb Artemus, living alone
in the dark, in that house, except when he came spying on Marie.

So what if he was her father? He had no sense, was cruel, if the truth be told, to living things. With those traps and his hides and his brute strength. And his strange dumb animal eyes.

Prudence had come back inside. She was sitting in the living room when the rocker stopped and the talking, more like whispering, began up in the attic. Aveline seeking wisdom from her runaway father. Old silver streak. Where was he? Never a word. Aveline insisted he was dead, had been murdered. By whom? Where was the body? Prudence waited for the footsteps on the stairs. They came soon enough, once she had hidden her piece of wood wherever it was she hid it. More than once Prudence had searched for it. She heard Aveline coming down, turned so that she would be facing her daughter when she arrived at the bottom of the stairs.

"Talking to your father, Aveline?" she asked.

Aveline looked at her mother coldly.

"If you must know, yes."

"Any news from the other side?"

"Nothing you'd believe."

"Try me."

Aveline stared at her.

"I said there was nothing."

"Did he tell you to throw away your shotgun?"

"*He* told me to buy it."

Prudence shifted so that she could face her daughter full on and not from an angle. She did not want to be looking over her shoulder for what she had to say.

"I've told you, Aveline, time and again. I don't like guns in this house." She moved her hand. "I want them out of here. Especially that shotgun. It scares me."

Aveline started walking away.

"You listen. This is *still* my house."

Aveline stopped.

"I don't want your damn house."

Prudence, shouting now, pointed a bony finger.

"That, Aveline, is something you won't have to concern yourself with. Believe me." She paused. "Where's Marie?"

62

Aveline lay looking at the ceiling, smelling the air coming in through the screen. Every now and then she heard the sound of a car and when she listened to the car she thought, as always, of Andre. It had been years. Still the thoughts came.

She had no real control over them. A sudden breeze, the sound of wheels screeching, and she would be off, thinking about the last time she had seen her brother. Her father had told her, through the Ouija board, that Andre was in another part of the other world. She believed the board. She believed it was her father speaking. Who else could it be? Who else would care so much about Marie? At the thought of Marie, Aveline remembered she had not seen her daughter that entire evening. Where *was* she? Out with another of the young men who kept coming and coming, to linger at the swing out back, all with an eye for the girl with long red hair, hair like Prudence. Eyes like Prudence and mouth and gait. It was as if Prudence were the mother, her blood ran so obvious in the girl. But Prudence was not. She was, Aveline. Her only child. Her only ever child. There would be no more. Not at her age. She heard a cricket and smiled to herself. She heard an owl, felt reassured, and hearing something else, she sat up.

"Marie?"

Marie was always lurking. She would come in through the open windows, any of them on the first floor, but especially through the windows off the front porch. She liked it there. They all liked it there. This time, certainly, she heard something and she turned toward the window.

"Marie?"

It was not Marie. It was a huge shape she knew to be Artemus and he stepped in through the window, pushing aside the screen, before she could say a word, before she could get up and get to the shotgun, which stood leaning against the bureau just out of reach. He stood staring down at her from the foot of the bed, saying nothing—he could say nothing—this giant, with long straight muscled arms that hung almost to his knees. She could see he was shirtless. She could see nothing else. Not his eyes, nor even much of his face. The moon was on the other side of the house. Artemus stood, waited for her to move. Aveline knew. It was too late to move.

"What are you doing here?"

He made a sound. What did the sound mean?

"I told you to keep away from here," she said, her voice low. "I told you never to come back."

He fell to his knees and began to beat the sheets with his fists, all the time making a mewling, crying sound. Was he crying?

"*Artemus*, you goddamn moron," she hissed. "Get the hell out of here. Dammit." She was trying to move off the bed. "And keep away from the girl. You frighten her." She watched him, every move he made. "She doesn't even know who you are." She stopped, almost out of bed. "I don't even know who you are. You know, you might not be her father. I think it was Billy Boy. You know that? Billy Boy, your dead brother." Swinging her feet to the floor. "I had him too. Did I tell you? No? Well, I'm telling you now. Why am I telling you, Artemus? I'm telling you so you can keep yourself the hell away from her. Hear me, you dumb bastard? She's not yours. Never was." Her feet hit the floor and she raced to the shotgun and tried to work it but couldn't and took it by the long barrel and swung with all her might at the still kneeling shape at the foot of the bed and heard a sharp cry of pain when she hit and she hit again, the back of his head this time, and Artemus stood, growling, squealing, and he went for her in the dark, throwing out his hand. "Sonovabitch," she swore, dodging him, but next time she had the gun and she tried to work the trigger, tried to blow his head off, but he tore the gun from her before her fingers could reach it and shoved her down. He stood over her, mewling, the shotgun dangling like an extra arm in the shadows.

"Get the hell out of here."

He turned from her and put the gun on the bed and then turned and grabbed at her with one of his arms. She slipped away. He cried and hit her with his huge fist, dazing her. She thought she would lose consciousness, but she did not and was almost on her feet when she felt herself being lifted, one long arm on her throat. She marveled at this display of strength, her eyes wide with fear and astonishment.

"You're hurting me," she got out, but the words, in her own ears, sounded distorted, the voice of another. "Put me. . ." She could not get out the words and now the other huge paw was at her throat and she felt herself being scraped against the wall. She could hear her nightgown tearing, feel her skin being abraded, as Artemus stretched out his arms until he held her—by the neck—against the wall and she looked down at him as from a great height and saw below her a dim but mad demon, all shape and shadow, without eyes, voice, words of any kind.

"You . . ." she started.

Again, she could not finish. Then something new. A pressure of some kind, squeezing, forcing her eyes out. She *knew* they were sticking out. In a minute she would be able to turn around and look at herself. Something snapped. She heard it. A chicken bone. She thought no, not a chicken bone. They're in the barn. Me. It's me who's cracking, and she felt a tear from her pushed-out eyeballs running down her cheek and then the world turned to shadows and a dream where a white owl perched on a wicket stretched out his wings and welcomed her to his kingdom.

He carried her like a doll in his arms, tears running down his own cheeks, along the corridor to the cellar stairs. Quietly, he opened the door, quietly closed it behind him, making his way in the dark to the floor below and once there to the hatchway, where he let Aveline down to the floor while he slid open the door to the tunnel. He looked briefly at her—like a broken doll in her white nightgown. He took a flashlight from his pocket and aimed it at her head and when he saw it in the light he made a choking sound and then shuddered before he bent down and lifted her again, her broken neck dangling, and tried to work both the light and the body down the ladder to the tunnel. He got down two steps before he trembled and almost lost the light and the beam, for one brief moment, lit both his and her face, and in that moment, just before he slid back the door and the room went dark, the girl, Marie, hiding in the corner, shaking with terror, saw her mother, dead, and the man who had killed her. She opened her mouth to scream, but no words came.

EIGHT BOXES/
POSTMARK MARBLEHEAD

1965

63

They are back upstairs, sitting in the living room, positioned as before. A chill wind howls outside. Over Sweeney's shoulder, at the edge of the dark sky, like a sliver of beaten gold, is the lower cusp of a full moon. Sweeney concentrates on his pipe. He puffs away. Then he puts down the pipe and for the first time that evening brings his free hand to his bright yellow sweater and fingers the ansate cross he wears hidden underneath. No one has noticed. Each of the others is busy with his own thoughts, his own explanations.

"I think what happened is clear," Sweeney asserts. "The dwarf came up through the trap door and took the head, once he realized it had been discovered." He smiles at Adrian. "Your leaving the door open, I suspect, gave him that piece of news."

Adrian is chagrinned.

"Sorry."

"Nothing to be sorry about, Adrian," Marian says, matter-of-factly. "You were frightened."

"I didn't mean that as an accusation," offers Sweeney. He muses, puffs his pipe. "I wonder what he wants it for."

"It could be evidence," suggests Boylan.

Sweeney nods.

"That's possible."

"Why didn't St. Loup come right out and say he was murdered and who did it?" comments Welcome. "I don't see why he has to be so, so..."

"Circumspect," offers Sweeney.

"Right."

"Who knows?" asks Boylan. "Maybe he's enjoying himself. You know, having a good time. Being enigmatic."

Sweeney raises an eyebrow at the word.

"You were going to say something about one of the panels on the quilt," Adrian reminds Marian. "Just before we heard the groan." He stops. "Remember?"

Marian slowly nods her head.

"I think it was, if I can remember," she begins, "the next to last panel. It's simply a square with a woman with long red hair. In a rocking chair. Looking out to sea."

"Yes," says Adrian.

Welcome jumps to his feet.

"That's right."

Marian is puzzled.

"So?"

"St. Loup," says Welcome. "He said 'save Marie'. She's in a house by the sea. That must be her in the square."

"That *is* right," echoes Sweeney, who stands. "You *said* he wanted you to save Marie. You said nothing about a house by the sea, though." He gives Welcome a displeased look. "Any other details left out of this tale?"

Welcome is sheepish.

"No, sir."

Sweeney looks at Marian.

"Where could she be?"

Marian looks up at him and holds his gaze. He knows what she wants to suggest. He wants it too. But the boys? It is a quandary for him, but he does like them and if she, who insisted Adrian stop, is for it, where could be the harm? He stares at her dark eyes and turns and sees Adrian and his dark blue eyes and then Boylan and Welcome. All their shining eyes. He looks again at Marian. Is he reading her correctly? Something has made her change her mind. But what? He senses she is certain it is the right—the necessary—thing to do next, and he can see also in her eyes and the way she sits when she sits next to Adrian that there exists some kind of bond between them and that, perhaps, the existence of this bond, now confirmed, has emboldened her and made it possible for her to take the chance.

And she would be in control. It would be her, not Adrian. Together they might even be stronger. That is the last thought he has. He has made up his mind.

"I'll get Wedgwood," he says.

Boylan inquires:

"Wedgwood?"

Marian looks at him with serene dark eyes.

"Every tripod has a name."

64

Sweeney comes back and motions for the boys to pick up the two Queen Anne chairs at the edge of the living room and move them into the dining room, where there are three others like them. The dining room is large and like the living room has a fireplace. After he puts the Ouija board down on the low glass-topped table at the back of the dining room, he tells Boylan and Welcome to help him with the fire. In no time at all he has a fire going. They stand in front of the gate, watching sparks fly, while Marian and Adrian sit at the low table looking down at the Ouija board.

"We're ready, Jim," she calls out.

Sweeney has not explained to Boylan and Welcome what he is doing with a Ouija board. Both boys have the same thought: it is the reason he listened to them. Talk of the spirit world is not new at Sweeney's house. They wait for him to say something, but he will not. They give up expecting an explanation. When all of them are settled in around the table, Sweeney, now that he has them in *his* power, with the bright fire and the warm house and the wind outside, at *his* table with *his* Ouija board, becomes bold enough to tell a story he never thought he would be telling students. He does not flinch. It must be told.

"I found this," he points to the board, "up in the attic." His eyes move to the fire. "Truth is, I'd been hearing noises. A bit like that groan we heard before, but sometimes worse. A high-pitched wailing." He pauses. "I think it was shortly after Rufus came for his visit I decided to give the place a good once over. He made me suspicious." He senses everyone is anxious to get going. "To make a long story short, I found this hidden behind a panel." There is a twinkle in his eye. "Quite a find."

The boys are surprised. Had they learned this earlier, before finding the head, before St. Loup and the tunnel, they might even have been stunned. As it is, they only see Sweeney in another light. The board gives him an extra dimension. They approve.

"Have you reached St. Loup?" asks Adrian.

Marian answers.

"We have, Adrian. First we reached Aveline, who claims to be the mother of Prudence. Prudence is Andre Doucet's, or St. Loup's, wife." She waits, to see if the boys understand. "Prudence herself was the mother of two children, as we know. One of whom had the name Aveline."

"After the grandmother?" asks Welcome.

"So it would seem," replies Sweeney.

"What about St. Loup?" asks Adrian.

Marian nods to him.

"I'm coming to that," she says. "Part of the reason for the turmoil we feel through the board is that Aveline, the grandmother, committed suicide. She hung herself."

"No," exclaims Adrian.

"We're pretty sure," she says. "Aveline tends to be vague. St. Loup, as you know, is elliptical."

"That's the word," agrees Adrian. "It's like he's having fun." He looks across the table at her. "Know what I mean?"

"Yes," she says. "But it's not fun. And it's not a game." Her eyes stare at Adrian. "This is real. How St. Loup presents himself to us has a lot to do with what he has in mind. Being clever is a good way to disarm people. He might also have had a sense of humor in life." She stretches her hand out over the tripod. "We'll never know. All we get is what the board gives us. His link." She begins to rotate her hand. The tripod moves in response. "Don't be startled," she says. "I can do that."

The boys stare down speechless.

"I want you all to close your eyes," she says. "It will better our concentration. Make us stronger." She waits for them to close their eyes. "Think of something good. Someone you love, perhaps. A

color. A nice piece of music. Something that calms you." She begins to hum 'Beautiful Dreamer.' "Hum along if you know the song."

At first they feel foolish, then something changes. The humming gives them a sense of power and serenity. It helps them leave
the world. Soon they are humming; before long they forget they
are.

"Is anybody there?"

The humming stops.

"Is anybody there?"

Sweeney opens his eyes. It is his job to take down the letters. He
watches her, then shifts his gaze to the boys. All of them have their
eyes closed. Marian stiffens. Out of the corner of his eye he has
caught the movement. It is as before. She seems to go into a deep
trance, to actually become an avenue between two separate worlds.
He grips the pencil tightly.

The tripod, untouched by her, spins and wheels. Sweeney writes
it down, one letter at a time. Then he reads:

I LIK UR TUNE

"St. Loup? Is it you?"

HUM THAT TUNE WE SPIRITS CANT SING

"You haven't answered me."

I AM THE WOLF

At this, Marian shudders. Sweeney watches her carefully.
"The dwarf. What about the dwarf?"
There is a mad jumble of letters, which Sweeney takes down.

SMITE HIM

"How?"

GIV IT SOME THOUGHT

"Should we have him arrested?"

AH NOW I C U A REAL LADIE

"Should Rufus be arrested?"

THE NAM MAKES MY WOUNDS ACHE

"What should we do?"

TURM HIM IN2 A SOUP OR BETR BONE HIM

"Where is he?"

HIDING

"Where?"

WHO KNOS HE HIDES THAT IS HIS WAY

"What must we do to capture him?"

FIND MY HEAD THE HORIBLE GNOME TOOK IT

"Took it to where?"

HAR HAR HIS LAIR

"Is he in the Wicks place?"

THE NAM ANOTHR ACHE I WIL HELLP BE UR GUIDE YR FAMILIAR U LOK SO LUVLE TARRY A BIT B4 U DIE IT IS SO DANK IN HER IT CUD THO B THE DAY THIS NIGHT STICKS TO MY BONES ACH THE DAMNABL DWARF HE ISNT FAR

"Is he in the tunnel?"

HAR HAR TUNL HIS MUSIK IS THER

"Can you explain?"

HE WHISTLS A SCARY TUNE

"Is he the one who makes the groans?"

THAT CD B THE MAD BITCH I HAV THE CROWS ON
HER

"Aveline?"

THE SAME

"Did she kill herself?"

IT DOES SEM SO

"Was she murdered? Which?"

2 MURDRS AND SHE IS NT 1 OV THEM

"In this house?"

AH MY ACHING BONES

"Where are the bodies?"

MOULDERING

"Who is Marie?"

AN UNFORTUNATE CHILDE SAV HER

"Who is her father?"

THE DISML APE

"Who?"

U WIL KNO HIM

"How?"

HE IS A BEAST

"How many beasts are there?"

THEY SEM TO COME IN PAIRS

"Are they both alive now?"

SAD TO SAY

"Where?"

U SAID IT YERSELF THE WICKS PLACE THEY R BID-
ING THEIR TIME BT THEY DO NOT KNO THEIR TIME
HAS COME THE WOLF WIL HAV HIS DAY U MES CHERS
WIL HELLP AH IT IS SUCH GODS WORK CD U BEND A
BIT I WONDR IF UR HAIR IS GOLD

"My hair is very dark brown," Marian replies.

ACH THES WINDOWS

"Who is Marie?"

THE DAUGHTR OF MY DEAD DAUGHTR

"How did your daughter die?"

MURDR MOST FOUL

"Who killed her?"

IT BREKS MY HERT

"Who?"

THE FIEND A FOUL TEMPRD A ROGUE SHORT ON BRAINS THEY ALL LOK LIK FLIES FROM HER YOUD THINK THEYD HAV SOME LITE IN HEAVEN A CANDL FOR AN OLD MAN BUT NO GOD IS SUCH A TIGHT OUCH EBN HER THER ARE THINGS I CANNOT SAY THOS DAMN FLIES WORK 4 ANY1 LIKE JUNE BUGS ONLE THEY STINK

"Please, answer my question."

SOMTYMES U COME IN GARBLD WICKS IS HER FATHR

"Where is she?"

SHE SITS FIND HER

"Where?

A STONS THRO

"Where, exactly?"

COME FOLOW ME

"Now?"

TIME WAITS 4 NO 1 I FEEL IT IN I WD HAV SED BONES BUT AS U KNO THER ARE NO BONES IN THE STARS COME CATCH THE DISMAL DWARF I AM STRONG I

HAVE MY BIRDS A THOUSAND STRONG AND OF COURSE MY EYES MY STRIKING FORCE

"Striking force?"

A MANR OF SPEECH

"Where do you want us to go?"

U KNO THE WAY

"The tunnel?"

EVEN AS WE SPEK THEY FLEE COME BE QUICK ABOUT IT

"Should we bring the board?"

I HAV NO NED OF IT

"What should we do with your head?"

USE IT FR SOUP

"Dammit," Marian hollers. "Why are you being so difficult? Should we bury it?"

NOT IF UR GOING TO BE ANGRY ABOUT IT

"We're going to bury it."

A GUD BONY HEAD WD MAKE GOOD SOUP

Marian smiles. "Are you trying to be funny?"

HAR HAR LISN I JUS HEARD THIS OZYMANDIAS IS A STONE HEAD MANY MORE WHERE THAT CAM FRM

"We are going to leave and go to the Wicks place," Marian says, opening her eyes.

PARTING IS SUCH SWET SOROW

She stands. There is a final rush of letters.

ACH I C MARIE I SEE HER SHE IS SO SAD U MUST HELLP ME SAV HER

"Where is she?" asks Adrian. The tripod freezes, then:

AH MES ENFANT MES CHER I DID NT SEE U GOOD 2 HAV U ABORD I SEE U R EXPERIMENTING WITH A NEW VEHICLE AVELINES HOW DOES SHE RIED THE LADY UR COMPANION HAS LUVLE BREASTS THEY STICK OUT TO ETERNITY

"Be quiet," orders Marian, opening her eyes.

KIS ME U FOOL

"We're leaving."

DON LEAVE ME WE MUS TALK

"I think we're done," she says. "You won't tell us where Marie is. We've nothing more to discuss."

I ENJOY THES LYTL CHATS

"You're the one who wants us to go."

U HAV UR WITS ABOUT YOU

"*Where* is Marie?" demands Adrian. There is a long pause.

I BELIEV IT IS CALLED ARRERHEAD

"Arrowhead?"

THER U HAV IT

"Thank you," says Marian.

THANK U ACH I SMELL THE DWARF THE NEMATODE

"Come on," says Marian. "Time to go. "

SAV HIS HED 4 ME I HAV PLANS FOR IT

"We'll have to see," she responds.

ONLE 4 A WHIL HE HAS IT COMING

"We shall see."

AT LEST THE EYES

"Why?"

FR MARBLS

They all sit back and look at Marian. She appears a little tired, but her eyes flash with excitement. She says nothing. Sweeney rises, then she gets up. The boys stand.

"Boys," Sweeney declares. "Stay here. Marian and I are taking a little walk. Going to visit a neighbor."

"But, sir," protests Adrian. "It's dangerous."

Sweeney has already made up his mind.

"There's a chance, but not much. Think about it. If Rufus really meant us harm, wouldn't he have done something by now?" He seems to be weighing his words. "He's trying to frighten me. Maybe he wants me out of this house. Why? No harm in asking." He begins to walk through the living room. "Moreover, we think he took the head. St. Loup tells us he did. Don't you think we should see if it's there? Or should we sit around and wait for someone else?"

The boys are crestfallen.

"What if he killed St. Loup?" asks Welcome.

Sweeney raises a hand.

"We don't know that."

"St. Loup practically told us," insists Adrian.

Sweeney smiles.

"But not specifically," he admonishes. "We don't know what happened. We do know that the fellow with some of the answers may be across the street." He stops talking. "Right now."

The boys look to Marian for help.

"You're going over there?"

"Why not?" she returns.

"You could get hurt."

She smiles.

"I don't think so. My real concern was St. Loup."

The three boys are puzzled. They cannot understand how the two adults can be so cavalier about going to the Wicks place. Not with the possibility Rufus is there waiting. And maybe not alone.

"It could be a trap," suggests Adrian.

Both of them smile.

"Too many late-night movies," rejoins Sweeney.

No one has any response to that.

"What should we do?" asks Boylan.

Sweeney looks at Marian.

"Wait here. If we're not back in an hour, call the police." He pulls open the front door. "We'll be back." He and Marian step through the door, then Sweeney steps back. "See if you can't locate my cat."

The boys watch from the door as Sweeney and Marian, arm in arm, go down the path and gradually disappear in the darkness. Then Adrian closes the door and the three of them return to the dining room and sit at the low table and stare down at the Ouija board.

"Damn," mutters Boylan.

Welcome gives him a look.

"Don't you start."

"What?"

"You know what I mean."

Adrian gives him a quizzical look.

"What *do* you mean, Andy?"

Welcome has a puzzled look on his face.

"Don't even think it."

"Think what?" asks Adrian, all innocence.

"You know."

Adrian shakes his head.

"No, I don't."

Welcome gets to his feet.

"I want no part of it."

"What?"

Welcome storms into the living room.

"What's eating him?" asks Boylan.

Adrian stares at his friend.

"You know."

"What?" says Boylan, with some exasperation.

"Do I have to tell you?"

Boylan gets up.

Adrian looks up at him.

"Har, har." He stretches in his seat. "Isn't it strange the way the two of them went off?"

"How do you mean?"

"I mean," Adrian says, "that if Sweeney were really Sweeney, he'd be calling the cops. Not like him at all."

"What isn't?"

"To play the hero."

Boylan looks down at him.

"Say what you mean."

Adrian stands up, moves close to Boylan.

"I think they're under a spell," he says. "St. Loup has them. Didn't you see the way she looked? Pale? But her eyes. They had this sheen to them."

"There was nothing different about her eyes."

"You didn't see it?"

Boylan seems flustered.

"There was nothing to see."

Adrian studies him superciliously.

"If you say so."

"Don't give me any reverse psychology horseshit, Sparks," says Boylan, his voice rising. "We're not going over there."

"Who said anything about going anywhere?"

Boylan shakes his head.

"You can be a real shithead."

"Look," says Adrian, putting his arm around Boylan's shoulder, "what's to keep us from looking in a window?"

"The house is dark."

"They took a flashlight."

"We wouldn't be able to see a thing," Boylan protests.

"We could see the light."

"Not if they were in the cellar."

Adrian nods.

"Good point, Blazes." He pauses. "Maybe we should approach the house through the tunnel."

Boylan frees himself from Adrian's arm.

"*Nothing*," he says emphatically, "gets me *near* that tunnel."

Adrian flashes him a smile.

"Do I have to go alone?"

65

"It was tough on the boys to leave them there," Marian declares, her face chilled by the wind. "I know we had to do it. I just wish there were some other way." She looks up at Sweeney. "They were a big help. We couldn't have done it without them."

Sweeney is holding her arm.

"I know," he says. "Especially Adrian. All of them actually. It took guts for them to come to my house like that. On Halloween of all days." He steps through some leaves. "Justin Martyr's a rigorous place. Any infraction and you're out."

"A visit?"

"Not permitted," answers Sweeney. "Unless requested by the teacher. I do it as a matter of course. I like them over for tea and chit-chat. Some of the others, though—they'd see a boy sacked for dropping by."

"Sounds cruel."

"It's a Jesuit school."

They can see the outline of the house up ahead. It stands, dark against dark, solid and foreboding. The wind whistles and the leaves kick up at their feet.

Marian stops him.

"We have to be careful in there."

"I know."

"I don't mean the dwarf," she declares. "St. Loup could be about."

"Meaning?"

"Just what I said. Be careful."

"Maybe we should call the police," he says.

"It's something to consider," she agrees. "But what could they do? If they found Rufus, they'd arrest him for trespassing. I don't see how they'd connect him to the tunnel or to your house." She takes a deep breath. "We want to find out about St. Loup. They knew each other."

Sweeney interrupts.

"Hated, I think, is the correct word."

Marian nods.

"That too."

He begins walking toward the house.

"I really don't feel afraid of him," he says. "I think he's menacing. But he's so small. No bigger than a child." He stops to get a better look at the house. "How could he hurt us?"

"He may have a weapon."

Sweeney unhooks his arm.

"Why? He doesn't want to kill me, us. I'm sure of it."

Marian takes back his arm.

"I'll agree with you there," she says. "But let's be careful. Keep quiet and don't use the flashlight unless we absolutely have to."

"I get it," smiles Sweeney. "Sneak up on him."

The moon, full now, brightens everything. Leaves, what few are left in the trees, shimmer, and the willow tree, its branches lashing the ground, shudders in the wind, which is rising. There is a stiff cold breeze. The house, caught in moonlight, seems to be stealing light from the glow in the night sky. Nothing seems to reflect. The windows are like black holes, the rotting shutters creak, bang against the windows. At the same time it is eerily quiet, preternatural. There is not a single light in the utterly dark house. But for the moonlight it would be difficult to see at all. Up above, in a tree, a tall red beech, an owl hoots. Sweeney looks and sees nothing, but then catches a flash of white in the moonlight. He can make out, sitting, watching, way up, a great snowy owl, immaculate. They stand under the tree and stare at it.

"You rarely see them here."

"He's gorgeous," says Marian.

They move on to the house.

"Do we knock?" he wonders.

"I thought you had this all worked out."

He looks down, stops walking.

"Doesn't look as if anyone's home," he comments.

She walks to the door herself.

"Think it's open?"

"How do we get in?"

"There's an open window on the side," he says. "Remember?"

"Right."

He leads the way. They walk past the brackish pond near the willow tree, past driftwood and a battered doll, its plastic shining lifeless face staring up at the moon. He stops at the window, takes out a flashlight and turns to Marian.

She holds up another, smaller flashlight.

"It's now or never."

Sweeney grins, uneasily. He hesitates at the window.

"I guess."

"Go on," she urges, "get in."

He turns on the flashlight, steps over the ledge and waits on the other side for her. She follows quickly and stands next to him.

"Which way?" she whispers.

Sweeney takes her arm.

"Do we have to whisper?" he asks, his voice low.

"Whisper, Jim. It makes me feel better."

She feels him nod approval.

"This way, I think."

She holds his arm as he leads her out of the bedroom into the long hall that will take them to the living room, the large room on the other end of the house with bowed windows. They will begin there. As they pass the rooms, through the windows moonlight, acting as a guide, helps them along. It is bright enough, in spots, not to need the lights, but eerie, very dank and cool. They stick close together and marvel, in silence, at the height of the ceilings, the enormous size of the place. The rooms are like hollow caverns and they echo. There is dust, even some leaves on the floor.

"In here," he says.

There is a sudden sense of something wrong once they step inside the living room. There is no name for it, but they can feel it.

Sweeney swings the beam about the room, starting with the shuttered bay windows. He sees nothing there. He swings it to the huge fireplace, then to the mantle above.

"Oh," he gasps.

Marian shudders at his side.

"Good Lord," she exclaims.

Her beam finds its way to the mantle and stops there. Illuminated in the twin beams of unsteady light is the glass cylinder and in the glass, like some horrible Gorgon, the head of St. Loup, its dead dull empty eyes looking right at them.

"God," groans Marian.

Sweeney puts his arm around her.

"Well, well," says a thin reedy voice from behind. "What have we here?"

They both jump.

"Rufus?"

They hear a quick chuckle.

"How about that, Artemus? He remembers my name."

Sweeney finds Rufus with his light. The dwarf shines.

"Easy, now, your honor. Light hurts my eyes."

Sweeney keeps the flashlight exactly where it is.

"Your honor," says the thin voice. "Move away that goddamn light, or I'll pith you like a frog."

66

Sweeney tries to quell his fear. He has been unnerved by the head in the jar on the mantle, further unnerved being taken by surprise by Rufus. He makes sure to keep Marion close to him and tries to keep her in sight, while he focuses on the small man in front of him in the large dim room.

"Why are you here?"

Rufus titters.

"Talking to me, your honor? Or my friend here?"

Sweeney looks and sees in the half-light behind the dwarf a huge shape hidden away in shadow.

"You, Rufus. I'm talking to you."

"Well," Rufus begins, his voice sounding disembodied. He can barely be seen. "To get right to the point. I came for the gold."

"What gold?"

"That's my secret."

"Is that why you're trying to frighten me?"

Rufus giggles. The sound is startling, the way it echoes.

"I want you out of the house, Mr. Sweeney. When I came last time I expected the place to be empty. You have no idea how bad I felt not seeing a 'For Sale' sign on the front lawn." He stops. "Took me longer to get up here than I thought. Then I found you," he says the word distastefully. "You were a great disappointment." He turns to the shape. "Light some candles, Artemus."

"Why did you murder St. Loup?"

Rufus turns back, hesitates.

"Who said anybody killed anybody?"

Sweeney presses.

"You did, didn't you?" He takes a guess. "Over the gold you still think is hidden somewhere in my house."

Rufus doesn't say a word. Not for what seems like minutes, but can't be that long. Artemus, having quietly gone off, returns just as quietly. In the silence they can hear him shuffle over the floor. His pants seem to rasp against the wood and one of his shoes has a flapping sole.

"Over there, over there," they hear Rufus bark. "You got some interesting ideas, Mr. Sweeney. Interesting." He moves a step closer. "I'm short, Sweeney. Not stupid. You say there's gold in your house? You say you found gold?"

"I've found nothing."

Marian speaks.

"What are you doing with that head?"

Rufus laughs.

"I came across it in my travels." He makes a vague movement with his hand. "Sorta catches the eye."

"Was it you who put those animal heads in the jars?"

Rufus moves ahead another step.

"That was Artemus. He likes to cut."

Sweeney remembers what St. Loup said.

"Marie's father?"

Rufus goes quiet a long time.

"You're good, your honor."

"Is he?"

"He may be. He may not."

Suddenly, a candle flickers to life near the window. Sweeney and Marian see clearly, for the first time, the huge shape known as Artemus Wicks, all six and a half feet of him. His face stares at them, lurid in the candle light.

"Close the damn shutters!" barks Rufus.

Artemus does as he is told, making a mewling sound as he latches them shut. They can see he is dressed in rags.

"What's wrong with him?"

Artemus moves to another window, checks to see if the shutters are drawn and lights another set of candles. Rufus cautions him.

"This ain't a damn ballroom."

Marian repeats.

"What's wrong with him?"

Rufus, his eyes glinting in the still dim but brighter light in the room, stares hard at her. His eyes make her uncomfortable.

"He's sex-starved."

At the sound of the word, Artemus turns about. He stands motionless and for the first time they can hear him breathing, a heavy, broken sound. He seems to fight for breath.

"He's mute," Marian says.

Rufus responds.

"Mute, yes. I don't know for how long, but he is now." He looks over at the huge shape in the window. "Not very bright," he says, "but he takes orders pretty good." He chuckles. "Me and Artemus have a kind of military union."

Sweeney wonders how long they have been in the room. He has no idea and he worries the boys might be calling the police, which is something he wants to avoid.

"What about Marie?"

"What about her?"

"Where is she?" asks Marian.

"What's it to you?"

"We want to help her."

"Who says she needs help?" Rufus spits back.

"We want to talk to her," Marian says.

Rufus laughs.

"Marie's another one." He points. "Like him. Not much interested in words."

"What do you mean?"

Rufus sighs, sits down in the middle of the floor, folding his legs together beneath him. He looks at them, small darts of light from the candles reflected in his eyes.

"Why are you so interested in Marie?"

"She sold me the house," says Sweeney.

"So?" mutters the dwarf, seeming to lose interest.

"I want to talk to her."

"Marie don't talk. I told you that. And she ain't sold anybody anything," he says.

A sound like a croak comes out of Artemus.

"Is she at Arrowhead?" Sweeney asks.

Rufus rocks back and forth.

"Tell you what, Mr. Sweeney," he says. "Tell me what you know about the gold. I'll tell you what I know about Marie."

"I don't know about any gold."

Rufus gets slowly to his feet

"I was afraid you'd say that."

Marian moves even closer to Sweeney.

"What does that mean?"

"Mean?" repeats Rufus, his voice rising to a near shout. "Get the goddamn rope."

Marian gasps. Artemus goes by close enough to touch on his way out of the room, following orders.

"Like I said, Mr. Sweeney. You found the heads." He shifts his weight from one foot to another, waiting for Artemus to return. "You might've found something else."

"I didn't."

Rufus grins.

"That could be your misfortune, Mr. Sweeney."

Sweeney is beginning to become genuinely afraid of the little man in front of him. He is also certain he has learned all he is going to learn. And he certainly isn't going to wait for the mute's return. He takes Marian by the hand and steps toward the mantle.

"We'll be taking this."

Rufus shouts.

"Hands off!"

They turn around.

"That's right, take a good look." He points a huge revolver at Sweeney. "Don't do anything stupid." He moves the gun to Marian, aims at a point near the heart. "You either."

67

"I could swear I saw a light," says Boylan.

"Where?" from Adrian.

Boylan points.

"Over there. There's a shutter missing."

"I can't see anything," says Welcome. "You're hallucinating again, Boylan. Better watch."

Boylan makes a fist.

"It's not there now," he says. "But it was."

"Listen," orders Adrian, holding up a finger to his lips. "Hear anything?"

The three boys lean toward the house, cup ears.

"I can't hear a thing."

"Maybe we should try the other side," suggests Welcome. "We haven't tried *that* side," he points to the south, "and the back. They could be in the kitchen."

"I doubt it," from Adrian.

They walk to the south side of the house, listen, peer in through a pane of broken glass. They see and hear nothing.

"We *know* they're in there."

Welcome and Boylan look at Adrian when he says this, doubt in their eyes. Adrian sticks his head in through the window pane, pulls it back out.

"They *have* to be in there," he says.

"We didn't actually see them go inside," offers Welcome.

Adrian sputters.

"Maybe they went out for ice cream."

"Or got took by Martians," says Boylan, grinning to himself. "I've heard of things like that." He looks up at the moon. "People go for a walk and get snatched by a probe from the sky. Like that couple in New Hampshire."

"I say we go in," Adrian suggests.

No one says a word.

"Why not call the police?" Welcome asks.

"And tell them what? We can't report them missing," replies Adrian. "Tell them about the Ouija board?" He looks at the house, ominous in the moonlight. "A missing head? Be serious, Andy. It's us or nothing."

Boylan shows his shining teeth.

"Again, the talons of Adrian. The hooks, the lies." He is still smiling. "You get us to agree to look through a window. All of a sudden, here we are on our way inside. Just like you planned."

"That's not true," Adrian protests.

Boylan raises a hand.

"Please, it hurts my ears."

Adrian waits.

"They could be in danger."

Boylan and Welcome are of the same mind.

"We may need a flashlight," says Welcome, his deep voice thudding against the splitting clapboards. "It's dark inside."

Adrian pulls a small flash from his pocket.

"Well, well," from Blazes. "I know. Don't tell me. You always carry one."

A grin from Adrian.

"Walk back to the other side and go in through our little empty window?" he asks. "What do you say?"

"I suppose," from Welcome.

They go back past the bay windows, the front of the house, the brackish, shimmering leaf-covered pond, weeds, detritus. Their feet swish through the leaves. They turn away from the scraping willow and move to the window. In goes Adrian's head.

"All clear," he whispers.

He is about to step over the ledge when a hand, Boylan's, grabs him by the shoulder. He wheels, questions in his eyes.

"A plan. Is there a plan? This house has three floors and a widow's walk. A basement. They could be anywhere."

Adrian raises a finger.

"Stick together," he says. "Listen. We *should* be able to hear them, especially if we keep quiet. We'll go room by room," he declares, "and we won't use the flash unless we absolutely have to." He looks over Boylan's shoulder, sees the moon. "There should be moonlight, at least through the window."

"And," intones Welcome, "assuming Sweeney and the lady are in danger, have been captured by the nematode—I do like that word—we will have to sneak up on them." He adjusts his horn-rimmed glasses. "We are shining knights, come to save." He pauses. "I relish the role." He catches himself. "Though, to tell the truth, I'm scared." He looks at his legs. "There they go again."

Adrian, at the window.

"Come on, come on."

In they go. As before, a shadowy room, leaves on the floor, high walls with wallpaper falling, a dampness. The air is dank, still and though they try to creep silently over the wood, there are creaks and a hollow muffled echo of every step they take. They crouch as they walk, Adrian at the point, his light still off, relying on moonlight. He switches the beam on when they come to the dark long narrow hallway, but only after listening for voices. They start at the kitchen, in the rear of the house, and work their way forward, room by giant room. They arrive at the last room on the first floor—the bay-windowed living room at the front of the house.

"Smell that?" whispers Adrian.

Welcome sniffs.

"Candles."

"Go ahead," hisses Blazes. "Turn on the light."

Adrian switches it on. He moves the beam about the room, wall to wall, fireplace, mantle, window to window.

"There," points Welcome.

A candelabrum in one of the bays. Gingerly, they tiptoe to the window. Boylan brings a finger to the wick.

"Still warm."

They stare at the candles.

"Why did they leave?" muses Adrian.

68

"You must be mad."

In the cellar Sweeney and Marian are tied to chairs, she with a wide piece of duct tape over her mouth. The room is illuminated by a single lightbulb, hanging from a beam, the power drawn from Sweeney's house through a series of linked red extension cords. A kerosene heater, off to the right of the chairs, warms a small circle. Rufus, his foot on the rung of Sweeney's chair, toys with a knife.

"Remains to be seen, your honor."

His flat eyes try to sparkle.

"Really," begins Sweeney, with a look to Marian. "I don't know a thing about any gold."

Rufus works up a smile.

"You found the heads." He turns to Artemus. "Where'd you put our friend?"

Artemus steps out from the shadows, ducking under a beam. He leans, shuffles to the tunnel and steps inside. He returns, carrying St. Loup.

"Bring him here, Artemus. Bring a chair." He faces Sweeney. "Might as well have St. Loup give me a hand." He waits for Wicks to bring the head and chair and set them up. "There, now. A feast for the eyes." He runs the knife down Sweeney's cheek. There is a thin line of blood. "There are some people," he says, "who might be inclined to think this is the very knife, your honor, that put that head in the jar." A pause. "Now, I'm not saying it's true." He smiles, revealing a row of decaying teeth on the bottom. "But you should give it some thought."

Sweeney, finding it nearly impossible to take his eyes from the head in the jar, forces his gaze up into the grinning dwarf's eyes.

"I'm telling the truth."

Rufus whirls, hurls the knife into the center of a beam.

"Like I said. You found the heads." He grins down at Sweeney. "You also found the Ouija board. Artemus remembers that particular item." He turns toward the giant. "Don't you?"

Almost a howl from Wicks.

"How do you know about that?" asks Sweeney, surprised.

Rufus walks to the beam, takes out the blade, walks back to Sweeney, returns his right foot to the rung of the chair and stares down.

"We have our ways," he replies. "Mostly, though, the tunnel. Once Artemus showed me that, my plan began to take shape."

Sweeney says nothing. His eyes dart about the chamber.

"There are things I could tell you," he says, "that would knock your socks off. Clear across the room." He smiles: it is like an accident. "Rufus Quick, your honor, one of the century's great detectives."

"Really?" from Sweeney, playing for time.

"Yes, sir. I didn't just *happen* to come here. No, sir. I *found* this place. Took some considerable effort, but I did."

"What made you come here?"

Rufus takes back his foot, squats, places both hands on his thighs and laughs. The laugh is like a squeal. Marian, at the sound of the laugh, takes her eyes from Artemus, whom she has been trying to locate in the shadows. He is the one who frightens her more.

"That would be the gold." He stands up straight and puts his foot back on the chair rung. "Which brings us back to the matter at hand." He pauses. "Either you tell me where it is, or Wicks over there," motioning toward the shadows with the blade, "gets a taste of your girlfriend."

There are birdlike shrieks from the dark.

"You wouldn't," exclaims Sweeney, turning quickly to Marian. He can see the fear in her eyes. What can he do? "All right, let her go. I'll tell you where the gold is."

Rufus cackles.

"Why don't I believe you?"

Sweeney gives him a baleful glare.

"I'll tell you something, you dwarf," he yells. "St. Loup is after you. He's come back."

The flat eyes go wide.

"Keep your voice down," warns the dwarf. But something has changed. "If you're talking about the whispers and the groaning, my friend," he says, "I wouldn't count on it. That was me. My tape."

Sweeney shakes his head.

"Don't you think I know that? How do you think I know the name St. Loup? How?"

Rufus stares.

"I did wonder about that."

"He's after you."

Rufus chuckles, but looks at the head.

"Seems to me, my friend, that the man you're talking about is pretty much finished up in this world."

"I'm not talking about *this* world."

Rufus shifts his eyes to Sweeney.

"You talking ghosts?" He shows a thin bloodless smile. "Don't much believe in spirits, friend." He turns to look at Wicks, hidden somewhere in the shadows. "Hear that, Artemus? Man tells me a ghost is out to get us." He turns his attention to Sweeney. "You been playing with that damn board too much." He taps his head. "Soft."

There are squeals from the shape against the wall.

"Quiet, Artemus," cautions Rufus. "You'll get your chance." He moves his eyes to Marian. "Can't say as I'd mind some myself." He holds out his knife, then points it at Sweeney. "Time to even you up." He leans closer. He hesitates. "If the decoration don't suit you, your honor, there's always fingers and toes." He tilts his head at the jar. "Heads too."

"You're insane."

Rufus blinks.

"Never looked at it that way," he says. "Figured I was too short. Not short on brains." He gives Sweeney a patient smile. "Why don't you tell me about the gold you found?"

"I never saw any gold."

Rufus sighs.

"You're lying."

"I'm not."

"Then where is it?"

"That's what I'm telling you. I *don't* know."

The dwarf moves the knife back and forth from his left hand to his right. Sweeney follows it with his eyes. He begins to shift it faster and faster. He is going so fast Sweeney can barely keep up with his movements.

"Quite a trick, no?"

"What good is it?"

Rufus stops.

"You hear something?" he asks. He turns very slowly. "Artemus, you hear anything?" He stands, forgetting Sweeney for the moment. He suddenly turns on Sweeney. "Who knows you're here?"

Sweeney opens his mouth.

"No one."

"Liar!" the dwarf shouts.

He takes a step toward Marian.

"Artemus," he hollers, but his eyes are on Marian. "We ain't got all night. See what the hell made that noise."

69

The boys watch in a trance the macabre scene unfolding before their eyes. They are stiff with fear. Hidden away at the far end of the cellar, they watch and hear Rufus and are powerless to stop him when he takes the blade and cuts into Sweeney's cheek. Welcome can feel his knees knocking together. Adrian and Boylan are frozen in position, too shocked to do anything but watch. When Rufus begins to move closer to Sweeney with the knife, Adrian squeezes Boylan's arm. He squeezes so hard Boylan almost cries out. "We've got to do something," he whispers.

Welcome tugs on his sleeve.

"Run and get the police," he whispers.

Adrian shakes his head.

"No time."

"What?" hisses Boylan.

Adrian wants to cry.

"I *don't* know."

"Shhh!"

There is a silence, then Adrian points to something.

"What's in that box?"

The other two make empty gestures with their hands.

"Take a look," he orders.

Welcome crawls off. While they wait for him to return they watch in terror as Rufus begins to toss the knife back and forth. They are filled with dread—and fear. Sweeney has his back to them, so they can't see him, or Marian. She is tied and facing the same way.

"Ball jars."

Adrian feels a shred of hope.

"How many?"

"I don't know. A box."

"Get them."

Welcome doesn't hesitate. He crawls away and returns, carrying the small box of empty jars. He puts them down and rejoins the other two in the shadows.

"Here's the plan," says Adrian.

"Hurry," whispers Boylan.

"Me and you, Blazes, each take two jars." He nods to the lighted area up ahead. "Sneak up on Rufus." He makes a fist. "We have four shots to knock him out." He takes Boylan by the shoulder. "What do you think?"

Boylan, his eyes wide with fear, forces bravado.

"If I get close enough to that fucker, I can take him out," he whispers. "Sure." He pauses. "What about Frankenstein?" He takes two jars from Welcome. "He's between us and the tunnel."

"Something'll turn up."

"If he's slow," whispers Welcome. "We can get around him." He taps Boylan on the arm. "Where's your knife?"

He touches his pocket.

"Where it always is."

Adrian takes his two jars.

"Give it to Andy. He can cut the ropes."

Boylan does as he is told.

"For the first time in my life," says Welcome, "I wish I was on the baseball team."

Adrian smiles.

"It is fear that gives us strength."

Boylan smirks.

"You mean terror, nitwit."

They begin to creep toward the light. They keep close to the earthen floor, trying to move as quickly as possible. Adrian, in the lead, suddenly stumbles over an old piece of wood. They freeze. Up ahead, they see Rufus stop shifting the knife and look their way.

"Artemus, you hear anything?"

Slowly, they creep forward.

"Who knows you're here?"

"No one."

"Liar!"

At the shout, they are within range.

"Artemus! We ain't got all night. See what the hell made that noise."

Before the shape even reaches the light Adrian and Blazes are ready. Adrian fires first and the jar sings over the head of the dwarf, who is too startled to do anything. Boylan's first pitch catches him on the side of the head.

"Shit!" he yells.

Rufus is stunned, but still conscious.

"Hit him again, Blazes."

He can't miss at the range. The jar smashes against the head of the dwarf with a crack. He sags to the floor.

"Damn!"

Adrian, desperate, throws his second jar at Artemus. The jar hits him on the upper chest, just below the neck. It bounces off.

"Had to expect this," says Welcome, waiting for his chance to get around the giant. "Create a diversion," he whispers.

Boylan stares at the towering giant.

"Look at the size of the bastard."

Artemus comes toward them, slowly.

"At least he's no sprinter."

"Get ready, Andy," says Adrian.

"I've *been* ready."

Artemus stops. He brings his hand to his throat.

"You hurt him," says Blazes.

Adrian is confused.

"I don't know."

"Delayed reaction," offers Welcome.

Artemus yowls in pain.

"Something's got him!" exclaims Adrian.

"What?"

"I don't know. I can't see it."

"Don't sound so goddamn happy."

They watch Artemus fall to his knees, his hands still fighting something that has him by the throat.

"Let's go," urges Adrian.

Welcome leaps ahead, the knife in his hand.

70

Marian is freed first.

"Hurry," she gasps.

Welcome races to Sweeney. The knife is sharp, the bonds come loose easily. Sweeney talks the whole time.

"Did you call the police?"

Welcome, busy at the rope:

"Sir, you said an hour."

"It's not an hour?"

"No."

"You boys. You're crazy to…"

"I know, sir. We thought something was wrong." He steps back. "You're untied."

Behind them, on the floor, still kneeling and struggling with something unseen, is Artemus Wicks. Marian and Sweeney, who are watching this for the first time, look on in stupefaction, and terror.

"What's going on?" Sweeney asks.

"I have no idea," she replies.

Sweeney steps around the dwarf.

"Where's the gun? Better find the gun in case he wakes up or the big one comes after us." He studies Rufus. "Where did he put it?"

"Check his pants. He may have a holster."

Sweeney does as good a job as he can going through the pockets of the unconscious man. He finds no gun.

"All the more reason to be quick."

The five of them stand in a circle above the dwarf. They pay him no attention. All of them stare at Artemus.

"Wait," says Adrian. "Look."

He points at Artemus. There is no need. All of them can see. Around the neck of the giant, a pair of claws, large, can be seen tearing into and squeezing his throat. There is blood. Then not just claws, legs. Artemus pulls at the legs, has been pulling at them before, when no one could see them. To no avail. The beast has a grip of iron. A white body, feathered, begins to appear.

"A giant bird," says Welcome.

"No," Adrian demurs. "An owl."

"Right."

The snowy owl has fully materialized. It has eyes only for Artemus. There is a deep gash in his neck that the owl tears at with its claws. Blood begins to spurt in an arch. The owl is covered with it. Artemus bends to the floor, still struggling, but with less strength. He is losing too much blood. He is making horrible rattling noises with his throat.

"We have to stop this," says Sweeney. "Look for that gun. It has to be near."

There is a dreadful gagging sound from Wicks, then no more. He lays still on the dark ground. The owl flutters its wings, lets go of the neck. It stands on the head of the giant and begins to screech. The screeches make their hair stand on end.

"Too late," says Boylan.

"What about us?" asks Sweeney.

"It's not after us." Marian asserts. "It's after them."

Sweeney bends down to the dwarf.

"We can't just leave him."

"You can't shoot that owl," she says.

Welcome bends down, retrieves the gun from under the chair, along with the head of St. Loup. He hands the revolver to Sweeney.

"We can try."

Sweeney cocks the trigger and aims the revolver at the great white owl. There is some hesitation.

"No," says Adrian calmly. "You can't shoot the owl, sir."

Down comes the arm.

"Do you know what you're saying?"

"I do."

"If the owl comes after Rufus we're practically accessories to murder."

There is a long silence. The owl hasn't moved from the head of Artemus Wicks. It seems to be clawing at the eyes.

"Ugh," Welcome chokes.

"Sir," says Boylan. "Leave the gun with him." He points at the supine form below. "Let's go!" He looks at the bird. "I can't take any more of this Cheshire owl."

The owl screeches ominously when Sweeney drops the gun at the side of the dwarf.

"We should wake him," he says.

Adrian, who has been staring at the owl, bends down to the dwarf. He slaps him, gently.

"Wake up."

"Jesus!" exclaims Boylan, forgetting he is in the presence of Sweeney. "What're you doing? We gave him the gun."

"It won't do him any good if he's unconscious," Sweeney reminds him. He approves of what Adrian is doing.

Rufus begins to stir.

"We can't just give him the gun," protests Boylan. "Not if we're still here."

He waits for a response.

"Let's go," says Marian. "Run."

The owl begins to screech. They run to the tunnel entrance, turn a last time when they get there, see the great white owl flapping its wings in the air above the dwarf. They enter the tunnel. Halfway down the tunnel they hear a long screech and then a short screech and then a high-pitched scream.

71

They arrive at the boxes.

"I can't believe this," Sweeney mutters, bending down to inspect the crates in the light from a single dangling bulb. "To think that all this time," he muses, not finishing the sentence.

Boylan has put up the ladder.

"Who's first?"

There is a second horrible scream from back in the earthen cellar. Then a gunshot.

"At least he has a chance," mutters Sweeney.

Boylan is exasperated.

"Which is more than we'll have if he kills the owl and comes looking for us."

The others wonder: can this owl be killed?

"Marian," says Sweeney, taking her by the arm. "You should be first."

She resists.

"Andrew, go ahead."

Welcome needs no encouragement. He climbs the ladder, slides back the trap door and vanishes into Sweeney's basement.

"Blazes."

Up he goes, into the dark hole above.

"Adrian?"

Adrian, his foot on the first rung of the wooden ladder, steps away. "I can't," he says.

"What do you mean?" demands Sweeney.

He looks at Sweeney.

"We left the head."

A week ago, a month ago, a year ago Sweeney would have forced Adrian up the ladder. Now he hesitates. Now he knows the truth: they cannot leave the head of St. Loup. It is what they have come for.

"What do you propose?" He sighs.

"I'll go back and get it."

Sweeney grabs him before he can take off.

"No," he says. "I'll do it."

Adrian stares at him.

"No, sir. I can do it." He stops. "I *have* to do it."

"Why?" asks Marian.

He looks at her.

"I promised."

Sweeney is in a quandary.

"I'll go with you."

Marian steps up to him.

"No, Jim. I'll go."

"You might get hurt."

She shakes her head.

"The owl means us no harm," she declares. "I'll go back with Adrian. You go upstairs. Or you can wait here."

Sweeney is perplexed.

"I'll wait," he agrees. It is not the ideal solution, at least to him. "Hurry up."

Adrian and Marian run back into the shadows. The cellar ahead is silent and each wonders what awaits them. Each is afraid, but not of what will happen to them. They are afraid of what they will see when they get there. It does not take them long to reach the opening.

"Oh, Jesus," Adrian groans.

On the floor they see the headless blood-soaked corpse of what was once the dwarf. There is blood everywhere.

"The jar, Adrian. Move."

He runs to the chair. He is not even there when be falls to his knees and starts throwing up. He holds his stomach with his left hand. With his right he points to the jar.

"Adrian," Marian calls from behind. Then she is next to him, holding his hand, brushing back his sweat-soaked hair. "Come on. Go back to the opening."

She gasps when she looks at the jar.

"Oh, God."

In the cylinder, not the head of St. Loup. The eyeless head of Rufus, bobbing gruesomely in rust-colored liquid.

"Let's go," she says. "We tried."

She helps Adrian to his feet. He is shaking and crying and needs her support. She is trembling herself. She forces herself to be strong. It isn't easy.

They stumble back through the tunnel. Sweeney, who hears them, comes halfway with his flashlight. He sees them, says nothing. He knows when to be quiet. He helps lead Adrian to the ladder, helps him up. He helps Marian up. He goes last, taking a final quick look down the secret tunnel, then is pulled through by Boylan and Welcome.

It is cold and very late in the evening when they move from the living room onto the veranda. The air is crisp. They can smell the leaves. There is a touch of winter. Adrian, Sweeney, Marian sit in the swinging chair. Welcome and Boylan sit alongside in two white wicker chairs. They are all too shocked to speak and stare over at the Wicks place, a grim shape limned in moonlight. They hear an owl hoot, and it chills them to their souls. A flock of geese squawk past the moon. They look up. The sight and sound of the geese is a good sound. They watch and listen until the birds are completely out of sight. Then their eyes go back to the house.

"Look!" cries Marian. "Fire!"

They first see flames at two, three, four windows on the ground floor. There is a flash and a boom and the entire floor is ablaze. There is an orange glow in the sky. Another boom, the sound of breaking glass. The house seems to shake.

"I'll call the fire department," shouts Sweeney.

He runs inside. He returns after he makes the call.

"Unbelievable," he says, walking straight to the railing.

Glass continues to explode. The wind begins to roar, or it could be the sound of the fire. There is a loud hissing, popping, the sound of great beams cracking and falling. The earth itself seems to shake and ring. In the sky above the house is a yellow band. The dark sky is brilliant with color, alive with it. There is a great bang, a groaning. The entire side sags, tumbles to the ground. Fire rages on every floor.

"What a fire," exclaims Boylan.

"I've never seen anything like it," remarks Sweeney.

It is a fire from the other side. St. Loup has set it. He has made a bonfire. The house, like a sculpted, angular stook stabs at the sky, stabs, dying, at the moon. There is no saving it. Sirens wail, at first from a distance, then closer. They see an engine, then another. The street fills with them.

"Good luck!" from Boylan, the only one besides Sweeney who has a voice.

More glass shatters and now water, great plumes of it from two, three, four separate hoses rains against the house. Clouds of steam and vapor rise, contend with showers of sparks and flames under a yellow moonlit sky. There is a roaring, another shaking of the earth. All of them stand now, join Sweeney at the railing. The old Wicks house is an avalanche of smoke and flame. It shudders, seems to bow out at the sides, ready to explode. The hoses, one by one, are called back, rolled up. Black-hatted firemen, tiny characters in a play, watch the flames, their own forms outlined in contending glows from earth and sky. Neighbors are out. All Gloucester seems to be out. It is like a great bonfire on Halloween. Voices carry, even above the flames. There are shrieks and the dull sound of people far off all talking at once. It is a kind of nightmare. There are flames, flames and stars, an orange sky and a big yellow moon. It is a harvest moon. Logs crackle and hiss. A sea of shapes and voices watch as the house of Wicks vanishes into flames.

72

It is Sunday, All Saint's Day. Adrian has been summoned back to Sweeney's house. He does not know why. He walks across the Justin Martyr campus under a cerulean sky. He notices the leaves have all been raked up, and that only a few remain in the trees. Winter is well on its way. The sun glints against the cool dark windows and he looks up at the Gothic towers, the arches of the old buildings. He thinks of himself as a boy walking down a long wide avenue in New York with his mother and father. It was a day like this. He thinks of things he plans to do. A letter to his mother, to his brother, a postcard to his father. He passes through the gate, steps out onto Old Beach Road. The ocean is somewhere off to his right. There are gulls in the air. He can hear them.

He looks at Graves Island.

It is not a long walk and soon he can see, in the distance, the still smoking ruins of the Wicks place. A few defiant timbers stand, charred and hopeless. The house is a pile of rubble. A small group of people stand in the street, talking, and pointing. He stops to take a last look, then moves down and around the corner to Sweeney's. He walks slowly up the walk, up the stairs to the veranda and rings the bell. Sweeney opens almost immediately.

"Come in."

Marian is sitting, drinking coffee.

"Morning, Adrian."

"Hi."

"Did you sleep?"

He shakes his head.

"No."

"Would you like some coffee?"

"Sure," he says. He wonders whether he should wait to be asked to be seated. He decides against it. He sits.

"How are you feeling?"

He groans.

"Don't ask."

Sweeney comes in with a silver tray. There is a cup of steaming coffee, a corn muffin, cream and sugar. He places it down on the end table next to Adrian.

"Help yourself."

Adrian thanks him, takes the coffee, black, and begins to sip. Remarkably, it does make him feel better. He takes a bite of the corn muffin. It tastes good.

Sweeney studies him.

"Are you ready for more adventure?"

Adrian, given to monosyllables, replies.

"No, sir."

"This one isn't dangerous."

Adrian holds out his hand.

"I'm still shaking, sir."

"Drink the coffee," Marian tells him. "You'll feel better. And finish the muffin."

Sweeney sips his own coffee.

"We're going to Arrowhead," he says, catching Adrian by surprise. "We thought you'd like to come along."

Adrian looks at him.

"You know where it is?"

He nods.

"Yes."

"What is it?"

Sweeney frowns, glances at Marian.

"A mental institution."

Adrian's eyes go wide.

"Marie's in a *mental* institution?"

Sweeney puts down his cup.

"So it would seem."

Marian watches the cat walk into the room. It comes directly to her, jumps into her lap, begins to purr.

"Adrian," she begins. "If you don't want to come, don't. You don't have to. We can drop you off."

Adrian sits in the chair, thinking.

"I'll go," he says. "I should go."

"I've been saying that all along," smiles Sweeney, who seems to be in a very good mood, almost his usual self.

"I have a question."

"Yes?" from Marian.

"Is St. Loup evil?"

He waits for an answer. It is not long in coming.

"It's hard to say, Adrian," Marian replies. "We don't know what Rufus did to him. Not that that would make what he did justifiable. He *murdered* two men."

"Then he's evil."

She shakes her head.

"We can't apply our standards to a world we know nothing about," she says. "Who knows what life is like in this parallel world? Is it a hell? A purgatory? We don't know." She pauses. "Keep in mind that Artemus Wicks murdered his daughter. In St. Loup's eyes, he was settling an old score."

"You don't see what he did as murder?"

"I'm saying we don't have a name for what happened. Who would believe it?"

"What happens if they find the bodies?"

She shakes her head.

"I doubt very much that will happen."

Adrian sips quietly at his coffee, going over in his mind what he has been going over for hours: the events of last night. He knows he will never forget. He has been altered. There *is* another world and he has gotten a glimpse of it.

"Why did he need us?"

Marian looks at him. Her eyes are dark and serene and eloquent. There is a world in them. She knows so much. Adrian thinks she is the most intelligent and wonderful woman he has ever met, or is likely to meet. He thinks of the kiss he is owed and flushes with embarrassment.

"We don't know for sure," she replies. "But I think what we said before is true. He drew his strength from us, some of it. Our belief made him more powerful."

"Is he gone?"

Sweeney breaks in.

"I should hope so."

Adrian looks at him.

"Will he be back?"

Marian answers.

"Who can say?"

Adrian sighs.

"More coffee?" asks Sweeney.

"No thanks, sir."

"Another muffin?"

"Thank you. I've had enough."

Sweeney stands up.

"What do you say?"

Adrian nods, stands.

"I'll go." He smiles weakly. "I do want to meet her." He looks down at Marian, still petting the cat. "Marie is what this is all about."

"That's right," Sweeney agrees. "I'll get my pipe and we'll be off." He looks around. "If I can find it."

He does. In the ashtray. He takes and stuffs it into his pocket, grabs his tobacco pouch, makes sure he has his car keys and leads the others to the door. At the door he gives the ansate cross beneath his sweater a careful, surreptitious touch.

73

"In there," directs the doctor. "That's her by the window." They stare into a small, sun-filled room with blue plastic chairs. Inside are three women, two of them older, and Marie, long, thick red hair draped about her shoulders, sitting in a blue chair looking out at the ocean. She is transfixed. She clutches an envelope in her hand. It is unopened. The two older women turn at the sound of voices in the hallway. Marie never looks away from the sea. She is wearing a dark blue dress, almost black, her hands, and the envelope she holds in her fingers, rest in her lap. Her face is without expression.

"Just like the quilt," comments Adrian.

Marian agrees with a quiet nod.

The four of them enter the room and walk up to her. The doctor touches her on the shoulder. She does not respond. He brings them around in front of her and introduces them one at a time. He retreats into the background. They stand, looking down at her, not knowing what to do. Sweeney squints to see the envelope and the postmark, Marblehead.

"Does she read?"

"Not that we know," replies the doctor.

"Who sends her mail?"

The doctor answers, quietly.

"Her grandmother."

They all look at one another.

"I'll leave you," says the gray-eyed doctor. "Don't be long."

They watch the doctor leave. An awkward silence follows, especially for Adrian, who has no idea what to do. Speak to her? She doesn't answer. It all seems now, at least to him, to be such a bother to her. He tries to catch her eyes. They stay on the sea. Her face, he sees, is extraordinarily pretty. She has bright green clear eyes, but pale skin, which is wrinkled about the eyes. She wears no makeup.

"Marie."

It is Sweeney.

"Marie," he repeats. "We know."

No response.

"We know who your father is," says Sweeney. "Would you like us to tell you? Do *you* know who your father is?"

She turns, slightly, brings a porcelain finger to the side of her nose, scratches, brings her hand down and joins it to the other in her lap. There is nothing in her eyes.

"Artemus Wicks," Sweeney says, whispering, as if the name is not a name others should hear. "Aveline was your mother."

Not a trace of a response.

"Marie," Marian begins, quietly. "We want to help. We think you saw something terrible." She waits. "Marie, we know."

Adrian thinks he detects a flicker in her eyes.

"Marie," Marian continues. "We know what you saw."

Adrian, watching, sees the eyes taking note. He feels an exhiliration. Marie is being saved. He stares into the green eyes. He wants to say something, but what? Sweeney and Marian, let them talk. He has not been brought along to talk, but to watch. There is a silence. Sweeney and Marie have stopped. They have said, he thinks, all they are prepared to say.

"Marie," says Sweeney. "Do you understand? We *know* what you saw." He looks at Marian, hesitates. "There is no danger. You hear? No danger. You are safe. No harm can come to you."

Adrian thinks: say something.

"Marie, please, listen to us," declares Marian, squatting down so that she and Marie are at eye level. "We've come to help." She pauses. "Don't you want to get out of this place? Go sailing? Out on the water instead of just looking through these windows? Don't you?"

Adrian turns away from Marie and looks out at the water. It is bright blue. There are brief shadows from passing clouds, whitecaps from the wind. In the distance, there are sailboats, chasing the wind, orange, red, yellow, green sails, spinnakers billowing. He can almost hear them, the sound of the rippling canvas, the rush of water. The sun is brilliant, the sky is clear but for the few clouds that race, wind-driven, over the water. She should see this, feel it, put her hand in the icy water. She should want to be alive.

"Marie, Artemus Wicks. We know he is your father."

Adrian thinks. He watches Sweeney and Marian step away to confer, leaving him at the window near Marie. He looks down, bends, kneels and takes her hands in his. He stares into eyes as green as emeralds and squeezes her hands.

"Marie, listen to me. Marie?" She stares back at him. She seems to be staring right through him. "Marie," he says, feeling an emotion in his voice so strong his voice is wavering. "He's dead. Artemus Wicks is dead. *That's* what we came to tell you." He implores her. "The man who killed your mother is dead."

A shudder passes through her.

"Marie," he says. "You're free."

There *is* something in her eyes. She shudders again and begins to sob. He does not release her hands. She looks at him with understanding, squeezes his hands.

74

They are back in the car.

"Was that true?" asks Adrian from the back seat. "What you said about what she saw?"

"We really don't know," Sweeney replies. "The doctor told me on the phone there was no physical reason for her silence. She's normal. What else could it be? Something traumatic." The car glides into a turn.

"How do you know she saw her mother murdered?" asks Adrian. He does not understand.

"We don't."

Marian turns around in her seat.

"We took a guess. It may not even be right. What she responded to, I think, was the news that Artemus was dead. She was afraid of him. *That* we were right about."

Adrian falls into silence.

"Where are we going?" he asks after some time has passed.

Marian turns around again.

"Jim's not saying," she says "It's a secret."

Adrian suddenly remembers.

"Her grandmother is alive."

Sweeney looks at him in the rear-view mirror.

"That's right."

"She must be a hundred."

"Or very close," suggests Sweeney.

Adrian looks out the window, watches people walking their dogs, joggers. He sees a newspaper boy, remembers his own days of delivering papers.

"You *know* where she is?"

Sweeney laughs.

"That I do."

"How?"

"The postmark," Sweeney replies. "Once I saw the postmark, I knew. Couldn't be anyplace else."

Up ahead they can see a large wooden house with a porch, up on a hill, surrounded by great green lawns. After a time they see a sign: "The Willows Rest Home." They turn onto the driveway. Sweeney finds a parking space. They get out, walk past another sign with the same name, see another sign, "Visitors Entrance." They step inside. A young woman at the desk looks up when she hears the door close.

"We're here to see Prudence Doucet," declares Sweeney, addressing the woman. It is dark in the waiting area, in spite of the bright sun outside. The windows have shades.

"Prudence?"

"Yes."

"Her lucky day," the woman remarks.

"Lucky?" from Marian.

"She *never* has visitors."

She puts down the pencil she was using to do the crossword puzzle in the *Globe* and gets up. "Whom shall I say is calling?"

"Jim Sweeney. I bought a house from her."

"All right," she says smartly. "I'll go tell her."

She departs, her white shoes making no sound on the carpeted floor. After she is out of sight, Sweeney turns to his companions.

"Go ahead," he says. "Tell me what a wonderful sleuth I've turned out to be."

Marian and Adrian grin.

"You're wonderful, Jim."

"Adrian?"

"I agree."

The woman has turned the corner on her way back to the desk. They try to read from the way she is walking whether or not Prudence will see them. Sweeney hopes his name means something to her. It was she who signed the papers for the house sale. Not Marie.

In that the dwarf was right. It was Prudence, kept hidden by her cat's paw lawyer.

"Prudence will see you," the young lady informs them. "If you'll just follow me, I'll take you to her room." On the way she tells them, quietly, "One thing you should know. Her eyes are sensitive to light. She must wear dark glasses or draw the blinds." She stops at a door with a number. "Today she has drawn the blinds."

75

They look into a room that is dim, airless, a place of twilight, and see, doll-like, her feet off the floor, an old, old woman, sitting, staring up at them from an oversized rocking chair. She rocks slowly, the chair barely making a sound on the carpeted floor. When the rocker goes up, her feet come off the floor. Now, used to the shadows, they can see her better. She is small. Her hair is tied in a tight white bun at the back of her head. The chair is too big for her.

"Prudence Doucet?" Sweeney inquires.

"Mr. Sweeney," comes a voice arid as dead leaves. "We meet at last."

"You remember, I bought your house."

"I remember."

"From you, not from Marie."

A dry chuckle; the rocker stops.

"You've been to Marie," she says, her voice now a monotone. The rocker starts again. "Sit, sit, please. There are chairs. Bring them up, so I can see you. Sit close."

They enter the room, take three folding chairs that have already been set up in a half circle, move them even closer. They sit, an audience. The old eyes take their measure.

"Looking for gold?" she asks.

She sits rigidly, waiting for an answer, the rocker unmoving, her milky green eyes staring, picking over each face. There is a thin smile that comes and goes and her hands, almost translucent, stay flat against the long arms of the rocker when it is still. They clutch tightly when she rides, rocks back and forth. The rocker, again, begins to move.

"We're not interested in gold," Marian replies. "We didn't come for any gold you have." She studies the old woman, sees that, even now, traces of beauty remain in the thin lined face, the large hollow eyes, the long straight nose, although her mouth does have the sunken look of a woman of age. "Do you remember making a quilt? A memory quilt about the house Mr. Sweeney bought from you?"

"I remember making a number of quilts," she says dryly.

Marian presses.

"You would remember this one," she insists, her voice quiet and remorseless. "It contained nine panels," she says. "The first panel was Andre St. Loup riding into town, the second the building of the house in 1885, the third, the birth of your son, Andre."

"I remember," Prudence says, her voice slow and deliberate. "Where did you find it?"

"I bought it in Maine," answers Sweeney

"It was a very dear quilt."

Sweeney nods.

"I've thought about that quilt," the slow words come, "any number of times. I thought it got left behind. Now I know what must have happened." She smiles wanly. "Marie put it in with the others." She stops. "We had to sell them."

"Why would Marie do that?" asks Sweeney.

The old voice sounds.

"She's in it. Too much in it."

Sweeney takes his eyes from her face.

"It's still beautiful," he says.

Again, the rocker stops.

"How did you find me?" she inquires. Is there a flicker of amusement in the eyes? Did they flash and fade?

"We were visiting Marie at Arrowhead," he replies "I saw an envelope you had sent. The postmark. I knew you had to be here—it's the only place like it on the North Shore."

They hear a dry laugh, like a moth's wings fluttering.

"That was clever of you," she says, her voice carefully gliding over each word. The eyes close, then open. "I get tired easily these days. You'll have to excuse me." A withered sigh. "And how did you come to find Marie?" A quick, unexpected laugh. "Don't tell me you looked her up in a phone book." The thin lips part in a smile. "Keep in mind—I only half believe what you said about the postmark."

Sweeney draws a breath, exhales.

"It's a long story."

The rocker begins to move.

"I don't mind a long story," she says.

Marian begins.

"Prudence," she says. "The Ouija board," her clear blue eyes imploring, "what do you know about it?"

The reply is long in coming.

"You're not going to tell me you found Aveline's board, wherever it was she hid it." The old eyes brighten and fade. "Is that it? Aveline's board? You found it?"

From Sweeney:

"Yes, I found it."

A dry cackle.

"Good for you, Mr. Sweeney," she says. "I never could. And I looked. If I had found it, sir, you never would have. I'd've burned it." Her head tilts, slightly, to the left. She rights it, quickly. "Aveline, poor girl. Talking to that thing day and night telling me her father spoke to her. Said he told her to buy a gun." A stare, steady. "Lot of good it did her."

"Prudence," Marian says. "He came back."

The old woman gives her a long blank puzzled stare.

"The colonel?"

From Marian:

"Yes."

No pause now. Quick.

"Why?"

"To help Marie," offers Adrian.

Her eyes wander to him.

"Marie?"

"Yes," avers Sweeney.

The old mind is still sharp.

"Why else? The gold?"

A pause. Then Adrian:

"No. The dwarf."

76

"The little man who came to see me?"

"If his name was Rufus," answers Sweeney. "Yes."

The old head, again, tilts left. Prudence, quickly, centers it. All now realize she has difficulty keeping her balance, even sitting. Her mind, though, is clearly in working order.

"I don't recall the name he used," she says. "He said he knew the colonel. Called him colonel. So he must have. No one here ever called him that. No one knew." The eyes close, stay shut, snap open. "Why did Andre come back for him?" Then, almost sleepily, "*How* did Andre come back? The board? What Aveline said was true?" She stops. "Tell me."

"Yes," replies Sweeney.

A laugh, short, dusky.

"A ghost story," she declares. "A real ghost story." Her eyes, just for a second, twinkle. "Tell me, was Andre on a silver charger? Did he come riding up onto the lawn? Or did he stay out where the tall grass used to be, waving his hat?" She gets serious. "How did he come back? How? I don't believe it." A sly wink. "The dwarf told *you* about the gold, Mr. Sweeney, and sent you here. Is that it?"

Sweeney, cupping his hands.

"We have *not* come for any gold."

"Then why?"

"To help Marie," replies Sweeney.

"So you said. Whatever gave you the idea to 'save' Marie? What is it Marie is supposed to be saved from?"

Sweeney looks over at the drawn blinds, shut tight. Barely enough light gets through the edges, the cracks, to make the room twilight. It is twilight in this room all the time.

"The past."

The eyes, like a doll's, shut, snap open.

"What has the past got to do with it?" she asks, her voice brittle, caustic, deliberate.

"I think you know," replies Sweeney. "I think you know your daughter was murdered. I think you know who did it, if not know, then suspect. You put him in the quilt."

They can hear the old woman take in air.

"Mr. Sweeney," a monotone, "either you are a mind reader, or a most capable detective." A long pause, during which the green eyes measure them, go over each of them in sequence. "I am an old lady. I have little patience, no time for games. You say you have come on some kind of errand of mercy. I'm willing to go along. I'll bestow some trust. I won't play games myself." Her eyes seem to glimmer at Sweeney. "What you suspect, or indeed know, I don't much care which, is what I have known in my heart a long time. Aveline was murdered. By Wicks. He was a dumb boy, a mute. Aveline toyed with him. Took him to bed with her when he was a boy. Got herself pregnant, by him I suppose, although there's no real way of knowing. Aveline liked men." A deep slow breath. "Marie was born in 1930. Aveline kept on with Wicks for years, years. He came in through the tunnel. She would meet him there. I know—I could hear them. And then it stopped. Who knows when, exactly? Just stopped. He kept coming around. He'd never had another woman, and, Lord knows, no one as pretty as Aveline would look at him twice. Of course, toward the end, she was old herself," tapping her head, "and going crazy. Took it into her mind that he was danger-ous, that he wanted Marie, wanted her for sex." She moves her hands from the sides of the rocker to her lap, entwines them. "I didn't know whether she was right or wrong in that. I never felt that about him. Just a poor dumb overgrown child, although there was talk and Andre hated him so. But that was because of Aveline."

"Why did Artemus Wicks shoot Aveline?" asks Marian, taking advantage of her sudden silence. "Why would he want to shoot her?"

Suspicious, wary green eyes move her way.

"What makes you say shoot?"

Marian is surprised.

"The quilt. There's a shotgun in the panel with the tombstone marked Aveline," she replies. "In the corner."

There is a flutter of amusement in the eyes.

"The gun was never fired," she says flatly. "I put it there because it was her gun and I found it on her bed the night she disappeared. She either couldn't get to it or couldn't pull the trigger. Take your pick. Although I'd say she couldn't get to it because I sincerely believe she had it in her to shoot a man."

"Then what happened to her?" Marian inquires. "What made you think she was dead?"

The old woman shakes her head.

"I didn't, at least not at first," she replies, in that slow, still voice. "I thought she ran off, that she'd had enough of the girl and me and that fool man coming around and she took off. I saw the gun and all, but I didn't think. I even found the girl downstairs and still didn't realize. It took some time, a long time. I finally believed that Artemus did it and that the girl saw him do it or saw enough of what he did to lose her tongue for fourteen years."

"Did you tell the police?"

Again, a dry chuckle.

"Tell them what? My daughter was murdered? Where was the body? Believe me, I looked. I do believe if I could have found her body I would have done something, called the police maybe, if it made sense to take family matters public. I don't know. I was, I think, eighty-three," hesitating, "eighty-four? when Aveline vanished. A bit old to be bothered going back and forth to a police station, or to court, especially when I knew, supposing it was Artemus that had done it, that nothing would happen." She taps her head with a long, surprisingly long, bony finger. "He wasn't of sound mind. He wouldn't have been punished." A pause. "And what about the girl? What about her? They'd've dragged her into court. She couldn't talk. What good would have come of it?"

There is a long eerie silence. Prudence closes her eyes, seems to fall asleep, wake with a start. Her green eyes go wide and she gasps. It is as if she has lost sense of where she is, what she is doing. But then the eyes are clear, even sharp. Like the woman, they seem to fade in and out.

"What about your husband?" Sweeney asks, his voice urgent. He does not know how much longer Prudence can go on.

A flicker of a smile.

"That's the same question put to me by the ugly little man," she declares. "What did you say his name was?"

"Rufus."

"Him. He wanted to know what happened to the colonel, wanted to know if I knew." A pause. "I knew all right. He ran off. Built a fire and ran off. Left me down there with some old woman. Getting my fortune told." She smiles vaguely at the memory. "I would live to be old. I would outlive my children. That's what she said. And that very night Andrew took it on himself to run away." A sharp dry cough. "I've never been able to figure it and I've given the matter considerable thought." A wan, almost serene smile. "I never really understood the man. Maybe that was why." The smile goes away. "Came back, you say? What did he have to say for himself? Did he tell you why he left?" All in that slow, deliberate voice. "Why he deserted me?"

"Yes," from Adrian.

She swings her eyes to him.

"What is your name, young man?"

"Adrian, ma'am."

"Adrian," she repeats. "Well, what is it you have to say for yourself? Seems like you have something on your mind."

Adrian looks quickly at Marian and Sweeney.

"Your husband, ma'am, the colonel," he says, "he was murdered."

A long silence. The rocking chair moves forward, her feet touch the floor. It moves back and her feet come up. The chair comes forward again and halts. There is a glassy look to her eyes. She sighs, very quietly. It is barely audible. It is like something leaving, an idea going and being replaced.

"How do you know?" she asks, sharply, wanting and not wanting to know, but wanting to believe. In the voice—everything there is left to Prudence. "How?"

Adrian takes a deep breath.

"He told me, ma'am."

"Told you?"

"Yes, ma'am. He talked to me through the Ouija board."

She leans forward, seems to be trying to get closer to Adrian, to touch him. She tugs on her chair.

"Come closer, boy, I want to see you."

Adrian, with another glance at Sweeney and Marian, moves his chair forward. Prudence makes him move it even closer. His knees are close enough to her knees to touch, but they do not. Prudence, with a move surprisingly quick, takes his hands in hers.

"Oh," escapes from him.

"I won't hurt you," she declares. "What I want you to do is look me straight in the eyes. Straight, and tell me again. What you just said. Again."

"The colonel was murdered."

"Who told you?"

"The colonel. Andre St. Loup."

Her eyes widen at the name.

"Who did it?"

"The dwarf. Rufus."

"Why?"

"Greed, ma'am. He said it was greed."

"The gold."

"Yes. Gold."

She stares hard at Adrian, holding his hands tight in her own parchment-like fingers. Then she lets him go and gently raises a hand to his cheek and runs her fingers over it, twice.

"I believe you, young man."

Adrian, his own eyes wide, shining, feels his pulse racing. He looks at her, is afraid to take away his eyes, afraid to smile—in re-lief—afraid to ask. But he must. He must.

"Can you tell us? Tell us about the colonel?"

77

She moves her hand to the faint triangle of lace at her breast, a delicate gesture, leaves it there as she thinks of how to tell the story she has never told but has never wanted to tell until this moment and it is the boy who brings it out, that and his news, his true news, that the colonel was murdered, had not run off, not neglected her or deserted or left without saying goodbye while she was down at the bonfire watching the sparks fly up to the stars and then over at the pig roast wondering what was taking him so long, with half a mind to go up and get him, and half to stay put and be mad and now all that madness, that anger and unfulfilled aimless pointless rage, gone. And in the words of a smooth-faced young boy.

"He was elegant in the saddle," she begins, her voice serene, flowing, the words deliberate, chosen carefully. "I remember when he rode into town how elegant he was, how tall and the horse such a proud silver mare—who wouldn't be, carrying such cargo? He came at night, alone and then after that a wagon came, driven by a boy and an Indian. They brought the boxes. I remember the first time I saw him. I was with my mother and she pointed him out to me and I said, 'Oh, how handsome.' Mother told me. 'He's too old for you.' But he came courting anyway. Too old never stopped a man like Andre St. Loup."

Her voice does not cease. It simply seems to vanish.

"He told me he loved green eyes and that if I promised to have children, progeny he called them, with green eyes like mine he would someday ask me to marry him, but first he had to build himself a house. That was his dream—to have a house. He set out, him and the boy and the Indian and they cleared the land, put in the foundation and when they were ready he called in hired men who did the rest. He watched them all the time. I would ride out with my mother and watch him watching and he would doff his hat, he was *such* a gentleman. Anyone could tell, although he remained a mystery to everyone in town, except me. He told me things. He told me he came from Tennessee by way of France and that he had fought in more battles than he could count. He was a hero and General Lee himself gave him a medal after his head was almost cleft in two by a Union officer who left him for dead. But he rose again and when he healed there was a silver streak right where the saber cut him, a mark that set him apart. After that he told me he believed he could never be killed in battle, so he fought like a crazy man, never stopping, never leaving a battle until they had to half drag him away. Men feared him. They were afraid to fight with him. Both sides. The North hated to fight against him, the South alongside. He was a brutal fearsome man those days, but he changed. He was a good husband and a good father and I think, truly, none of what happened to Andre and Aveline would have happened if that evil little man had stayed away. Why did he come? Who was he? How did he know about the gold?"

"He knew," answers Sweeney. "Somehow."

"The gold belonged to Andre," the voice returning, like a stream, into and out of an interval. "The others were all dead. General Cleburne, Irish Pat, shot and run over, and the other man, dead, whose name I never knew, but I did know the gold was his and that soon as the war was over he took the eight boxes—only one of them was gold—and rode north into Ontario, where he stayed until he came down here. He knew the North was going to ruin the South and he wanted no part of it, so he stayed away until he felt it was time to return. He changed his name because he had fought for the South and even though the war was over, it hadn't been over that long and there were any number of graves he felt personally responsible for. I kept his secret. I never told. But I knew who he was."

Like a river turning a bend, the voice vanishes, returns.

"He built the house, we married," she intones, her voice rising and falling. "A lovely wedding. The whole town turned out. Lasted an entire day. We moved in, mother, Andre and I. Those were happy days, the three of us, then when the children came there was so much happiness it's a wonder none of us burst. I remember him in the morning, with Andre, riding off through the tall grass on their way to the open pasture. He'd always turn at the end and wave his hat before he disappeared into the trees. Those mornings, they were the nicest, and in the afternoons we'd come and sit on the porch, on the swing, and listen to the June bugs and the birds and smell the forsythia and lilac. You could smother in it." There is a long wistful sigh. "I guess it started to fall apart when mother got sick. Something happened," points to her head. "A fall, or an injury she never told about. She would sit up in the attic in a rocking chair, all day, and just rock. Then one day the rocking stopped and Andre went up and he found her and she was dead."

She takes a breath, a rest, the lids of her eyes fluttering and now the chair begins to move, slowly, imperceptibly.

"The gloom came in 1914. After that nothing was ever the same. Until this afternoon I thought he had vanished, run off and left me. Now you say he was murdered and I'm glad, not that he was murdered but that he didn't run away, desert me and the children. None of us knew what to think. The boy, Andre, was something of a problem—he drank to excess—although you could hardly call a man of twenty-eight a boy, which was his age when the colonel was killed. Aveline, too, became strange, introverted, after her father disappeared. You could say that Halloween day in 1914 was the worst thing that happened to us all and you'd be right. Indirectly, it led to Andre's suicide. I know the coroner was kind and wrote it up an accident, but it wasn't. Anyone who knew him knew that he drove that car straight into the ocean. Then Aveline withdrew even more and took up with the Ouija board, but that you know. What you're probably wondering about are the eight boxes and the gold and what happened to it, even if you didn't come here for that."

The rocker moves. There is a low, quiet laugh from the almost ghostly twilight form in the flowered dress with lace at the wrists and neck and small black shoes with pointed toes that come to a stop an inch above the floor when the rocker swings back. The laugh becomes the voice.

"All gone," she says, "every bit of it, except for one bar and that belongs to Marie if she can use it. There was gold in just one of those boxes, the others all had paper money. Yankee money, so it was good. Two built the house, five kept us going. We lived like kings and none of us ever worked, the colonel especially, with his horses and gambling. The money held out for a long time, going on seventy years, and we never wanted, never went without a thing. Then with the colonel's investments—he about owned half this town at one time—we did all right. There isn't much left, with my up-keep and Marie's and it won't be long before it's all out. One gold bar, though, and that's all and enough cash to keep me here until I'm a hundred and five—if I should live that long—and Marie until she's sixty. After that she'll have to fend for herself or throw herself on the mercy of the state. I don't know which. But it's gone, spent, especially that gold, which we held until last." A dry chuckle. "That little man said, 'The boxes are all empty.' God, he was furious. Furious because he didn't find out about the tunnel until it was too late and furious because he suspected that in 1914 the gold was still in the tunnel, which was true. Untouched. A whole big box of gold marked 'Dynamite'."

A long dry laugh and the rocking stops. She takes an audible breath. There are footsteps in the hall.

"Marie," she says. "Tell me about Marie."

Adrian, still close, takes *her* hands.

"I told her he was dead," he says solemnly. "Wicks was dead and she was free, that there was nothing to be afraid of."

The head tilts, the eyes seem to close, but snap open. Prudence fights to stay awake, aware.

"And?"

"She sobbed," Adrian replies, "and squeezed my hand."

She reaches out to touch his cheek.

"You're kind," she says. "Sob? A sob?" She smiles wanly. "Good. It's a start. She'll be back. She'll be all right."

She takes back her hand.

"Prudence?" says a voice from the door.

"Hello, Carol."

"How are things in there?"

The dry voice, learning to speak again.
"Fine, everything's fine."

78

He tries to read. He cannot concentrate. There is too much to think about. His eyes wander about the room, touching on what belongs to Boylan and what to him and he wonders about St. Loup and what he did to Artemus Wicks and Rufus and the house itself and the great power it entailed. What was the source of that power? When he thinks of what happened with the Ouija board and especially the events of Halloween and the fire he knows he is thinking of events that, like all events, will fade with time. Can he keep them fresh, these things in his mind? Can the garden be watered? Is it a garden? In the top drawer of his desk is the Ouija board. Will he use it again? Will he be afraid? Are there other spirits waiting to make contact? He is tempted to open the drawer, just to look at it. He hesitates and decides against it. Not for a long time. The spirits can wait. He has had enough. His heart has had enough.

"Greetings, chum," offers Blazes, entering the room. He slams the door behind him. "Where've you been?"

"I went to see Marie."

Boylan stops what he is doing and looks at him. He gives Adrian a very even, very measured look.

"Well, well."

"She hasn't said a word in fourteen years. I think we got through." He watches Boylan, who has resumed looking through a pile of socks in his drawer. "I think she'll be able to talk."

Boylan is exceedingly noncommittal.

"Good," he says.

Adrian plunges ahead.

"We saw Prudence."

Boylan stops poking through the socks.

"I hate it when I can't find the mate," he mutters. "It drives me crazy."

"Did you hear me? I said we went to see Prudence."

Boylan looks up.

"I heard you," he replies. "Who's we?"

"Mr. Sweeney and Marian and me."

"How come you? What about me and Welcome?"

Adrian gets to his feet.

"He called me, Blazes. I wanted you guys to come." He walks to Boylan. "I got the impression they didn't want lot of people."

Boylan snorts.

"Right. *Now* we're a lot of people." He looks at Adrian. "Wasn't too long ago you couldn't make a move without us."

"Come on, Blazes. You're making like it's my fault and it's not." He stops, reaches into Boylan's drawer. "Here. The mate."

Boylan rips it out of his hand.

"Thanks."

"I had no idea what he wanted when he called," Adrian says. "If I knew, I would've *insisted* you guys come along."

Boylan scratches his head.

"*Maybe* I believe you," he says. "Just maybe."

"Have I ever lied to you?"

Boylan snickers.

"Far as I know you lie to me all the time."

Adrian throws up his hands.

"Give me a break," he exclaims.

"I had a compass," says Blazes, going back into his drawer. "Any idea where it is?"

Adrian looks down at the drawer.

"No."

"It might be in my gym locker." He shuts the drawer. "Want to walk to the gym with me?"

"It's dark, Blazes. We're not supposed to be out."

"Oh, yeah, right. School tomorrow."

"Right."

Boylan points a finger.

"Seems to me, Sparks, anytime you want something done, it's a good idea. When I do, it's not."

"I ran into the headmaster an hour ago," Adrian says. "He *told* me to get to my room. *Told* me. He's probably up in his window with binoculars waiting to catch me going out."

Boylan walks to the door.

"No time to argue, Adrian. Got to get my compass." He opens the door. "I'm lost without it." He laughs and steps out into the hall. He sticks his head back in. "Har, har."

He shuts the door and leaves.

Adrian goes back to the chair and tries to read. He stares at the same page for a long time. He still cannot concentrate. He gets up and opens the desk drawer and sees inside the Ouija board, the planchette resting quiet and still on top of it. He reaches down, fingers the tripod, then takes back his hand. He is afraid. He closes the drawer and just as it closes he hears, outside, the hoot of an owl. He goes to the window, opens it wide and peers out.

"Hoot."

There, in the gray light, perched on a wicket, he sees an enormous owl, whiter than snow. He stares and the owl stares back at him with unblinking yellow eyes. He moves his eyes down to the claws of the bird and sees nothing unusual. No sign of blood.

"Hoot."

Why is this owl staring at him? Why has it stopped at the wicket, near the red maple? Why does it stare?

"St. Loup. Is it you?"

The great bird blinks.

"Hoot."

Then, like before, he sees it start to happen. The feet begin to fade and then the legs and lower body. Out go the wings. The upper body and then the outstretched wings and then the head, beak to crown. His last image is of two great staring yellow eyes and then nothing. The owl is gone, leaving behind an empty wicket in gray light, silence.

79

Finally it is night and Adrian is in bed. He has been thinking since he watched it disappear about the snowy owl. He cannot take his mind away from it. No matter what he tries, nothing works. The magic bird has been branded into him, has in some way become a part of him, of what it is that makes him Adrian Sparks and not anyone else on the planet. He wonders about the world where St. Loup exists. Is it existence? Or is it a floating, a coming into and going out of? What is it like there? *Is* it the afterlife? Or another step along the way to immortality? St. Loup gives the impression it is a place of crows and spirits, of dim, dank things with glowing eyes and the ability to inflict pain. Is it a place of fire? A world of pain? Will he go there when he dies? At the very least he knows it is something rather than nothing, a dimension, a parallel world, a stepping stone, an alcove on the way to eternity. He sees in his mind the smoking ruins of the Wicks house, the charred beams and shattered windows sticking up, into the air, with nothing to hold them, nothing to bend them back into the shape of a house. They just point upward. A grim acrid smoking ruin St. Loup left behind. He rolls on his side and looks over at his roommate.

"Blazes? You awake?"

He gets no answer. Even if Boylan were awake, he would get no answer. Not a word or a grunt or a don't bother me, which is his way.

"Want to know a secret?"

The form on the bed shifts, but no words escape from it.

He wants to tell Boylan that there is a hereafter and that it is a democracy, a democracy of ghosts, not all of whom are bent on destruction. They live under a set of runic laws. There are good clean spirits and there are tarnished spirits out for revenge. Some are proud and driven, little Lucifers. Others are penitent. He can feel the cool autumn air coming in through the open crack at the bottom of the window. He can smell the leaves. And he can see himself in them, in the rushed piles under the trees. Dead Adrian! But he will not be back, not be formed anew in some distant future spring. Unless! Unless somewhere out in the beyond, where there are no stars and planets, where God works in a strange vortex and where time is as malleable as the atoms he is made of, something happens. Then he will be back. Or try to be back.

Will he find a boy with a board?

Adrian drifts off, does not hear the scratching in the drawer or see or know the words.

AH MES CHER MES

The scratchings continue. He is in a dream, Adrian. He is on a silver horse, in uniform, making a charge. He yells and screams.

TH GATES THE DON BE SAD

Over the breastworks, a great flying leap. He sees ahead another figure on horse, a familiar figure. The head turns slowly and he sees, like a razor in the sun, a silver streak.

AU REVOIR ADREN

For other fine titles from
VIVISPHERE PUBLISHING
visit
www.vivisphere.com

or call for a catalogue:
1-800-724-1100